Dark 1

Dark Pines— Copyright © 2016 by Shay Lawless

ISBN-10: 1-940087-20-1
ISBN-13: 978-1-940087-20-7

21 Crows Dusk to Dawn
Publishing, 21 Crows, LLC

Shay Lawless

Chapter 1

Taking Pictures of Dead People

"Can you do me a favor?"

I don't know why Abe Starling even bothers to ask me that question while he rolls his window down six inches, and stuffs his face into the open crack. I am juggling my camera in one latex-gloved hand, my tripod in the other, and trying to talk to him at the same time I give instructions to two buff cops trying to mask the dead man from view of the newspaper crew and bystanders, but not cover it from mine.

"I am doing you a favor, Abe," I grumble. "I'm taking the crime scene photos for you."

He is sitting inside his car five minutes into a loud, dramatic gagging fit. I can't see more than his silhouette in the murky depths of the car settled into what little shade there is beneath a landscaped lilac tree sparsely covered in dead flowers. He's got a long nose, big blue eyes, and shoulder-length, brown-red hair. The baby fine hair, he's always shoving into a man bun on top of his head. Every model he hires looks at him like he's some kind of a god. He's got one in the car with him now, all smooshed up to his side and clinging to his arm. She keeps peering past him at the dead guy and giggling at my full-body protective suit, telling Abe I look like I'm on zombie patrol.

I just don't get the fascination. He's more eccentric than my Great Aunt Lilly who's got seventeen ill-mannered, carpet-peeing pugs running wild around her RV that's permanently parked in a campground in northern Alabama. Maybe it's because he's such a big wimp, I get turned off by him. I'm not so into guys that can't give me a firm handshake. He's got one of those loose, finger-holding clasps. And he's got a stash of hand sanitizers he keeps tucked into the pockets of his jeans which I'm sure he's doused his entire body in by now.

I'm ten feet away. It was misty-cool where I stepped on to the plane and dry-hot here where it landed. I'm an hour and forty minutes from Houston, Texas. I'm thinking that maybe he wants me to use the toe of my tennis shoe and shove the dead body I am standing over slightly to the right and just enough so the angle doesn't allow any blood to be showing. Maybe he wants me to dig the bottle of perfume out of my backpack I use as a purse and spritz the air with it to avoid the dank bit of stink. The dead guy weighs about three-hundred pounds and he's sprawled spread eagle in the Timber Jack Grocery Store parking lot. He's got one gunshot wound to his chest and one to his head. Why the local police let him lay this long in wait of crime photos is beyond me. It was a five and a half hour flight for me and another hour drive from the airport. I've never had a case where they didn't want the victim bagged and tagged and out of the eyes of the public in less time than it takes to stand under a short, cold shower. Surely anybody with a camera can take the same shots I'm getting right now.

I sigh. Maybe not. I'm a walking medical equipment supply room because I've been taking crime scene photos so much lately. Evidence markers, scales, body suits and modified tripods are always stuffed unsystematically in the trunk of my rental car. I lug my own around because half of the places I take these pictures don't have fresh in stock. Or they don't have any supplies at all on the scene. And as slightly macabre as it may seem, I find it almost as entertaining finding new gadgets to use at the scene as it is to buy new clothes and camera equipment. Oh, and I hate to admit it. I spend a lot of time by myself, so what the heck else do I have to do?

"I'm already doing you a favor. I came to take the pictures for you, Abe," I say flatly. "Why do you bother to tell the cops you'll come and take crime scene photos if you nearly faint when you see someone in a hospital gown? I mean, honestly, they've got people on staff that can do what I'm doing right now."

It annoys me. I have no doubt in my mind that agreeing to do him a favor will, ultimately, come back to bite me in the ass. It always does. There's always an ulterior motive, a concealed agenda with my boss. However, a rejection would do more harm than good. That's why I left Washington State at three this morning in a half-daze dancing into my fluffy boots before I took a flight to Houston, still wearing my pajama shorts and t-shirt.

"I don't know, Piper. They called. I didn't want to tell them I couldn't do it."

"Well, you *can't* do it," I mumble. It is a losing battle. Trying to tell Abe he should turn down a job, no matter how far out of his comfort zone, is just as easy as trying to convince a two year-old that the tantrum they are already five minutes deep is a waste of time. His daddy was some big television journalist during the 1960s. He not only knew just about anybody that has anything to do with police work, but he was a huge TV personality for the six o'clock news during the 1970s. Everybody recognized him. Now, they all know Abe who is quick to hand his hopeful next client his business card that proudly states: *Abe Starling Photographic Agency. We represent a catalogue of photographers who can cater for clients in commercial, editorial, and the private industry.*

So I'm sure he whined his way into holding some local cop off using his daddy's name until I got there just like he whine-talked me into coming.

"I know. It's gross. You want me to start calling Delta Raines for the contracts? Because she's got two things you don't got, Piper, and I wish I didn't always have to point them out. One, she'll do it without giving me lip. Because whatever is in that blood of yours, that redneck-whatever, leaves me with a bad taste in my mouth sometimes. And two, she's a risk-taker. You won't take chances. And we both know you wouldn't still be stuck with me if you hadn't restrained yourself time and time again."

Delta Raines. I cringe inwardly. She's Abe's go-to girl for all the easy stuff now. I get the crappy dead people jobs. I know for a fact Abe Starling can sniff out the feral scent of irritation creeping past the aroma of my baby powder roll-on deodorant I rubbed under my armpits right as I got off the plane. Delta Raines is America's sweetheart of teen magazine photography. She's won so many awards, it is nearly sickening. She's bubbly with short blonde hair. And she's tiny. Abe's been dancing on the air since she contacted him six months ago. She was exploring the idea of finding jobs more adventurous than sitting in a studio and taking photos of spoiled movie stars. I ignore his remark in the same way I used to ignore my mama threatening she would take my sister to lunch after church instead of me if I didn't get dressed on time for the first hymn.

"It's not gross. He's just some poor guy who figured out his wife was meeting somebody a hundred and fifty pounds lighter than him."

"How would you know that?" he asks me. "You got some kind of sixth sense or something? You're not still talking to those dead people, are you? It creeps people out when you take pictures and do that, you know that right?"

"Dude, it was on the Channel 4 News this morning. His name's Jack Keenan. His wife was having an affair with her yoga instructor." I shake my head. "The yoga instructor confessed he hired a man to knock this guy off. He didn't think the job was done yet. The police couldn't figure out which parking lot he was supposed to be at. They were an hour too late—" And yes, I do talk to dead people. Where I grew up in the Southern mountains, we still held wakes in our house for days at a time when I was little and sit around with whoever was dead. We'd talk to the dead person just like they were alive. I vaguely recall, one time, my big brother saying something offhand about my old Uncle Ben after he died. He said he was nothing but a drunk. Mama's eyes had gotten as wide as two ripe tomatoes and she'd said: *Don't speak ill of the dead. They might hear you in heaven.* It was just how it was done. It's not like they ever talked back.

"So you'll do me a favor?" Abe interrupts my thoughts.

"Is that what this is all about?" I give Abe stink-eye, scrunch up my eyes as small as they get and let my lip twitch. Still, it's difficult to look mean with my almond-shaped eyes. They are already small like I'm smiling all the time. I've got what's called *hooded eyelids* in the fashion industry. There's a hundred tips online about how to fix them with makeup, disguise them to look bigger. It's just too much work. Besides, the nice thing about them is their size and shape covers up the abnormal shade of burnt orange of the iris.

Abe doesn't notice. Nor does he care about my eyes. Yeah, he doesn't answer. But he knows. Abe's got a smug look on his face while he rolls the window down and presses his wrist against his nose to protect it from the reek of dead body. Now I know why the cops waited five hours for my flight to come in.

"Pretty much. Somebody owed me a favor who

happened to be this dude's half-brother *and* a cop. And I told him if he was going to use this little rookie cop he had come in with one of those cheap cameras from the dollar store, the chick was going to miss something. Then, whoever killed him was going free." He shrugs it off. "If it was his sister-in-law, I understand now why he was willing to pay for your flight. He ripped her from one end of Texas to the other. Regardless, I told him you never miss anything." He doesn't even take a breath when he finishes with this: "Hey, while you're here, I need you to go to a few farms and take some pictures," he tells me while I flip my sandy-colored hair from my eyes.

"Here? In Texas?" My bangs are long. Ask me why. It is because I don't have time to get a hair trim. My hair is halfway down my back and the few strands of cotton candy pink highlights are starting to look like a four year-old's first stab at finger painting.

"No, it's farther north, a few hundred miles away."

"That's not here."

"I didn't say it was."

"Yes, you kind of implied it was here. You said: *while you're here—*"

"That's not what I meant, Piper. Will you do it or not?"

"Abe, I do nothing but favors for you. Every cruddy job you don't want to turn down ends up in my lap," I snap at him. A couple cops standing outside the yellow police tape eye me cautiously.

"Do you want me to send them to somebody else?" he asks me snottily in return. "Because I can. I've got a hundred photographers begging me to give them a chance."

"To take pictures of dead bodies while you sit in the car and gag?" I ask, but he's right. He's Abe Starling. If he put a call out for someone to take pictures of dirty diapers tossed on to hot August highways, he'd have forty people lining up to take the job. I would swear there isn't a magazine on the face of the earth that hasn't used one of his photos. I've seen hundreds of e-mails from professional photographers begging to work for him on one of his projects. "I just landed from the last job, Abe, that you handed me from the bottom of your pile of the worst jobs a photographer would want to take and that was taking pictures of old abandoned farm machinery at a junk yard outside Lansing, Michigan. I stepped into my apartment and the phone rang. It was you."

So while I stand there in my pajama shorts and fluffy boots covered by baby blue protective overalls and footies so I look like a giant baby in a paper onesie, I recognize Abe knows I jumped like an eager pup at a bone when he called and so much so, I didn't change my clothes. He is laughing secretly at me for kowtowing once again to his needs for one main reason—I am alone. And I hate to be alone. And he also comprehends I won't ask where he is sending me. That would suggest I might turn it down if it is something beneath most photographers.

"So ask me what it is, Piper."

"Um, what is it, Abe?" Yeah, I'm like a little fish poking at his baited hook.

"It's right up your alley. Midwest Farmers Magazine is run by Farmer's Outlet." He holds out his hand and dangles a magazine in front of me with the image of a cow's face on the cover. "They're wanting something fresh, something that appeals to the farmer and still sells their line of clothing. Jeans are in style, boots are in style, organic farming is in style. Their magazine is *not* in style. Look at this crap. An eighth grader in the yearbook club could do better. Sell us to them. They're looking for a new account, new ideas."

"I see a cow. Is this a joke?" I am actually wondering if he set this up just so he could pull a prank on me, make me the butt of some joke for nothing more than to entertain the bored, silly model sitting with him.

"No, I just know you came from a farm. You can do this, Piper, you're so artistic. If you can take a picture, you can write a story about it. Easy-peasy."

"Dude, that's like saying Picasso could write a horror story as good as Edgar Allen Poe's just because he's, well, imaginative. Painting and writing, photography and writing—they are two different things. And you're the only one who knows I mucked a million barn stalls so I'd like to keep it that way." I feel a tickle in my nose. I start to scratch my nose and realize I can't. It makes it itch worse. "I'm not a journalist, Abe. I'm a photographer."

"Did you not take journalism classes?"

"A few."

"And if you do this, I will be your best friend." He smiles with a teasing grin. "So you'll do it?"

"Of course, you know I will," I say with a smile and hide the terror I feel inside—I'll never have enough courage to break free from this idiot and step out into the unknown alone.

"I'll get you a flight and a car rental." He stops long enough to wag a hand at the driver. "By the way, it's in Kentucky."

"Kentucky? That's considered the South, right?" I snap my head up, take a few steps to follow the car as it slowly eases away. No, not Kentucky. I don't even want to work in the neighboring states around it for the fear that it is anywhere near the place I grew up.

"Well, they want it to start at the farthest edges of

what people might consider Midwest and work its way northward. They've got a lot of consumers in the surrounding states who buy farm clothes and supplies. For marketing purposes and because of the number of buyers for the magazine in the borderline states, they consider Kentucky in the soft South, so it can go either way."

"Where—in Kentucky?"

"About twenty-five minutes from Hazard."

"No." I'm shaking my head. "No, no—" But it is to the bumper of Abe's car while it speeds off. I toss my hands into the air, let them drop to my head and turn.

"Hey!" I turn to the sharp voice, see a cop poking his finger toward my feet.

"Oh, sorry, bud." I step back. "My bad. I suppose it sucks being stuck like this. I'll hurry, get it done." I almost trudged right over the dead guy. "I suppose your day's been worse than mine."

I look up just in time to see the cops snapping their eyes away. One leans into the other. I roll my eyes. I can imagine how crazy they'd think it was if they knew my Aunt Jeanie used to tell the bees in her hive everything that went on in our town, including making special visits to tell them of any deaths. Her little bees were supposed to help lead the dead in the right direction. "They just don't get it, do they, Jack?" I ask the body. Maybe he does. Maybe he doesn't. Regardless, he doesn't answer in return.

Chapter 2

Whispering Hollow, Kentucky and the Mystery Behind a Boy in an Old Photograph

I have frizzy, fine and long blonde hair and freckles. I'm five feet and eight inches and best described by my papaw as scrawny as a winter chicken. And although I'm a bit of a tomboy, I like to wear expensive dresses because we could never afford them, nor was it an option of buying them growing up on a mountain farm. It was always hand-me-down jeans, t-shirts, and cowboy boots. So now, while I'm donning an Ellen Crane Original little black slouchy dress and ankle boots, I stick out like a sore thumb in a room full of conservative farmers and Kentucky cowboys which is where I'm at right now executing Abe Starling's favor. It is the Whispering Hollow Community Building in downtown Whispering Hollow, population 1,210.

It is twenty-two minutes after standing at the little wooden podium and explaining to the small crowd settled in old metal chairs, that Spitfire Media Group is searching for a small town and farm to do a national photo shoot for a Midwestern magazine. There will be a media festival, thereafter, that is supposed to bring in over four-thousand tourists. Because the area is settled into a huge forest, Dark Pines, once mined for coal and then reclaimed as federal lands for public use, it has become a magnet for tourists and a goldmine for tourism businesses. It is also the type of area attracting wealthy retirees wanting to finally make their dream come true by buying a bit of property for a horse farm or cabin rental business or simply, to live the high-end rural life. Such, it is the perfect place for a growing farm clothing and supply company to set up shop and gain new upscale customers.

I am here to collect a list of farm owners, tourism agencies, and towns interested in hosting the event. Once I receive their information, I will visit and take photos of the farms and communities so Spitfire can choose which area to use. Well, that's what I tell them. What I don't tell them is I am supposed to recommend a farm and send Spitfire a detailed report and proposal, justifying my submission. Considering I had gotten mobbed at the first town I stopped in when I announced my intentions, there was no way I was making that mistake again.

I'm standing at a little card table that Mindy Greene, a county commissioner, set up for me. In front of me is an open lined paper notebook with thirty-eight lines out of the sixty-two filled with names. There is still a line of about twelve people waiting to sign up.

"So there's this many people trying out for the job?" There's an old guy standing in front of me with my pen in his hand. He introduced himself as Josif Landowski, didn't shake my hand. He's wiggling the pen back and forth with hesitation over the paper. He took off his hat when he spoke to me, a spotless cowboy hat that he's holding in his left hand at his chest. He's got thick, gray hair and blue smiling, shy eyes. He's wearing the kind of conservative, upmarket brand of camping and farm apparel that city people who have retired and moved to the country buy from the magazines selling high end clothing—designer flannel-lined khaki chinos, an expensive flannel button up, and duck boots. I'm sure he's probably wearing knit stockings even though it is deep into spring because, well, it is fashionable. He keeps staring timidly at the sheet, tapping his finger on the table.

"Yes, sir," I tell him. "And that's from here in Whispering Hollow. I've got one-hundred and forty-two farms and homesteads on my list from six other areas I've visited this week."

"Oh, so the odds are slim we'd get it."

"The odds would be approximately one-hundred and eighty to one, Grampa, including our town, give or take."

I let my eyes veer to the left of the man and one step behind. The voice comes from a younger version of the old guy. He's twenty-something, tall, toned and angry-eyed like a pit bull pup that just got its toes stepped on. He's one of probably thirty white collar twenty-somethings I've had to deal with this week. They all look alike, act alike, and have a haughty air about them.

"That's my grandson," the old man tells me with a grin and a proud tip to his chin. "He's smart, he is. He teaches at the high school here in town. He's a good boy. He's helping his old grandpappy out this summer instead of visiting with his mom and dad in Ohio like his younger brothers. The rest of the family moved up there last summer. My Ben, he stayed."

"I couldn't move, Grandpa, I had a job."

Grampa's favorite grandson has on a cowboy hat just like the old guy he's tapping with his knuckle. It disrupts my thoughts for a second. I'm not used to seeing cowboy hats on young guys even this far south. Oh, yeah, *soft* South.

I shrug. "Regardless, your odds would be the same as everybody else's." I let my eyes veer back to the older man. "Of course, they might better if you've got the type of property they are looking for to shoot."

"I think you'd have better chance of return of your money by tying a dollar bill to a helium balloon and releasing it in China," the younger man says and shifts, taking a step toward me, "*and* hoping it would make it to American investors in California, than banking on whatever company this woman's trying to hard sell us."

"I'm not really sure what hard selling is, but—" I start to defend myself. Is this guy an idiot? I'm not advertising a product, I'm giving them a chance for free publicity for their stupid farms so they can make a buck.

"High pressure salesmanship," the younger man interrupts. "Like a used car salesman with a bunch of lemons on his lot or a—"

"Listen, bud—"

"Benyamin, my name's Benyamin Landowski."

"Well, listen Benjamin Landowski—"

"It's Benyamin, not Benjamin—" he corrects me hotly. "Just leave it at Ben."

"Well, Benyamin or Ben, I'm a photographer. I'm here to take the pictures of the properties. I'm looking for people interested in renting their property for the pictures. I'm not a salesman. I'm not selling anything. I'm not even buying. I'm offering for free—"

"It sounds like you should be nice to this young woman." There's a second young man coming up beside Ben. He's standing just far enough away and with just the kind of business-suit strut I would expect from a city boy who has given up his city job to move to the country and start a bed and breakfast. He's probably hard strapped for paying off the loan and he's eking out the last of his mama's inheritance so he can tell his buddies back at his old haunt that he's got it all—life in the country, an ATV, and a wildly great investment that he'll pay off in three years so he can retire in Hawaii by thirty. "Hi, you're Piper LaRue?" As if I could have changed my name in the thirty minutes between the podium and table. He shoves out a hand, waits for me to shake it. "I'm Conner Williams with Williams Rental Properties. My family owns about five-hundred acres of rural property, each with cabins and cottages on the lots. We've got farm rentals, hunting cabins, and even barns with stalls for horses. I'm sure we don't even need to sign up. We're the answer to your prayers—"

I want to tell him finding the perfect property for the photo shoot is not even remotely close to something I would go so far as to pray to God about this week while I watch the two men in front of me turn and gaze at him. Honestly, if I felt that haughty, I'd ask for just one hot, home cooked meal and an entire night's sleep without the sound of trucks screeching down the highway and rude tourists banging their suitcases against my hotel door and screaming at their kids to be quiet. And unless he's carrying a plate of meatloaf and mashed potatoes in his handbag on his shoulder for me, he could take a hike—

I sigh. I don't say that. I just smile. "Regardless, Conner, you do need to sign up and fill out an application." I poke a finger at the paper in front of me. "I'd love to take a look at your properties. I'm an independent contractor. My opinions do not reflect the views of Spitfire, so they will be having the final say anyway. However, they will never get the chance unless you put your name right here."

"C'mon, Grampa, she's not even with the company," the grandson, Ben, mumbles while he tugs on the old man's arm. He's got that creamy, sweet Southern boy accent. It's as thick as frozen butter and deep like talking through a pipe. Home. It reminds me of the boys back home I grew up with and I can't help but feel my belly make a wistful jerk. "She doesn't know what she's talking about."

"Excuse me?" I bring my own head up, glare at Ben and his stupid accent. I'm tired. I love taking pictures. I hate trying to talk a snarling pup out of a bone he doesn't even want. I've spent two weeks driving from town to town, staring at ugly hotel ceilings and trying to gulp down gas station food. I've been staring at the same people over and over again. They just have different names, live in different towns. This dude is pushing me over the edge. "I know what I'm talking about. I have an eye for the product they are trying to obtain. Don't talk to me like I'm an idiot. I'm not. I took six years of college to learn what I do including two years with forensics and criminal science—"

"It took you six years to learn how to hold a camera to your face, focus, and press your finger to a button so it takes a picture?" He sniffs a chuckle under his breath. "Give me a camera. I can do that right now without a college degree."

I look left to right and nobody seems to think anything of this jerk verbally accosting me. One lady shifting papers in the line just rolls her eyes at him and gives me a knowing smile.

"What does a degree in photography have to do with police stuff?" There's a third young man to the left of Josif Landowski. He's another twenty-something but he's not another younger image of the elderly man. He's got sandy-colored hair and green eyes. He's smiling softly, though, looking from Ben and then to me. He ignores Conner Williams. "Yeah, I hate to admit it. I'm with Ben. Don't hold it against me. Are you a cop?"

"No, I'm hired by cops sometimes to take pictures of crime scenes."

"You've taken pictures of dead people?" He seems to chew on this a moment. He's sweet Southern boy, has his hands stuffed in his pockets. "That's pretty cool."

"It's not cool. The people are dead, Bucky, or dying, or a victim of a crime." Ben sighs. He's shaking his head, pulling his grandpa's arm. "So she's smart. Whoopee shit," he leans into the man and mumbles. "Is she going to take pictures of dead people here?"

"I heard that. I'm two feet away," I spit back. "And

although it may not be up your alley which is farming or working at the local feed store—"

"That's insulting," he remarks. "Is that a part of your job too?" He's got short, black hair and he rubs a hand across it, turns and seems to take in the door behind him like he's looking for an escape route if he needs it.

"I thought you worked at the feed store on the weekends, Ben," Conner has this little scrubby beard that he tugs on right then. He winks at me like I'm in on some joke, and he gives me a nod. "And you farm. So she isn't insulting you unless you are simply slighted because she's like holding your puppy head down to a puddle of pee because it is the only thing you've accomplished—"

"You're the photographer?" the older man quickly slips between myself and his grandson. His head shoots up. "A professional photographer? Can you look at a picture?"

"Um, I suppose." I'm still blinking at Conner. I am stunned he just said those words to Ben. I realize I've got my mouth slightly ajar in surprise. I slap it closed quickly.

"I mean, can you give me your honest opinion of a picture that might have a ghost in it?"

"Huh?" Oh, the picture. No. I groan inwardly, smile outwardly. "I mean, I have to be truthful, with photo manipulation programs nowadays, you can superimpose images—"

"This is an old one."

"Well," I feel like all eyes are on me. I usually have an eyebrow ring I tug on nervously in these situations. It isn't there. I took it off thinking I might alienate people here in the same way I tucked in the small section of pink hair I've got. "They could do it even back in the nineteenth century. In the 1860s, there was a photographer who took ghost pictures. He would take a photo of a living family member. After he processed it and showed it to the family, there would be one of their dead loved ones hovering above the person in the photo. It was thought he broke into the homes of people who'd recently had a death in the family and stole their old photos of the dead. He'd then take a photo of the living family and during development, insert the photograph of the deceased into the picture."

It doesn't deter the man from shifting a bit to the left, reaching into his back pocket and tugging out his wallet. He ignores the deep sigh of his grandson and opens the billfold wide and tugs out a small, black and white photo.

"This is my family from Germany. It is from 1941." He pokes a finger at a family posing on a yellowed picture. There's one little girl with brown braided hair who is perhaps one or two. There are two little boys between five or six, one with blonde hair and one with dark. On either side of the children is a man and woman. Near the back, a grandmotherly figure is standing stoic and proud. "That is my father's mother." He points to the older woman. "In front of her is my mother and father and my brother and sister." He pauses, wiggles a forefinger at a little boy with a mischievous grin. "The brown-headed boy is me, Josif, when I was seven. The little boy to my left is Aleksander, my little brother. He was a year and a half younger than me." He pauses. "You see his face?"

"I do," I answer. I look at the little boys and then I look at the older man.

He holds up a finger and digs into his wallet again. This time, he takes out an aged newspaper clipping. He unfolds it carefully and pushes it under my nose. "This—this is a newspaper from the Louisville Daily Tribune. It's a picture to sell war bonds. It's showing the same boy, right? My little brother."

I look at the picture. Then I look to the newspaper. The image is of a sailor and a little boy sitting in a soda shop. The boy in the newspaper and the boy in the image look almost identical, both with dimples and fine, light hair. The newspaper boy is slightly older, his face has elongated. "I suppose it could be him."

"My little brother died at the Nazi-run Jewish extermination camp in Treblinka, Poland in August of 1942. We were both in the ghetto of Warsaw in Poland. Our parents had died and he was living at the orphanage. I lived on the streets. A friend of my father's said he watched the soldiers march the orphans to a train August 6th of 1942 along with their guardian, Janusz Korczak. My brother was among those children. But, this newspaper is from September 8th, 1943."

I don't know what to say. It is awkward and silent while I politely look from the newspaper to the picture he is still holding out. They are all staring at me, I can feel it, waiting for an answer.

"You're suggesting it is him?" I ask. I reach for my thick, black glasses in my backpack. With all the flying I do, it's much easier to lug around a backpack with a change of clothes and my most expensive camera equipment. However, it is nowhere to be seen. "Crud." I whisper more to myself than the older man. "Do you see my purse?"

I'm forever losing my things, setting them down and going completely blank when I do it. I look up just in time to see Mister Landowski nod. He pokes a finger to six inches from my left foot.

"Your purse? Is that it? The backpack?"

"Um, yeah." My cheeks are sprayed with red. I bend down, dig out my glasses, and slip them on my nose. Then I take the images in my hand, look closer at the tiny faces. "I suppose if you get me copies of the newspaper and the picture, I can superimpose one over the other and maybe even age the face in the picture for a comparison to see if the two match."

"You can't just tell by looking at them?"

"You're asking me to tell you if I believe in ghosts or I believe in miracles, Mister Landowski." I smile up at the older man while I return the two delicate documents. "I'm not sure I believe in either."

"I told you, Grampa," the younger man says, nods to the back door.

Conner Williams seems to take this moment as his way of barging back into my personal space. I see him take one long step to the right side of the card table, edge closer while I'm watching the backs of the two leave.

"Hey," I call out. I'm not sure if the old man will turn or not. But he does, pivoting on his right foot and eyeing me curiously. "I want to believe," I tell him and shrug. He gets this funny smile on his lips like he's going to chuckle, but he doesn't.

"So, let's do supper," Conner interrupts the moment and I tear my eyes back to him. "I'll buy. We can talk photo shoot." He's tall and thin and is obviously used to getting what he wants.

"Conner, I really appreciate it. But I have supper already lined up," I lie while I try to imagine where I'm going to find food in the middle of boondocks Kentucky again. "Maybe another time." But I'm sure it's going to be another gas station.

Chapter 3

I Can't Seem to Escape Dead People . . .or Actually Catch a Flight on Time

There's a knock on the window of my car. It's raining. There are tiny dots of water glistening on the windshield, dancing reflections of two, slightly bowed security lights wavering with the wind over the wet buckled-asphalt parking lot of the Whispering Hollow Quick Stop and Carry Out where I'm parked. I'm confused for a moment, a bit out of whack. Where am I? Oh, yeah, after I got done with the meeting, I got a text that my flight out of the Louisville airport was cancelled. It was late so I just camped out for a few hours before I got another flight to Houston to meet with Abe and give him the information I have so far. Then, I return for one and a half more weeks of pictures before I'm done.

I groan, push myself up in the seat. I blink at the shadow outside. It's still the dusky gray right as the sun is getting ready to hit the horizon. Flashing lights, cop lights. Crap. I was sleeping so hard, I didn't even see the police cruiser pull into the lot.

I roll down the window, blink against the drizzle of rain popping me in the eyes. I can see gray shirt and black pants, a police radio strapped on a shoulder and a gun belt.

"Yeah, I know. I can't park here." I yawn into the back of my hand. I make out the features of a middle-aged man with a round face and tired eyes beneath a deep green Smoky Bear hat. "I'll go. My midnight flight out of Louisville International got cancelled because of the storm—give me two seconds, I'll wake up and catch another one this morning—" This morning. I look out. It's oozy gray still and maybe pushing six-thirty a.m.

"Piper LaRue?"

"Yes." I scoot up in the seat. It alarms me. I don't understand how he knows my name and why he's addressing me that way instead of *hey, you* like I might be a random homeless person looking for a place to set up house, because that's probably what I look like. The back seat of my car rental is loaded with my camera equipment, duffel bag for clothes and an odd assortment of blankets, pillows and fast food bags. I'm in a pair of yoga shorts, a tank top, and a beanie cap. I see his eyes roll from the top of my head to the bottom of my knee-socked feet.

"Yeah, I'm with the Whispering Hollow Police Department. Bill Phillips. Detective Bill Phillips." He shoves out a hand between us. I take it, shake it, and feel his hard gasp. I'm pleasantly surprised. My daddy used to tell me a firm grasp is a sign of respect. Of course, he also told me: *if common sense was lard, most people wouldn't be able to grease a pan.* Still, I don't take a solid handshake lightly. "Heard you are a certified crime scene photographer. Is that true?"

"Huh?" I mumble. I reach for my glasses on the dashboard, slide them over my nose. I focus on the man. He's clean cut, late thirties or maybe early forties and lives-in-a-subdivision/business-suit attractive. He's got a ruddy complexion, deep red hair and he's working on having big jowls in another ten years or so.

"Josif Landowski's down at the police station. He said you've done crime photos, got some kind of a degree. That true?"

"Oh, yeah." I yawn again. It's hard to be professional when I'm in my car with a pink and white kitty cat blanket draped over my scrawny shoulders. "I do."

"You got credentials?"

I blink and nod, still half asleep. "Yeah, of course." I reach toward the glovebox, halt my movements in mid grope of the glovebox latch. "I hope this doesn't ruin our budding relationship." I look up at him with a slight cringe. "I've got a handgun inside. It isn't loaded. I keep my paperwork with it. I was just on a job. You can call the city of Louisville or Houston or Cincinnati. But I've been to Cleveland and—I got reference letters with phone numbers."

"We got a mess on our hands, a real mess." He sighs deeply, plays a little with his fingers on his gun. "Well, Dark Pines has a mess. They're the town next to us. Our department covers for them because they aren't really a municipality anymore. It's mostly federal lands with little pockets of houses with folks who can't afford their own police force. And we can't afford to fly somebody in for this one." He wags a finger at my hand. "Just move slowly." He gives me a bit of a teasing eye roll. "You know, kind of like a first date in high school, don't go grabbing anything too fast. Let's see what you got."

Thirty minutes later, I'm slipping into a crisp, new white disposable protective suit—booties, hoodie, overalls and latex gloves. I'm balancing myself on a steep hillside. Detective Phillips had made the call, spent four minutes looking over my paperwork before he gave a bull-wag of his head and then helped me load my equipment in his cruiser. Now I'm standing about fifty feet outside of the town proper of Dark Pines. It was properly named. The entire region is settled in an old growth pine forest with a lake running through the middle. Detective Phillips says the fog rolls in along the mountains and covers the valley every day. It's always dark here, always layered with a smoky mist above and below. The defunct town, itself, is tucked into a little valley and isn't much more than a couple blocks of old brick buildings and toppling, abandoned houses.

Here, deep into the forest and along the main route between Whispering Hollow and Dark Pines, I'm standing in muddy knee-high grass and just below an old, curving gravel road that has a dented and bowed guardrail. A stone's throw behind me, there is a ramshackle cabin with two sides buckled in. Where it is settled, is the only flat place along this section of hill.

"You can see where the mud's slipped away." Detective Phillips is pointing to a thirty foot section of hillside about three steps from where I'm standing. "We found three bodies there, nothing but skeleton and pieces of clothing. The fresh body was almost at the guardrail like it had been dumped quickly. Annie Lynn was coming through here this morning delivering mail and saw a part of a bare foot. One of the sandals was found tossed a little farther. It is a brown high heel, cheap like you buy at a retail store. Not too high. Kind of like the ones girls wear to church."

"Pumps."

"Excuse me?"

"They're called pumps," I repeat, look up and catch his gaze. "There's stilettos and wedges and platforms, to name a few—shoe heel sizes. She was wearing pumps."

"Oh, you had me there. Thanks for the fashion lesson." The detective rolls his eyes, smiles.

"Anything I should know before I start taking the pictures, Detective Phillips, other than you're a comedian?" I ask. He snickers, shakes his head. I'm placing my camera on a modified tripod with an adapter, a painter's pole, so I can get some shots directly above the body. I've got my bag leftover from Louisville. I come prepared. I'm sure most don't, or they get their gear from their police departments.

I, however, have found that most small town police departments don't have enough crime scenes to warrant the major investment in gear.

"You can call me Bill."

"I like to keep it professional," I tell him without blinking. He just stares at me with a funny tip to his chin like I'm kidding.

"Yeah, I know," he mumbles. "First date jitters, right?"

I laugh and shake it off before snatching up a handful of disposable cones with little rules on the side for measurement and bare sections to number evidence with a marker. I can see the body from where I stand. It is a young woman with shoulder-length auburn hair. She's lying on her left side like she's just started to roll over in bed. Her left arm is under her head and straight. Her right arm is settled limply at her side until it rests at her belly. She's wearing a jean skirt that my mama would say was *too short for church* and her white blouse is buttoned to just above her breasts and has smudges of dirt. Her right foot is bare and black on the bottom like she's been running through old dirt. I'm guessing her age is between twenty and thirty, her height at five foot and two inches, and her weight at one -hundred and forty. She has soft, elf-like features and a chubby frame. And she smells like she has been dead more than a week.

"Okay, Detective Phillips is fine." He sighs and nods. "As soon as the officer saw the pieces of bone, he backed out and called dispatch. There's a set of shoe prints leading to the bodies that belong to him." The detective holds his finger out so I follow it to the imprints. "There are also set of footprints that are not his. He wears a size 12 men's shoes. The footprints look considerably smaller, maybe like your size. He believes he saw three skulls, brown and old."

"Three. Okay." I smile and take one step forward, trying not to look up at the small crowd forming near a line of cars and being held at bay by local police. He stops me with a hand.

"Miss LaRue." He nibbles his upper lip like calling me that particular name tastes a bit unusual on his tongue. He lowers his voice. "You should know four years ago, there was a car wreck right here. A young woman was found dead in the car. It hit the guardrail, flipped along the roadway and burst into flames. By the time the fire department arrived, she was burnt so badly we couldn't even use the teeth to identify her." I see his eyes veer up over my shoulder to the roadway. I follow his gaze and quickly turn it away when I realize he's pointing me to Josif and his grandson, Ben.

"You think there might be more evidence I should watch for that might impact this case? Car parts—?" I ask him. And I'm not sure if he's pointing a finger at the two men up there. Should I be looking for a piece of their clothing among the skeletal remains? "I'm not sure where this is heading."

"No, it was the girl that was dating Josif Landowski's grandson who wrecked here," Detective Phillips tells me. "Benyamin's fiancé. Josif seemed to know who you were when he came down to the station. He got a phone call from the mail carrier. I wasn't sure how well you know the family. I just thought you should be aware of this."

"I really don't know them at all." I shake my head. "We just talked at the community meeting in town. Somehow during the five minute conversation, it came up that I did crime photography."

"Alright, I'm calling you Jane. Jane Doe," I'm telling the body of the girl in a soft voice. "Sorry I don't know your real name. It'll have to do." I suppose I observe things differently than most people considering I spend most of my time looking at life through a camera lens. I'm incredibly focused. "She's got ligature marks on her neck. Look." I point out the green-red bruises halfway between jawline and collarbone to Detective Phillips. "There's been a rope or a cord tied around it. Oh, this is weird." Strangely, there is a layer of foundation makeup covering it. I can see the smudges through decayed skin. Decayed. "Somebody tried to cover it with makeup. And, I've got to be honest, this girl looks like she's been dead a couple weeks."

I don't make lazy scans of my surroundings until my attention settles on whatever in my visual perspective is most interesting at the moment—the prettiest face in a crowd, the most expensive car in the parking lot. I'm constantly searching for the little things that stick out, the interesting things like the tiny smile on someone's lips when everyone else around them is frowning.

"Stop! Don't move that!" Or like the way a driver's license which appears to be laying haphazardly against a dead woman's left thigh might have been placed there on purpose. I see four sets of surprised eyes look up at me.

My voice was loud, but I needed the four officers to stop immediately. One was holding a tarp to roll the victim over so I could get posterior pictures. Three had sunk down to a squat. A fifth was vomiting four steps away. Yeah, it wasn't just the gut-pummeling smell of death, but a few black beetles slipping out of the woman's right nostril. I've taken probably four-hundred images, each carefully set for scale and resolution, and the proper angles—bruises on her thighs, lesions on her neck, and puncture wounds near her forehead which may be insects. A gold bracelet on her wrist. I've got seven evidence marking cones laid out next to the victim. Now, it is eight.

"What's up, Miss LaRue?" Detective Phillips is standing back. He's got his eye on the crowd and he's helping hold up blue tarps to keep people from seeing what we're doing. There are six or seven primly dressed women and a couple suits who are complaining that the site might be an old cemetery.

"Anybody up there going to take a shot at me?" I ask him first. One churchy-looking woman in a modest dress keeps pacing up and down, stern-eyeing me with pursed lips. Detective Phillips follows my gaze. Then he leans in and tells me that's the mother of Jody Mills, the girl who died in the car accident here four years ago. She's a little loopy, but otherwise the only thing he's ever heard she's done is complain to the public schools about provocative books. She gets online and gives scathing reviews to books she finds religiously offensive. "I'm serious. She does. I've heard she's got a thousand anonymous accounts and she's proud of it. God's work, she calls it." He laughs.

"The devil's work, I'd call it. She does realize that she's breaking one of the Ten Commandments, right?" I toss out to him. "Bearing false witness to neighbors—spreading false reports."

"Well," he answers. "She feels she's protecting them because she couldn't protect her daughter. How do you know that? You're religious, huh?"

"Not necessarily. I fly a lot. When you're six miles up in the air and it gets a bit bumpy, people tend to become a tad bit religious." I grin at him. "I've probably heard more confessions and prayers than a first year priest." Two of the women keep hailing the detective, pursed lips telling him they are going to call the mining union. From what I've gathered, the area used to be a part of a historical mining town. They don't want anything else dug up.

"What was it you wanted to show me—Miss LaRue?"

He stifles a grin, steps forward along the little path we've made to keep the evidence from being contaminated.

"I know." I hold my hands up. "Don't say it. My name sounds like a porn star."

"God," he says with a funny grin to his lips while he swipes a hand over is brow. "Piper LaRue. I wasn't going to say it. But, yeah, it does."

"I'm glad we got that out of the way." I feign a grimace, then turn my attention to the girl. He hasn't mentioned anything about me talking to the Jane Doe, although I did catch him eyeing me carefully.

"This is what I want to show you. Look, there—" I point to the driver's license right before I slip out another ruler cone and take six carefully laid-out shots. The license looks ragged, completely unreadable, like it had been skimmed across a file over and over. It is sticking to bare skin and it is aligned perfectly with what appears to be a palm-size black tattoo of a black cat, its mouth wide open as if holding the smaller end of the card in its teeth. It is standing with tail erect. The image is incredibly detailed straight down to the fur. The skill level is consistent with a professional-level artist.

I scoot back where the detective is now squatting next to me. "It looks like the cat's holding the card in its teeth, see? I don't think it was tossed with the body. It's laying up right next to a tattoo on her left thigh like she was laid here carefully, then the card placed on her thigh in the cat's teeth. If you look closely, I think it matches up with it."

"Yeah, I see what you're saying." He leans forward on one hand, squints hard. "You don't think the body was dumped? You think it was placed here."

"A black cat is a warning in these parts," I mutter, wishing I didn't have to hint I knew this area enough to know its traditions. Maybe it will bounce off the detective and he'll just think I know the history. "You know that right?"

"I've heard tell." Did I see some knowing in his eyes?

"Yeah, you ever heard this saying?" I nibble my lip, look up through my hood at the detective. "If a black cat is seen in the morning, it is trying to give you warning. If a black cat crosses your path in the afternoon, turn three times or it means doom. If a black cat follows you at night, death will come before first light."

"So maybe this is a warning, huh?" Detective Phillips chews on the same thoughts while he tugs at his chin. "She was found in the morning."

"Well, it is what it is. I don't think somebody could have tossed her out of a vehicle and the driver's license could still be stuck to her skin. I don't think it's coincidence. The license is right in the cat's mouth." I reach in my pocket, tug out a pair gloves and hand them to Detective Phillips. "Go for it. Before we move her, let's see if it's glued on or stitched on or just stuck to her skin by body fluids."

He doesn't pull his gaze away quickly, kind of lets it lag on my face. "I think you like this, LaRue," he mutters while he tugs on the gloves and shimmies up to the body.

"I guess, I do. It's interesting. Better than taking pictures of naked models. After a while, they all start looking the same."

"Now, I find that form of thinking interesting," he tells me and barely sticks his forefinger on the plastic driver's license. It's dirty and smudged. "You like the dead better than the living." It plunges to the earth below. He reaches out, wiggles his fingers for an evidence baggie and I watch it fall into the depths.

"When you put it that way, it makes me sound

creepy," I sigh, turn my head to him. "It's just that dead people don't stab you in the back or have grand expectations for you." But he's still staring at the body. I let my gaze veer back up the hill to the people milling around. "Do you know anybody in the vicinity who follows the old customs?" I wiggle my nose, twist my head to look up at him through the white hoodie. "You know, hanging a horseshoe on the porch or knocking knuckles on a door to keep ghosts out?" Why does my nose always itch when I'm in the middle of taking pictures of dead people and I can't scratch it?

"Like an itchy nose means you're going to get a visitor?" The detective reaches out with his pen and pokes my nose where I'm wiggling it up and down. "You're kidding me, right?" he answers. He scans the body, waves the crew with his fingers to come over and work the body around so I can take pictures of the back. "LaRue, you're in the mountains. Even I get up out of bed with my right foot first in the morning. We're superstitious. It's in our blood. Call it what you like, but it's kept me alive this long."

I giggle. I hate to admit it. I get out of bed right foot first too. "Dark Pines, dead bodies, and a black cat," I mutter more to myself than Bill Phillips. I sigh, look out over the hillside. I haven't even finished taking pictures of the first body and I've been here three hours.

"You bored?" the detective teases me.

"Naw, just realized I'm going to miss another flight."

Chapter 4

Trying to Digest a Mummified Hotdog at Whispering Hollow Quick Stop and Carry Out

"Alright, Abe, I'm done." I'm staring at Abe's just-got-out-of-bed face in super slow-motion on my laptop in the Whispering Hollow Quick Stop and Carry Out. It is an old brick building that was probably a restaurant at one time. It has rows and rows of shelves with canned vegetables, plastic bags of diapers, motor oil, and one old lemon-yellow restaurant booth I'm sitting at with paperwork sprawled from one end to the other.

"Yeah, Piper, you just told me you're finished getting the pictures." I did. I returned, took another week's worth of photos and feel like I've gone full circle coming back through Whispering Hollow to get one last set of Williams Rental Properties. This was Abe's choice. It took all I had not to run off the farm with Conner's fake Southern drawl and his patronizing attitude.

"No, you're not listening. I'm having a bejeebas crisis. I've had it with these damn self-righteous, condescending, haughty small town cruds that would just as well stab their next door neighbor in the back to get five dollar's worth of free advertising for their rentals." I'm poking a forefinger at what appears to be a dehydrated hotdog the guy with EDDY embroidered on his shirt told me had been there since eleven this morning. He smelled like he hadn't worn deodorant in three weeks and his face had broken out in a hundred pimples from the amount of grease in his uncombed hair. He didn't even bother to offer me a fresh one. He just told me to take it or leave it and gave me a creepy leer from my knees to the top of my head. It's raining hard or I would have run back out to my car to eat it. The bun is hard and stale. I'm working myself up to eating it. I've had worse, but I'm thinking if my flight got delayed once, it might get delayed again. I don't want to be throwing up from food poisoning when I finally get out of this hell hole. "Abe, please don't make me ever come back here again."

"Piper, really?" he laughs at me from his cushy bed with thick white comforters and a gazillion toss pillows. "You've been to the Philippines after a tropical cyclone and Anchorage after a blizzard. You're being silly."

"Silly." I sigh. "You think?" I ask him. It is seven at night. "After shifting gears for a day from taking pictures of just about every farm in a fifty mile radius whose family signed up for the photo shoot, I got to take more crime photos here last week. Then back to finish this project. I'm done being dehumanized—"

"That's being a bit harsh. Folks in Kentucky aren't that bad."

"Really?" I thrust at him. "And you didn't have a local travel and visitor bureau guy chase you down in his car and threaten to have a lawsuit placed against you because you didn't take enough pictures of his horse barn. Somebody scratched a hex sign on the door of my car of a half-moon with a snake on it."

"What?"

"They do it to get rid of witches and Satan."

"That's funny, Piper, you're a witch. Oh, or Satan."

"Not funny. To make matters worse, there was a murder a town over. I ended up taking pictures. I know they are going to call me back to court for the case if they ever find the person who did it. I think Kentucky wants to suck me into its little hell. I'm done. Fire me. I honestly don't care." It's been quiet in the store. I think once in a while somebody gets gas outside. Three people have bought groceries and stopped to stare at me a minute. But it's a one stoplight town and I think everybody here goes to bed at nine. "I have not seen the inside of my apartment bedroom in seven months. I'm paying seven hundred dollars a month rent and I'm living in crappy old hotels and my car so I can take pictures of dead people, models that don't even have enough ass to push up the underwear they are—modeling, and now, fence posts and old farm houses. I'm going back to taking pictures of babies in Howard's Retail Outlet if I have to do it just so I can have a hanger to fly into once in a while. Goodbye."

"Baby, please don't get mad. You're living the dream, right? You get to travel and—"

"Don't *baby* me. You're sitting in Costa Rica or some beautiful place while I'm in boondocks Kentucky in the middle of a monsoon." He knows I grew up here and I never wanted to come back.

"Do they have monsoons in Kentucky?"

"No, shut up. I told you something's sucking out my brain here."

"Okay, then you're done. I'll call you a hotel room—"

"That's what I'm saying, Abe. There is one hotel here and it is out in the middle of nowhere and more like apartment rooms they rent out. When I drove past, the cops were there breaking up a fight. It's a frigging billboard advertisement for bedbugs, rats, and roaches. Anything close to the airport is full. There's no way in hell I'm staying at any of the rentals here because it is so cutthroat in this area, they might knock somebody off thinking I'm accepting a freebee in return for giving them a good word with Spitfire." I throw back my head in a silent testimony to my weaknesses. There aren't any jobs for me out there. I poke at one of probably nine-hundred pictures I've taken over the last week. "No, please, Abe," I sigh. "I'm sorry. It'd just be nice once in a while if somebody said thank you and meant it." And now I know I'm going to have to lower myself to all sorts of humiliation to save my ass so I'm not living in a box under the closest highway viaduct. "I need to get out of this state. You know what happened here last time. I can't be within a fifty mile radius of this place. I need a frigging cup of homemade vegetable soup and a good night's rest."

"How about Cancun?" he says. I know he sees he's got my attention. "You finish this one for me and I'll find you a job somewhere south of the border with a pool and a masseur and a guy who'll paint your toenails. Look here. This will make you feel better." He holds up his phone. He's got a picture of a fox jumping up into the air on all fours with its head down. "Isn't that cute. I got that last week on a trip."

"You're kidding me, right?" I huff. "That should have been my shot. I'm the one who likes cute stuff." I lean closer to the screen. I can see myself in the upper left corner and I look like a cat getting ready to snap up a mouse. "What's it doing?"

"Catching a mouse. It catches their scent even when they are deep in the grass. That's what my guide said."

"Yeah. You know, Abe, sometimes I feel more like that poor little mouse. You take pictures of cute stuff. I get dead people."

"Yeah, well, LaRue, you've got a knack for the crime scene photo business. That's why everybody calls you. What is the saying? You've got it coming and going—"

I suddenly get this strange feeling someone is behind me. I crane my head to the left, look over to see the old man from the Whispering Hollow community meeting and probably his family staring at me from the candy bar aisle next to the cash register. Oh, yeah, there's his surly grandson glaring at me before he shakes his head back and forth, leans in and mumbles something to the old man.

"Shit, got to go," I tell Abe and close the computer. I don't know how much of the conversation they heard. I see the old man, Josif, wave his hand at me like we're best friends from junior high and it's the first time we've seen each other in ten years. I give him a sloppy wave in return, then look at the time on the phone. I would give fifty bucks to avoid them so I pick up a pen, open the computer again and pretend to stare at something there. I sort of skipped about ten or so applications I just didn't think had the right kind of property for the shoot. Okay, I just got lazy partway down the list and started skipping some. Josif Landowski's property was one of them.

"Well, lookey who is still in town." He must have taken my superficial, hand-wag acknowledgement as an invitation. Less than twenty seconds after, he comes trudging around a potato chip display and stops at the end of the booth. He takes off his hat, holds it at his chest like he did last week and bends over slightly above me. "Oh, I don't know if I would eat that," he tells me looking at my hotdog laying limply there.

"You think?" I poke it with the pen in my hand. "I've eaten worse." I shrug. "I lost a bet and ate slugs. I put them in tomato soup."

"How'd that work for you?"

"Aw, it was disgusting," I tell him. "But I put on a happy face and acted like it was the best darn thing I'd ever eaten and got my prissy sister to eat it."

"Sweetie, why don't you come home with us and eat supper," he offers softly. "No slugs, no prehistoric hotdogs, just a home cooked meal. When was the last time you had a home cooked meal?" His brow is furrowed and he looks over his shoulder at an older woman with gray hair and tired eyes who is smiling at us.

I laugh gently. "Eight years ago this September," I kid with him. "When I left home. I can tell you what it was—meatloaf, sweet corn, and mashed potatoes."

"We'd love to have you. We're just getting done from church and—"

"I can't, but thank you. It could be considered accepting gratuities." I sigh. "I've had six people call in and complain about me already because they didn't have one thing or another Spitfire is looking for and I told them they had been eliminated. And I've got a flight to catch three and a half hours away in Louisville at seven in the morning. I'm planning on driving to the airport and sleeping in my rental."

"Then just take our name off the list," he says. He wiggles his fingers at the papers in front of me. "Problem solved."

"I can't answer any questions about the crime that occurred on Dark Pines Road," I say flatly.

"And we won't ask any questions," he's just as quick with the reply. "You can land at our house for the evening and catch a few winks, then get up at three or so. Lisette will make you some vegetable soup."

"Oh, no," I grimace. "You heard that?"

"Yes, we're not all condescending and haughty. And it's Sunday night. The gas station closes at eight."

I scrub my hands over my face. "You know what? Alright."

I'm kicking myself for my decision two hours and two huge bowls of homemade vegetable soup later. It isn't the soup or the homemade butternut squash muffins raising the regret. Nor is it the light chatter when I sit at the table eating while Josif Landowski tells me about his farm while his quiet wife stares with soft eyes at me. Actually, it occurs twenty minutes later and a brimming mug of hot chocolate with whipped cream on top and me doing my usual dorky moves when I'm around an attractive guy who, for some odd and puzzling reason, appeals to the part of my brain that does not make intelligent, adult decisions.

You'd think I wouldn't be prone to being that goofy girl who laughs too loud or trips on air when she's around good-looking guys considering I'm always taking their pictures. But I professionally turn the silly-crush button off when I'm working with them. I've had this happen one other time in my life. It was when I was seventeen. That particular relationship spiraled downward so fast and crashed and burned so disastrously, I swore I'd never let my emotions rule me again.

I'm heading down a little foyer between two open living rooms, one on either side and toward the front door. Just then, Ben Landowski makes an entrance through the door. He stops just one step inside the door frame. I'm ten steps away and holding my breath when I see him. He'd taken a separate car at the gas station. I'd hoped to completely avoid him by hiding in the cabin Josif had given me for the night, then leaving at four in the morning.

"What are you doing in my grandpa's house?" He stands there, looks me up and down with a smirk on his face. "Are you stealing stuff?"

But I'm already working a quick pivot on my feet, looking at my cup like I just remembered I had to fill it or something—or something, because it was already full until I turn and smack right into the wall to the left living room.

"Crap." I look down. Hot chocolate is splattered all over my arms, wrists, and shirt. It's dribbling to the wood floor, splattering a cute little rag rug with brown speckles.

I hear laughter behind me, sense a blazing fire shoot up into my cheeks. Skin the color of canary cabinet file folders does not hide the shameful aftermath of trying to time travel away and then actually not vanishing at all.

"Are you trying to avoid me?"

"Does it show?" I ask trying to swipe away the tan-brown from my shirt.

"Maybe considering you'd rather try to walk through a wall made of solid oak than come face to face with me. Do you think I killed them, is that it?"

"That hadn't crossed my mind. Should it?" I blink. What is wrong with me? I'm usually so focused like the automatic setting on my camera. "I mean, should I be worried?"

"I can't believe you just asked me that."

"You brought it up."

"No, I assumed someone told you something down at the police station."

"I told you I can't talk about it." I feel myself starting to sweat. "Where's the other dude, Bucky? Wasn't that his name?"

"He's at his apartment. Why do girls always ask that after we meet?"

Because *you've* got a crappy attitude. Bucky does not. I don't say that, though. "Because when I walk into a room that you're in, and I've only done it maybe four times, I feel like I have to announce my arrival as your archenemy and tell you I checked my gun at the door because you've got your emotional gun pointed at me ready to shoot."

"Wow, you are really annoying."

"What is going on in here?" The pad of stocking feet and the deep voice belong to Josif. I hold my chin up, jab a thumb at Ben.

"He's scaring me, Josif." I swing my head around, glare at Ben, then give the grandfather a pitiful gaze. "Make him stop."

"I think he can sense your fear, sweetheart, like that little fox your friend was showing you in the gas station."

I get the analogy. He is like a fox. And right now, I feel like that poor little mouse.

"Thanks, Grandpa, for comparing me to a predator." Ben turns to me, shakes his head. "Did you just—tattle on me?"

"I—I think I did." I wince. I'm rattled. I'm discombobulated. I absolutely hate being rattled and discombobulated. Did I just stutter? Okay, he's hot. I try to tell myself I take pictures of hot guys all the time. Big, hot guys and little hot guys and lots between. But Ben Landowski, he's got it—what did Abe call it? Oh yeah, Ben's got it coming and going. I mean, he's not just guy-down-the-street good-looking. Not the kind of odd, off-beat model good-looking that makes it to the movies because they can act, but it's more the charm that gets the girls buying tickets to see the show. It's the type of attractive that's tucked inside the magazines and selling guy's underwear because it's the girls looking at them. And it is from head to toe on this guy.

"You're a real piece of work, Pippy—is that your name, Pippy?"

"Piper," I correct him while his grandpa mumbles something about going to get a towel so I can clean myself up. "Yeah and if anybody's a piece of work, it's you," I spat back and it sounds even more stupid.

"Yeah, right." He just nods while his grandpa hands me a wet towel and smiles smugly. "But you've got it coming and going. Isn't that right?"

Chapter 5

Basketball Therapy with Ben Landowski

Boom-boom-boom-pop. That's the sound of the basketball bouncing against a section of lawn dotted with gravel that has slipped away from the drive. I'm bouncing the ball, dribbling it between my legs and doing the solo basketball dance around and around, and taking the shots. It's almost completely dark when I step back and away and aim at the hoop with graying net screwed to the side of the barn. There is one small, security light leaving a flimsy glow of yellow. However, every time I miss the hoop and hit the barn wall, the light wiggles and goes out for a second.

I've got my jams on low, earphones stuck in my ears. I knew it'd happen. It does every time I got to take pictures of somebody's dead person. I look at their eyes. Dull and hazy or sunken and nearly gone, I realize they'll never look back at everybody they've met and loved or who they'll never meet. Then, at about one in the morning, I wake up with this incredible sense of guilt and all's I can see are those eyes. Hundreds of them that I've taken pictures of at crime scenes. But tonight, it is twenty-four year-old Kayla Delray's eyes. They identified her from her driver's license. The last time the cops can find anybody who looked into those eyes when they were alive was twelve days ago when she got out of class at Basin School of Business two hours away in Berea, Kentucky. She walked out on to the rainy pavement and simply disappeared until eleven days ago.

So I go for a run. If I can't sweat all those eyes out of my head on nights like this, I play basketball. There's always a hoop somewhere around. The sound of the ball hitting the pavement soothes me. Focusing on the hoop and getting the shot, it takes my mind off—the eyes. The music, it covers the bases when my thoughts creep out, start to wander again.

But eyes are watching me. And they are very much alive. I don't see him there at first. Ben Landowski's standing in the oozy light until I miss the hoop, hit the wall. The light jiggles and I see a t-shirt and sweat pants. It startles me. I just stop, tug my earphones out lazily while he reaches out and catches the basketball.

"Too loud?" I look toward the house. It's a big and rich people kind of charming farmhouse, freshly painted a bright white. There's a lantern porch light on the wrap-around deck and wicker chairs beneath the porch roof. The lights are still out except for one in the downstairs bathroom. It's a couple stone's throws away. To my left, is the small cabin where I was trying to sleep. It is one of six working down a long, tree-lined lane.

"I dunno." He shrugs and tosses the ball back to me. His dark hair is sticking up on top of his head like he just woke up. He doesn't seem to care and he doesn't smile. "Just shoot."

I do for about five minutes and each time, he comes out and grabs the ball when it goes through the hoop or misses. Then he takes a shot himself from wherever he ends up, then tosses it back to me.

"Play with me."

"Play with you?" He rubs away a snicker with his hand across his lips. "Isn't that what we're doing now? Or do you mean like you against me? I don't know if that's a good idea."

"Because I'm a girl?"

"You want me to answer that?"

I wiggle my fingers at him, bounce the ball in front of

me. "I had seven brothers. I was in the middle. It was sink or swim at my house. I preferred to swim."

"If you get hurt, you gonna tattle on me again?"

"I might."

"I'll tell you what." He comes up to about an inch of the ball, doesn't try to grab it. "I make a basket, you tell me something about you. You make a basket, I tell you something about me." He squints, reaches out and pokes my shoulder with a finger. "Oh, why are you sweating so much?"

"I ran to town and back."

"No, you didn't. That's ten miles, city girl."

City girl? Where did that come from? "It's been a rough week. Yeah, I did." I bring the ball up, wiggling it in my hands. He doesn't reach for it, so I drop it, dribble it between my legs. But if he has a nickname for me, I've got one for him. "Are you going to play or not, *Possum*? I kind of don't like you. I want to smoke your ass."

"Possum?"

"Yeah, that's what you're gonna be when I get done with you, a dead opossum, you know, a road kill." I rock the ball hand to hand. Crap and he snatches the ball out of my fingers just like I was holding it out to him.

"So are you having a bejeebas crisis?" he asks. I stop long enough to stare at him hard.

"Where'd you hear that?"

"When you were in the gas station eating. You were telling somebody on your computer you were having a bejeebas crisis. What's that?"

"It's something that sets me off, something out of my control that sends me over the edge, I guess," I tell him. "Are you making fun of me?"

"No, not at all," he huffs. "My mom's all *bless her heart* and *Lord willing and the creek don't rise.* You try to hide an accent. I hear it."

"Blue. My favorite color's ocean blue." That's what I tell Ben on the first basket he makes. He looks at me, rolls his eyes and tosses the dang ball over his shoulder and makes a second basket while he's telling me *whoopee-shit.* "Gimme something more. Something I can dig my teeth into."

Crud, he's good, real good. "Um, that's easy." I push past him, snatch up the ball. "My entire life is like a bone waiting for a mean little pup to snatch up."

"I'm that mean pup today." He nods his head.

"Yeah, so chomp down on this. When I got on my phone tonight, my ex-boyfriend sent me a picture of him and his new *boyfriend* at a bar in Mexico. What the hell? Who does that? And yes, the new boyfriend is cuter than me." It's true. I had this guy I was dating. His name was Romeo and he was all red hair and freckles and modeled jeans which meant most of the time he was working out so he had big pec muscles because he was shirtless in all the advertisements he did. "Okay, here's weirder." I snatch up the phone, pull up the picture and hold the phone out for Ben. "He looks like me, right? He's—the boy-me."

"You're kidding me, right? A boy version of you, ha ha." He laughs while I toss my phone toward the ground and make the basket. "That's funny as hell."

"You think?" I roll my eyes. "I should have recognized there might be a problem with our relationship when we went to the beach and he didn't even try to wipe the sand off my butt for me." I laugh and Ben laughs and snatches the ball. "I told him that. He thought it was funny too."

"You're still friends?"

"Of course. We haven't dated in a year. We just keep each other posted on stuff."

"You don't think that it didn't have anything to do with maybe—you're like smart or something?"

"Because I'm smart? What's wrong with that? Guys like smart girls. My ex's new boyfriend is smart. He said my replacement was finishing a master's degree in art."

"I don't like smart girls. You make me uneasy."

"Because you have to work at a relationship?" I ask. "It's easier when a girl's dumb. You just have to hold up a stupid conversation. Yeah, I suppose I like dumb guys too. Same problem. *Not.*"

"Okay, you got a shot, so here's mine," he says. "I can better it. I've got a girlfriend and I haven't even kissed her yet."

"No way," I stop, hold my hands out. "Possum, you got to be kidding me. Are you churchy?"

"A little. Not as much as not kissing a girl would imply."

"I don't think I like this game." I stop and push a forefinger to my head like I'm pulling a trigger to a gun. "We sound like losers, you realize that, don't you?" He shoots the ball. It goes right in the rim.

And that's how it goes for about forty-five minutes, back and forth until we're more fighting over getting the ball than making baskets.

"Alright, I got nothing left to tell." I am laying on the ground on my back. It was like one second, I'm scooting the ball around him, the next he's lunging forward and BAM! I'm lying on the ground.

"I knew I shouldn't play with a girl. And one wearing glasses." He reaches down, picks up my black framed glasses and holds them over my face. "I stepped on them."

"And you did play me and I trounced your ass." I didn't. Far from it. He's like six and a half feet tall. I'm five and a half feet tall. That's an entire foot he's closer to the basket. It doesn't matter. I now know Ben's favorite thing to watch on TV is motocross, he's got an ATV, and a horse named Big Black. He broke his arm when he was six. He hasn't kissed the girl because he still isn't over his fiancé, maybe, maybe not. He's not sure if he's ready to take the step. And he knows everything down to my bra size which he had the audacity to say: *You're lying*, when I told him it was a 34b.

"I played basketball in high school, varsity all four years and intermural in college five years."

"No kidding," I mutter to his hand he's stretching out. I grab it, let him tow me up.

"You okay about taking the pictures of dead people?"

"Yeah, of course," I tell him. "I do it all the time. What makes you think—?"

"Why else would anybody be out shooting hoops at two in the morning?" He rubs his arm across his forehead, pushing away the sweat.

I'm quiet for a minute, go over and sit down on a wall of cinder blocks laid up along the barn. I stare at my glasses. The lenses are fine. The bar between them is cracked and bent a bit.

"You have a backup, City Girl?"

I don't know this guy, really, I mean other than playing this strange, unfriendly footsie game of questions with him. "No. I really don't need them," I say. It's true. My eyes are twenty-twenty. "I guess it's weird. I've got this fear that I'm going to go blind. It's not a phobia. I just think if I'm easy on them, I won't. My aunt went blind. Since my work depends on it, being a photographer—"

"It's the scariest thing that could happen to you."

"Yeah."

"Almost as irrational as the fear of kissing somebody because you're afraid you're going to kill them if you get attached to them." He stops, lowers his voice. "Because you have this horrible feeling you did something as little as taking a step toward the bedroom instead of the kitchen to twist fate the wrong direction the day somebody you love dies. Maybe if you didn't take that step—" Ben just stops there. He's got the ball. He's holding it and I can see he's pale as a spring cantaloupe.

"Have you ever told anybody that?" I ask.

"No. You ever tell anybody you don't need glasses?"

"No. Alright, give me the ball. Round two of Piper and Ben's therapy session that shall never leave the court," I tell him, holding out my hands so he'll toss it to me. "This one's dedicated to you, to everybody who's arrogant enough to believe they've got enough stock in God to sway decisions on people's fate—"

"I'm arrogant?" Ben gives me a haughty laugh and throws me the ball. I shoot, miss. "You're kidding me, right?" He turns and snatches the ball, makes an easy basket. "Oh, you are so on. I'm going to wipe you off the map."

"If you actually believe you had any control over a situation that a woman was in at the time she got into a car and drove away, yes," I tell him, driving forward and snatching up the ball before he can get it.

"Well, I was more implying that you are the one with the holier-than-thou attitude. A city girl all decked out in city clothes and a city attitude. You walk into town like some princess on a white horse in your designer car—"

"It's a rental with dents in the bumper." I stop, stare at him and roll my eyes. "Oh and an anti-witch hex sign."

"—acting like you can make or break every little business in this town or the next just by choosing which one's going to be in that stupid shoot."

"Is that why you're acting like such a jerk, Benyamin?" Now he's making me mad. "Because you're afraid I can make or break your family—or *you*?" His expression just drops. He's got this glaze to his eyes, a smirk to his lips. And damn, those lips are pretty. I see him reach out, try to snatch the ball out of my hands. I step back in just enough time, his hands hit the air. I let the ball bounce—once, twice and the third time, he reaches out. I make a quick snap of it between my legs and turn. "Na na na na, boo boo," I say. I don't know why I said it. It slips off my lips like a third grade bully. My little brother, Will, used to taunt me with that one. He was almost five years younger than me, quiet and ornery just like me. I miss him the most and wish his face didn't come to my mind right then. He was always tagging along, busting his knuckle in my back or getting into my stuff in my room. The last time I saw him, he was a face full of bruises and a black eye from getting in a fight at school.

Ben whips around me, but not before I dunk the ball from where I'm standing ten feet back. It's a good shot and I'm expecting him to walk away. I'm thinking this guy's a real crud and he's mad, so he's going to slip off into the dark. He doesn't. He just snaps around me, grabs the ball. And he plays hard with me. I'm sure he's holding back, restraining himself. I'm also sure that by the inflamed look on his face, I don't want him to let loose whatever fury he's got going inside him.

"Okay, that's it." I finally wave a hand, lean over with my hands on my knees. I know it has to be four in the morning. I am wiped out. Ben walks over to a spigot by the front of the barn, leans over and turns it on, gets a drink from it. I follow, get a drink when he's done. When I look up, wipe my mouth with my wrist, he's just staring down at me, expressionless and sweaty.

"We need this, my family," he says to me softly. "I'm sure I just blew any chance even if Grampa didn't already by telling you to take our names off the list." He leans over, shakes the sweat from his head and stares at me again. "We refinanced the loan on the farm to add six cabins. People don't come to Whispering Hollow. It wasn't the most brilliant idea I've ever had. I don't know what I was thinking, what Grandpa was thinking." He sighs, looks to the house. "I don't know. It's not just the money."

I don't know what to say to him. I just nod which probably isn't the nicest thing to do. Then I shrug. "I'm not the one who makes the choices," I tell him. "I just take the pictures." Now he's the one staring at me.

"I get it.

"Maybe if you would have let me win," I tease him. "You know, things might be different."

"I know better than that," he answers. "Then you'd just be insulted."

"You're right." I look at his eyes. They're deep blue and contrast with the darkness of his hair. Even when he's angry, they have a bit of smile in the corners like he's just one step away from a grin. If he notices I linger on them way too long, he doesn't say anything. I don't point out he was looking at my legs earlier and trying to hide it. I figure when I lay down and the lights go out in a few minutes, maybe I can shove away the dead eyes and concentrate on his very much alive ones.

"What are you staring at?" He takes the ball, acts like he's tossing it at me so I blink and take a step back. He reminds me so much of my brother when he does that, it almost makes me homesick.

"Your eyes," I just say it, wiggle my fingers in front of my face.

"What's wrong with them?" Ben asks, looking back and forth between my eyes.

"They're just—" I sigh. "—so alive, I guess."

"You're kidding me, right?" He snickers and shakes his head. "If the eye is the mirror to the soul, then what you're seeing isn't alive. I feel dead inside most of the time."

What a strange thing to say. I tip my head to the side. "Why do you say that?" I ask. "Because I've seen plenty of dead ones and the ones I am looking in aren't dead at all, Ben. Maybe just a little bitter. That's what brought me out here. Eyes. Dead eyes. The eyes of those I photograph for crime investigations. Trust me, your eyes aren't dead. Your soul is very much alive. I can see the difference."

Ben Landowski doesn't say anything else. He seems to chew on my words before he bounces the ball and shrugs. "Goodnight, Piper, I'm going to bed."

Chapter 6

Sticking Around Whispering Hollow

"Hey, there's been a change of plans. I need you to stick around—where are you at?"

I rub my eyes. For a minute, I'm not sure where I am. I recognize Abe's voice on the other end of my cell phone. That's where it ends. Wood walls. Soft bed. The sound of nothing creeping to my ears. Oh— "I'm—I'm in Whispering Hollow—what are you talking about?" I blink hard at the little clock radio by my bed to get the haze out of my eyes. "I have a flight in— oh, God, is it really eleven in the morning? I gotta get up."

"No, you don't. I'm sending a couple models up. It is Marcus Keating and Tessa Youngblood."

"I thought you had them on contract for the shoot you're doing in Orlando."

"Sure, yeah, I'd like to see them set up where you are. They fit the bill there. You need to get them from the Louisville airport at six. Pick a place and settle on it. Take some shots around town. I'll send you a list of Spitfire's requirements and the paperwork for the business to sign. I'm sending Kim for makeup. Keep them busy for a week."

"Keep them busy? Am I babysitting somebody?"

"Huh, what?" Abe mutters. "Are you sleeping in your car again?"

No, I'm not. I'm three inches deep in a soft king-size bed in a cabin at the Landowski's farm. I could live here forever, doused in thick comforters with a beautiful view of the mountains outside the window.

"Naw, I'm just tired. I couldn't sleep last night."

"New boyfriend?"

"No, Abe," I grunt. "So who is paying for all this?"

"You are. I paid for their flight tickets. The rest, put on your card. I'll reimburse you."

I growl. Then Abe goes about telling me all the stuff Spitfire needs for the shoot, including a gazebo. It's a country theme for a new line of clothing in a farm type magazine. But they want it to be high-end like for rich, organic farmers. I halfway listen, slide down in the bed and wiggle my toes. Is there such a thing as a rich farmer, I wonder? I peer out at the leather couch and the cute crafty cowboy lamps and decorations. There's one bedroom where I am and the rest of the cabin is an open kitchen, a living room and a fireplace. I don't know when the last time was that I got to sleep in, not worry about bedbugs at a crummy motel, and just lounge in bed. By the time Abe hangs up, I'm nodding off again and thinking it's crazy that I'm not up by seven in the morning.

Then there's the knock on the door. I groan, hoping whoever it is will go away. They don't. I see two shadows when I lean sideways on the bed and force myself to slide out. "Shit on a stick," I curse and pad my way to the door in my socks. I look down. They have holes in the toes.

"Eek!" And that's the message I get when I open the door and squint against the early sunshine outside. The air is a little cool. The sun, warm. It's Ben and he's poking a finger at my head while his grandpa gives him a warning glare. "Grampa, she's scaring me," he goes on in a whiny, high-pitched voice

I reach up and rub my hand through my hair. And yeah, my hair is sticking up all over. I wish I was one of those girls that didn't care. I do. "I took a shower and went to bed, Possum." I glare at him, turn my head down to my duffel bag on the floor by the door. I can see my beanie hat sitting on top and snatch it up, slam it down over my head.

"There, better?"

"No, because I know it's hiding under there and pretty much everywhere," he pipes back, wiggling a hand toward my hat and then working down to my shoulders where it is now making frizzy rivulets to my back.

I shake my head. "You know you insult me with every word you say."

"I know, cool huh?"

I turn to Josif and force a smile. "I'm sorry. I slept in."

He gives me a grin and reaches out, pats my shoulder. "You've been a busy girl, honey. No shame in that." He's got a plate in his other hand. That, he extends toward me. "We brought you some breakfast," he goes on while I take the plate in my fingers. Scrambled eggs, two pieces of bacon fried to a perfect crisp and toast with jelly.

"We kind of figured you were from the city and stuff so you were probably a bunny rabbit, you know a vegetarian. But Ben, here, remembered you were going for that hot dog at the gas station."

"Yeah, I grew up with meat and potatoes on the table at every meal. It's a hard habit to break."

"Billy Phillips called from the police station. He wanted you to stop by on your way out." He doesn't fail to notice I'm stuffing the bacon in my mouth and reaching for the toast. "He's got questions about the pictures."

"That's really good," I slur my words through the bites. "Did Missus Landowski make this?" Home cooked meals. I never get them. They must think I'm crazy. Both of them are tipping their heads to the right, furrowing their brows. "Sorry, I'm starving. It seems like I get nothing but gas station food—"

"*I* made it," Ben says.

"It's not poisoned, is it?"

Okay, I shouldn't have insulted him like that. It just popped out of my mouth, much to the surprise of the young man in front of me. I also should not be startled when he simply snatches the plate from my fingers and turns.

"Screw you, City Girl."

"Oh, I'm sorry," I say and follow him with little padded steps. "Please, please, please don't take it away."

"Ben," Josif chastises softly. "Be nice to the guest."

He wheels his head around, looks at his grandpa. I see the roll of his eyes before he shoves the plate toward me again. I snatch it up quickly before he changes his mind.

"He teaches during the school year and now he's going to cook for us in the summer in return for room and board," Josif says quickly while I snatch up the second piece of bacon. "He teaches English at the high school and coaches basketball. Our grandson, he's going to be a writer, aren't you?"

It's almost like Ben is uncomfortable with his grandpa's words while I look up at him. His cheeks are red.

"I don't know," he grunts noncommittedly. "Maybe."

"You should be a cook," I say while I snatch up the toast. "This is good. Where's your buddy, Bucky?" I say it just to make him mad.

"Why? You want a date with him?"

"No, I just figured he could interpret nicely what you say that is mean. Then we might get along. Remember, I like dumb guys."

"Ha ha, you're so funny. Not—"

"He made the jam, too," Josif interrupts whatever tart remark Ben is about to say. Then he wags a finger at me. "Will you look into that picture of my little brother when you have time and let me know what you think?"

"Yeah. Uh huh," I mumble past the toast, wag a fork with my hand. "Bring them over. I'll scan them." My eyes are veering outward. The farm, it looks like a real farm, like the kind people see in books. I look out, I can see cows dappling the fields and a little copse of pines right before the mountain climbs upward.

"I went to the library this morning and made a copy of both." Josif looks at me proudly. He brings up his hand. He's clasping a tan folder which he thrusts at me.

I take it slowly, trying to juggle my plate at the same time. I opt for stuffing the folder between ribs and arm so I can eat. "So, I need two more cabins for a couple weeks. You got openings?"

"Sweetie, we are wide open."

"And how difficult would it be to build a gazebo back there?" I ask Josif just as my cell phone rings. I hold up a finger. "Hold that thought." Then I work my way back to the bedroom and snatch up the phone.

"Miss LaRue."

"Detective Phillips," I return. "And I know you're getting a goofy little smile on your lips and trying desperately to remain professional when you say my name."

"You are perceptive. You should have been a police officer."

"No, I have too much empathy, even for bad guys. In my mind, I'm always taking them back a few years and see them selflessly trying to save their families from dying of starvation and robbing banks and so, it seems okay whatever act of violence they've done. I'd make a really bad partner."

"Oh, well, with that in mind, I'd still like to pick your brain about something," he says. "You up for coffee?"

"I got to be at the Louisville International Airport by

five-thirty or six, Low Po, so I got to leave about two—"

"Low Po?"

"Yeah, Low Pro Po. Low Profile Cop. Good gosh, where have you been hiding? It's an undercover cop. I just shortened it. You know, police on the low. Or, I guess it could be *laugh our pants off.* Oh, nevermind. Well, I'll ride with you. We can talk."

"So does this mean we get to have the photo shoot here?" It takes Josif Landowski ten minutes to absorb what I meant about building a gazebo. "Or are you just staying here?"

"I'm sorry." I blink, realize I was in the middle of telling them when the detective called. "Yeah, yeah. Both. It's the perfect setting. I've got to leave to pick up a couple models for the shoot in about twenty minutes. They need a cabin each. For a week. Can you swing that?"

"Yes, dear." I think he's going to hug me. I must get a wild look to my eyes because he steps back. "This is awful quick. Is this the way things work in this business?"

"Yeah," I lie. Not about being quick, but about not telling them I think Abe has ulterior motives with this situation.

Still, not everybody is on board. I don't quite get to the front porch of the cabin when Ben jogs up behind me and stops with his hand on the wooden railing leading up the two little steps to the porch. "Yeah, I don't know about all this," he says while he turns his head, peers around to his grandpa walking back to the farm house. "He—he's a retired teacher and a farmer, Piper. He doesn't know about all the stuff involved."

"There's not much to it, Ben," I tell him. "I take a bunch of photos. You really don't do anything at all."

"We got muddy pasture and old barns. I know everybody else has immaculate settings. We can't afford to lose money, you get that right? We are like—" He sighs. "—Grandpa, he's living right on the edge of losing it all. I mean, this isn't going to bring anybody into our cabins. I know that. You want a gazebo? I don't know if he even has twenty bucks in his savings to get one. And I know he's going to go down to Billings Hardware and buy one on credit."

"Are you making the call, then?" I ask him. "I need to know right now because there are fifty other people out there that want this job. Conner Williams is probably top on that list—"

"Yeah, I suppose it wouldn't be a big investment for him. He's big city like you—"

"I don't want to work with him." I don't. I couldn't imagine two weeks of dealing with a rich, snotty brat. Ben just looks up like he's surprised and not sure I really said those words.

"You don't want to work with him?"

"I don't think he'd swallow his pride and let me win a basketball game against him at two-thirty in the morning," I grunt. "Heck, I don't even think they have a basketball hoop on their property."

"You're doing this because I played a game of ball with you in the middle of the night?" he asks. "And I didn't let you win."

"I don't know, Ben, I really don't know." I throw up my hands to my sides and shrug. "I just don't know. Just decide. I'm going to Louisville. Talk it over with your grandpa. Let me know. I'll leave you my cell phone number. Text me."

Chapter 7

The Story Behind Black Jack

It is actually twelve-fifteen when we leave. I tugged out the folder Josif gave me and stared at it long and hard after my shower and while I dried my hair. The boy is sitting on a barstool in a fountain shop or maybe a drugstore. There's a little sign above his head. I squint, try to make out what it says. *Fourth Street Diner.*

"Do you have a way to pull some pictures in a sequence from 1943?" I am asking a dull-toned woman who picked up the phone from the archives of the Louisville Daily Tribune. I get nothing. There's this long, drawn out silence.

"Are you still there?" I ask.

"You're kidding me, right?" she finally answers.

"No," I tell her. "It's from the Wednesday, September 8th, 1943 newspaper. It's a picture of a boy and a sailor in a diner. It says *Victory Starts at Home* at the top and *Buy US War Bonds* along the bottom."

"That'd be our advertising department."

"No, I've already been to them. Your history section sent me to them, advertisements sent me to you."

"Hang on."

Hang on. So I did sit there with bland music playing in the phone, thinking that surely this wasn't going to happen. Then a man picks up the phone where the dull-toned woman left off.

"Rita tells me you're looking for pictures from 1943. Albert Kline did all those advertisements, won some awards for them," he tells me. "All his shots are in his private collection. It was donated to the Hanes Historic Society."

"Are they open today?"

"I can get you the number."

"So they are telling me we don't have a serial killer," Detective Phillips tells me this while I hit the gas to get on Kentucky 15 twenty-five minutes later. It's a highway straight up one mountain and then down another. He's got on sporty aftershave and he's freshly shaved. "The skulls and bones you took pictures of were probably from an old cemetery there. Well, not actually a cemetery. Dark Pines used to be an old coal mining town set up by Black Jack Mining Company. Even though the mine was only around for about thirty years, the town's been around from 1867 to 1958. There were shacks all over that hillside for families. People back in the olden days, they just buried their own wherever they could. Don't even know if we could identify who it was buried there. Folks, they came and went and the company had maybe 200 or 400 employees at any given time."

"That's kind of big."

He wags his head over and gives me a funny grin. "Ask me how I know all that. No don't. Growing up here, there was only once place we took field trips every year from kindergarten through high school. It was the Whispering Hollow Historical Society Museum." He turns back to looking out the windshield. "But my point is this. In that little cabin, there were probably twenty or more families staying there over the course of the mine being open." He sighs, pulls out a folder and opens it. "The coroner just thinks the newest victim was dumped."

"Dumped." I shake my head. I'm wondering about my sanity letting him come along. Three hours of cop talk. I'm only a half hour into the trip. The first twenty minutes and while I felt my stomach lurch along the twisty-turny roads, he gave me the details on the autopsy the coroner had started on one of the three skulls found on the hillside with the body of Kayla Delray. I'm not sure if I get paid enough for this. Hell's bells, I'm probably not getting paid at all.

"What do *you* think?" I ask. Trucks are everywhere, slow up the mountains, fast down the other side.

"What do I think?" he laughs quietly. "I think I'd love to just move on, figure the girl was some druggie or gang member. Not so. She's a college student with good grades. Off the record, LaRue," he grins slyly at me when he says my name. "I wouldn't be surprised if it was a serial killer."

"What makes you say that?"

"Until I know differently, I look at everything like it's a crime. Until the case is solved, everybody's a criminal."

"That's nice to know," I say and flash him a smile. "Except me, right?"

"I don't know, you got an alibi for the three Jane or John Doe remains on the hillside?" he asks me, tries to appear stoic.

"Yeah, I wasn't born yet?"

"How old are you, LaRue?" he asks me. "What'd you do, start college at ten?"

"I started college at seventeen. I left home, got my GED, and went straight to school," I tell him. "I'm twenty-six."

"Damn. I was hoping you were older." He sits back in the seat and shrugs. "I guess you look young. It's the glasses."

"Why were you hoping I was older?" I ask, then realize that maybe the two of us riding together isn't just a prolonged business meeting. Ah, hence the aftershave, button-up shirt, and fresh haircut. "Oh."

He gives me a crooked smile and shrug. "So, after he started examining the first skull and felt it had been there at least fifty years, the coroner decided to leave the two remaining skeletal remains where they are," he says, switching gears suddenly. "He contends it is a cemetery and doesn't want to cause any controversy among the old miners, the churches, and folks that just want to see their kin rest in peace forever."

"Did he even bother to do an autopsy to see if there were any signs of a crime? Because two skulls had small square holes."

"No, he's not doing an autopsy. He says to leave sleeping dogs lay. I saw your pictures. I saw your evidence markers."

"And you've got no say?"

"The bodies have been there—anywhere from almost a hundred years ago to a few years ago."

"We don't know if the bodies have been there long," I tell him. Then I sigh. "Nevermind, I shouldn't get involved."

"LaRue, you're singing to the choir, here," Detective Phillips tells me. "There are three skeletons. I suggested that there may be more. I don't think they care if there are more. They don't want Dark Pines to get a bad name."

I laugh aloud and he looks at me strangely. "Dark Pines?" I ask him. "C'mon, it just sounds like someplace begging for a horror movie to be shot there."

"You don't know the story?" Detective Phillips leans back in his seat, gets a smug smile and rolls his eyes. "I'd figured somebody'd said something to you by now."

"Story?"

"So Dark Pines, it didn't always go by that name. It was Black Jack, you know for the mining company." He looks out on the road while I drive. "The Black Jack Mining Company was started by a man named Dexter Black. He came in and bought out all the land in the hollow there, Dark Pines Hollow, back around 1866. He built a house on top of the hill, brought his only kin out, a twenty year-old wife, to live with him there. People didn't want to sell, but he was very—coercive, kind of bullied them out of their homes with threats. All except one. There was one old lady that lived in the hollow in a little cabin with a bunch of cats and she refused to leave. She was a widow of the civil war and I guess her husband had left her the land. When Dexter Black sent some of his boys out that were building houses for the miners to threaten her, she started screaming she'd put a curse on them. She had this little doll in her hand she'd made of pine sticks and pine needles and she kept waving it at them saying she'd sent out Stick Man to get them."

"Stick Man." I chew on the words while I pass a truck, let my eyes veer toward Detective Phillips. I'd heard of Stick Man before. I don't tell him that.

"Her cats started coming up missing, well, all but one black one that always stayed on her porch," he goes on. "And one day, the little old lady disappears too. Now some folks believed she had a son that came and got her and she moved to Lexington. Others though, believe Dexter had her murdered so he could get her house. Because one night, his wife told him she saw a man outside her window."

"Oh, God, please don't tell me—"

"It was a dark-suited man that looked like he was made of sticks."

"Did she die?"

"She did." Detective Phillips makes an eerie whistle with his lips. I giggle. "So whenever somebody used to die in the mining camp, they'd say whoever died had a black cat cross their path the day before. On the day of the death, each person who died saw a dark figure at their window and blamed it on Stick Man."

"Well, I'm glad that the dead girl had a black cat on her leg and not a stick man," I sniff. I look over, take Detective Phillips in with my eyes. He's staring at the windshield. Then he tips his head.

"A black cat. Do you realize what you just said?" he asks me. "Piper—I mean, Miss LaRue. The black cat. I mean, I'm sure lots of girls have tattoos of cats on them. But what are the odds they get dumped in the exact place where this old legend originated?"

"I don't know." I shrug. "Did I tell you we're stopping at the historical society in Louisville before we get to the airport?"

"Lead on," he says, leaning back in the seat. "Anything's better than the single's meeting at Mount Laurel Unity Church. I'm not into mingling with a bunch of women I've known since high school and didn't want to date back then because they were ugly and chubby, much less now that they're a hundred pounds fatter and starting to wrinkle."

"Are we—on a date?" I let his callous words slip off me and focus on what he didn't say, but implied.

"I kind of thought this was like our first date." He gives me a silly, cocky grin. "I like to get things out of the way, you know the awkward dance, skip the crazy bullcrap. Then we can get down to business."

"Business?"

"C'mon, LaRue, you're smart, figure it out."

"I kind of like the awkward dance," I mumble.

"Um." That's what he says, *um*. What does that mean?

Chapter 8

Pictures with Clues

There's a box waiting for me at the Hanes Historical Society, a privately supported organization whose main job is to take old historic newspapers and images in Kentucky and place them in online archives. Detective Phillips and I have to wear white gloves to sift through the images. There are hundreds and hundreds of them categorized by date.

"Here, I found something." It is half past five when I dig out the fifth of eighteen images shot on a parade route along Fourth Street on September 8th, 1943. I don't realize they are a sequence of shots for a war bond parade until I hit the jackpot right in the middle with the exact picture from the newspaper of the boy and sailor. There are six or seven of the parade—military men marching along Fourth Street, then several of two little boys sitting on a curb watching the parade. Bingo. One of the little boys matches the boy in the Fourth Street Diner. I pan upward in the next image and there's a sign that says: Boston Shoe Company and across the street is Fourth Street Diner. The two boys are in the image, too, along with a nicely dressed couple who are standing behind them at the parade waving.

"So what are you going to do with your little clues?" Detective Phillips asks me after they've been scanned on a little travel drive for me. We're leaving at a fast pace, trying to get to the airport on time to pick up Tessa and Marcus. I'm a little suspicious Abe sent them to me for this shoot. They are mid-twenties and experienced, a bit older than what Spitfire is looking for in their article. They don't look country, they look like two magazine models for high end, hipster clothing. Everybody wants eighteen year-olds—no wrinkles, no fat, and they don't fit the farming bill.

"You're the detective, what do you suggest?" I toss back at him. He keeps eyeing the empty space between us like he wants to move over. I plopped down my backpack there hoping he took the hint.

"I dunno. I've heard Josif's story. I can't imagine an adult escaping a concentration camp and showing up in Louisville, Kentucky, much less a child." He is quiet, scrunches up his face like people do when they talk about things they'd rather leave unsaid. "And it was Treblinka where they took the orphans from the ghetto where he was living, the Warsaw Ghetto. Treblinka wasn't a concentration camp like some of the others, it was a *death* camp. They didn't take folks there to live. Josif told me they took people from the Warsaw Ghetto, promising a better life in the country. They put them on a train and it stopped at a little town called Treblinka. There, the Jews were divided by male or female, stripped down and told they were going to a bath house. They weren't bath houses. They were gas chambers."

"So you think he is looking for a ghost?"

"I want to believe he's not," the detective tells me. "I don't know. It just doesn't happen much in my field. By the time a story gets to me, it is the end of the road for the person I'm investigating. I start at the dead and work back. Maybe, Piper, it would be better to just leave it alone. I think that's what everybody kind of does when Josif starts talking. They kind of think finding the truth is worse than hanging on to the dream he's alive."

"Isn't it the truth people want, whether he's dead or alive? You've probably heard it— *At least we know now.*"

"Yeah, I guess. I haven't been there. I don't know how folks actually feel after they find out the truth when they are laying in their beds at night three months afterward or even ten years later. I'm sure it cuts whatever horrors they are imagining their loved one suffers in half—you know, maybe they are still alive and enduring some horrible fate. Now they know the person is dead and it only leaves what suffering they had to that point. But I suppose, too, it forces all that energy to the side of knowing the person is dead and focusing the attention on what atrocities occurred. I don't know if I'd want to relive the ten minutes from train to gas chamber over and over, imagining a child's face the moment they realize they can't breathe."

"You're not being very helpful," I mutter with a roll of my eyes.

"And I think your decision is already made, Miss LaRue."

He is correct. My decision was made the moment Josif Landowski stuck that newspaper article in my hand. We don't talk about it any farther. I know Detective Phillips wishes I would drop it. He knows I wish he would pipe up and give me a pointer or two on where to go from here. It isn't quiet in the car, though, while we drive to the airport. Detective Phillips likes Bluegrass music and he jams with it playing air guitar or air banjo while I laugh and dance along.

He's good company. At least, until we get the two models from the airport. And I can't say the same thing for Marcus Keating and Tessa Youngblood the moment they get into the car. He's blonde-haired, buff-skinny, and doesn't look up from his phone once to make eye contact. She's blonde-haired, bony-skinny, and always looking around to make sure she's the center of everybody's attention.

"What hell are you bringing us to?" Tessa giggles into her hand while she looks out the window when we finally get back on the highway forty miles from Louisville.

Detective Phillips has a goofy grin on his face and keeps looking into the back seat.

"So you're a real, live model like the kind in magazines?" he fires off at her.

"Yes. I'm on contract with the Gin Harper Agency for now," she answers. "I've been in two commercials and I've played a dead girl in a horror show." She looks over to Marcus and he's got his earphones on and is still staring at his phone. "I told my agent that I want to be in movies now. We're working on movies."

Small talk. I let them take over the conversation while I drive. My mind's on other things anyway—stick men, black cats, and dead girl eyes. And a little boy who can make or break an old man's dreams.

My phone wiggles on mute with a text. I'm scared to look at it. I'm not afraid Abe's left me a message to do another job for him between the ones I'm already doing. I'm not even scared that it's the police station in Whispering Hollow or Louisville and they need more pictures. I'm thinking it might be Ben Landowski to tell me we'd better find someplace else to stay for a couple weeks.

When I take an exit to fuel up, I check the messages after I pump the gas. There's one from Ben Landowski and I find it incredibly discomfiting that I'm afraid to read it. Why? I don't know. I guess I do. Because when I scan down, make out the words—*Hey. We're in*—I'm not indifferent like I always am with working one of Abe's jobs from hell that he's passed off to me. My tummy makes this funny jump-tickle.

"That's a mischievous grin if I've ever seen one." Detective Phillips passes me while I'm staring at the text, getting ready to open the driver's side door. I look up from my phone. He's sipping on a soda. "Good news?"

"Yeah," I answer. I'm smiling too. "I guess so."

Chapter 9
The Legend of Dark Piney Falls

"You ride horses?"

Ben is slapping a pair of tan, leather gloves on his knee when I come out of my cabin a stone's throw from the barn the next morning. He's just outside the barn, saddling up a huge bay quarter horse. He's got a funny grin on his face like he's getting ready to tell me a joke and the punchline's so funny, he can't hold back the laugh.

"Maybe."

"Yeah, right, City Girl." He laughs like he is holding off that punchline for as long as he can because maybe I won't get it and it's going to ruin the whole joke by explaining it. "You do know what a horsey is, right? Big. Four legs and hooves. This?" He pats the horse's neck and she turns, nuzzles his shoulder.

"You know what?" I let my face stay deadpan. "You're right. I haven't ridden one. I knew you'd make fun of me. So go for it."

"No, I'm not going to make fun of you," he says. "I just thought you might want to go for a ride. Grampa's got six dead broke horses so we can take our cabin people out for a ride. You know, that's kind of his thing. He advertises for people who want a real farm stay. Horseback rides. Country cooking. We've got a couple petting zoo donkeys, pygmy goats, sheep, a llama, and twelve cows we rescued from the slaughterhouse that are fat and lazy up on the hill. Oh and pigs. We've got five of them."

"It doesn't sound much like a farm stay if you're not going to milk the cows or make bacon out of the bulls." I use one finger to roll back my hair and cock my head like the silly girls selling sexy panties in the commercials do. He doesn't know I'm teasing him on purpose. I have to wonder the kind of dingbats he dates.

"Well, first of all, you don't make bacon out of bulls. You make bacon out of pigs." His voice is so condescending. "The difference between real farming and what city folk like you want to see is that we just have a bunch of animals that are more like pets than the reality of the situation. We don't want the humane society knocking on our door because we slaughtered a pig in front of the kids and marred them for life."

I grew up on a farm. I watched my papaw slaughter pigs and chickens and once a year, turkeys and a cow. I suppose for folks who haven't seen it before, it's a bit disturbing. But I was taught if you didn't kill them, you couldn't eat them. If you didn't eat, you'd die. Easy-peasy. I don't tell Ben this. Instead, I shake my head. "I'll pass. Thanks."

"Listen, you don't even have to ride on your own. You can ride with me. I'm going to the waterfall at Dark Pines. I'm checking the trails to make sure they're safe to take riders on. I asked both of your friends and neither—"

"They aren't my friends. They are the models for the shoot. You know, the marketing material."

"That's cold."

"Okay, no not really. They get paid to look perfect. No bruises, no messed up hair. No fat, no cellulite, and no wrinkles or they lose their job. They go to bed early, don't eat. It's not a lifestyle. It's a career. Just like your grandpa would lose his job if he slaughtered a cow for the company."

"Whatever. But our trails hook up with the federal land trails. You ever heard of Piney Falls?"

"No. Is this another joke?"

"No, it's not, City Girl," he laughs. "Bring your camera. It's beautiful. Maybe you can use them for your photo shoot."

My ex-boyfriend always told me I'm like one of the crime scenes I photograph. There's caution tape around my heart that says: DO NOT ENTER. I know he's right. I make a conscious effort of trying not to push other people away. Still, it is always there like the big, white elephant in a teeny weeny room. Like now while the horse digs his hooves into the worn dirt of the trail and tromps into a stand of thick, dark green pines.

"Would you quit squirming?" Ben has told me this four times in the last five minutes while I ride in front of him, my back to his belly and my digital camera banging hard against my chest. "I promise you we won't wreck." He thinks it's funny that I used that for the last excuse when I tried to scoot up and almost got impaled by the saddle horn. I can't help it. We're packed in like sardines on the saddle and he's close, way too close for me to be comfortable. His chest is pressed to my back. His man front is pressed to my woman rear. His arms are around me. In fact, I don't even know if I got this close to my last boyfriend and I tell him that. He laughs. "I'll keep that in mind."

What does that mean? I don't know. Ben Landowski discombobulates me. I'm around attractive people all the time. I'm not usually sidetracked by the way a person looks. I'm more concerned they fit the picture of what my clients are looking for in a product they are selling. Because truly, everybody has their idea of beauty. However, Ben, he's distracting me. He's not the usual, run of the mill pretty. He's got this charm, this slow Southern drawl. He's got these eyes that test me, lay into mine for a second before he peels them away.

"He's an idiot."

"Did you just call me an idiot?"

I did. I blink. I didn't mean to say it aloud. "No, I'm just talking about my boss."

"You work for someone?"

"Well, I do contract work for someone—Abe Starling. If you read a magazine or watch a movie and see a picture fly by in the credits, he's the one behind most of the images used for the storylines. He's the clearing house in his office. I'm kind of his go-to person."

"Like on the commercial with the horses playing in the Alaska skyline that flash through so fast, it's like a thirty second movie—"

"Buy-Right Across the Continent Flights," I nod. "Yeah, I did those pictures. It took me three weeks camping in ten degree weather with a sinus infection to get them. I hate winter."

"You got those shots?" Ben's voice leaves me with the impression he doesn't believe me.

"Yeah. Again Abe's in his office most of the time sorting through the images."

"Oh, my God, quit squirming!" he hisses. "What is it about city girls? You can't sit still, you're afraid of everything that isn't covered in cherry red lipstick and twice you've told me not to get too close to the trees, you'll get sap on your jean shorts."

Oh, I'm insulted. I feel my face flush with anger and I can't move to glare at him because I don't want to exacerbate the issue that I'm wriggling like a worm on hot asphalt being this close to Ben. "They are two-hundred dollar jean shorts, butthole," I grunt. "And I'll stop squirming when you quit shoving yourself up to me like we're conjoined twins in utero."

"You're weird, you know that right?" he says and my

heart makes that sliding jump downward. So I've got to be honest. I'm not star struck with the beauty of the people I take pictures of, however, I am horrible about pointing out my own superficial flaws to myself. My face must show it when I twist my head, peer up at him. "I don't mean the creepy weird, Piper. But you're really smart weird like—"

"Just leave it at that, Ben Landowski." I turn my head back. "I had a whole family that let me know on a daily basis I wasn't normal like them." Hence the caution tape around my heart.

"I'm just saying. You want me to go back?"

I breathe in, breathe out. And I don't answer. Where I'm ready to jump off this horse thinking that my sweat's mingling with this stranger's sweat, Ben's incredibly comfortable with pushing an arm around my waist when we go up a hill or resting his chin on the top of my head. Who does that with a stranger?

"So if I called your boss right now, he'd agree that you did most of his pictures?"

"No, he wouldn't. He takes the credit for them. Doesn't your boss do that? Why wouldn't you believe me? Of course—" Then I stop as we crest the hill and my breath is caught in my lungs. I had been hearing the sound of water splashing, the kind of rumbling resonance that is like bath water falling from the spout and into a full tub. Still as we crest the mountain, it is a hundred-fold, almost deafening the rich shower of water downward. But that is only second to the dark pines surrounding my view for miles around us so the mountains and deep valleys look like a black velvet blanket has been swathed across them. And before us, there is deep cut in the hill, a lake that is almost as black as the trees that surround them.

"Breathe, Piper."

I had been holding my breath. I don't appreciate Ben banging my back while I shift and start to dismount from the horse.

"No, no, no," he says quickly. "It's a long way down. Let me take the horse—"

"I can get off here."

"No, you can't. Stop, dammit! It is dangerous here."

He grabs my upper arm and stops me. It kind of hurts and I wrestle his hand away with a shake of my shoulders. "Let go. Fine."

I suppose if I would have looked around again to his face, I would have seen how pale he was right then. However, until he's got the horse tied and he's standing twenty feet away from the edge of the waterfall fiddling with the horse's saddle and trying to look busy that I realize he must have a thing about heights.

"So you're afraid of waterfalls, huh, cowboy?" I ask.

"I wouldn't tell you if I was," he snaps back like he's embarrassed. "As my archenemy, you might use it against me. I imagine a battle pursuing and you tossing me off up here."

"And you call me weird. Archenemy?" I spat at him. "I don't even know you. Why would you say that?"

"You said it first when you tried to be a superhero and walk through the wall at my grandpa's. Listen, I brought you up here to be nice. I usually take customers up the lower trail. Don't point out my flaws."

"Then don't call me City Girl. Don't act like I'm prissy and I haven't done anything. And quit being a know-it-all." I see a little white building tucked into the trees and point it out with my finger. "What's that?"

He looks over his shoulder, eyes the little building absently. "It's the old Dark Pines church. The cemetery is somewhere behind it. The church still gets used sometimes."

I make a stealthy walk toward the church. It's not much more than a well-made shack although it has been white-painted not long ago. When I try to jimmy the door with my hand on the knob, it doesn't open. When I peer in the windows, there are two lines of old wooden pews and a makeshift podium in the front. Along the far walls, there are boxes with blankets plopped on top. I don't see anything but a small chimney for heat. They still probably use the blankets to keep warm on chilly days.

I hear a soft swish of old autumn leaves. It is coming from the far side of the church and on the outside. However, I can see straight through from the window I am tiptoeing to see inside and across through the other. There's a figure. The glass is smudged, but I can make out a muddy form of a woman in a dress. The wind is blowing a bit. I wondered if she didn't hear us coming up the hill. Because now she is making that head wag toward the church like people do when they are startled and think someone is nearby. Then, I swear, I see the pale smudge of face hone in on mine from the other outside of the church.

"Uh oh." I'm not sure if she sees me. But one second, I'm slamming my face against the glass with my palms against it and then next, I see her doing the same on the other side. At the same time, I feel a hand slap down hard on my shoulder.

I gasp, turn.

"Did I scare you? You look like you saw a ghost." Ben is laughing at me.

"Yes, dumb butt, there's somebody on the other side. They were watching me through the window."

He rolls his eyes, leans his hand against the wall of the church and weaves his head back and forth. "There's nobody there, Piper, inside or out."

I stomp across the leaves and around the old building with Ben on my heels. There's an old cemetery, but no sign of a woman or anybody else.

"It could have been a hiker, Piper, or somebody fixing up the cemetery," Ben says and he's still chuckling under his breath. "You probably scared her just as bad as she scared you."

"You are the one who scared me, not her. And it was on purpose."

I suppose I should have just let it roll off my back. Of course, I don't. I take a bunch of pictures and seethe on it. I have this big brother, Lee. When we were little, he was relentless taunting me. He'd wet his forefinger, give me wet-willy-ears. He'd try to scare me all the time by jumping out in front of me in the dark. If there was a way to pester me, Lee would find a way. He'd kick me under the table, flick spit wads at me and lob me with a baseball if I looked away. I always took it. I am tiny like a scrawny kitten. Lee is huge like a pit bull. I'd let it sink in for a few days, his little sieges on my patience. Then when he was least expecting it, I would pounce on him from behind with some ornery payback.

Such, I wait for Ben Landowski to walk off into the woods to putter around. Then, I hop on his horse and start along the trail back the hour's ride to his grandpa's. Because I have ridden. I had an old mare growing up that used to buck me off about a mile from my daddy's house. I'm not a city girl. And even if I was a city girl, I would have ridden horses. I see him off in the distance when I cut down the path. His head is tipped to the side when I ride past him, my middle finger waving in the wind. I think he called me a really bad word. I just hear it far off and hardly above the waterfall.

So this is how it always worked with my big brother. He wasn't that smart so he was easy to trick. I'd add cayenne pepper in his root beer or unplug some of the wires in his truck so he couldn't drive it. I'd put a bucket of water over his door and when he walked in, it fell on his head. It was fun for a few minutes while we all laughed and he chased me around telling me he was going to kill me. Then Lee, he got this sad look in his eyes and he'd tell me I'd always get him in the end because I was smart and he was dumb. I suppose, in retrospect, it was actually his final blow to me so he'd win. Because he always did when I'd clean up the bucket of water off the floor or get him a fresh root beer at the grocery store.

It worked this way with Ben. I'm maybe ten minutes from the top of the mountain, weaving my way down the hillside. The guilt hits me. What if Ben trips and breaks his leg and can't get back. He did make a special trip up here for me. Blah, blah, blah.

"Hey." I must have said that twelve times when I found him on the rutted part of the trail. Ben, he doesn't answer, just goes around me and I follow behind.

"They still hang horse thieves in Kentucky." He isn't looking at me, just walking with his hands in his pockets and staring at the ground. "You can just keep riding. I'd rather walk."

"I'm sorry, but you were being a jerk."

He stops, his back to me, pivots on his feet. I haul back the reins on the horse, ease her to a stop. "You're kidding me, right? I think there's something wrong with you." He makes the crazy sign of his finger around his head. "You're like this tiny bee buzzing around my head just waiting to sting me over and over—"

"Bees only sting once, then they die."

Perhaps I shouldn't have corrected him. He just

glares at me, shakes his head. "I don't understand why you're like this, why you're attacking me—"

"I'm not attacking you. I'm just calling you out when you're a jerk. You're just not used to people doing that because you're pretty. I deal with it all the time."

He holds his hands out, shakes his head. "Go away." Ben turns around, starts his walk again.

"I'm sorry."

That said, he stops. It's like he's thinking it out for a second while I bring the horse to a halt again. Then Ben just turns, walks up to the horse and climbs back on behind me. "Where'd you learn to ride?" He shifts, situates himself and shoves himself against my back again while I turn my head to look up at him.

"City girls can ride horses too, Ben."

"Why are you looking at me with that goofy grin?"

"I don't know. You're like tickling me with the buttons of your shirt." That's a lie. I could ride like this for hours shoved up against him. Even if he is rigid, this is warm and cozy. It's something I haven't felt in a long, long time when I remembered piling sleepy-puppy style with my brothers on the living room floor to watch a movie. I won't admit it, of course.

"Okay, so do you want to hear the legend about the Dark Piney Waterfall?" Ben says while I try not to focus on his heartbeat against my left shoulder. "Because you were standing at the opposite end of the forest. If you made a straight line walking about a mile or so, you'd hit the road where you took pictures the other day."

"I got wind of the witch and the coal mine owner, Dexter Black. Detective Phillips told me how some witch cursed the land because he made her sell it and Dexter's wife died after she saw a stick man at her window."

"Did he tell you how she died at Dark Piney Falls?"

"No, you probably won't be surprised that there wasn't a melodramatic ending to his story. It was condensed and really, really undramatic to the point it played out like a dull police report."

Ben chuckles. "You crack me up when you use big words." I start to retort. He has the audacity to push a hand over my lips. "Stop. I'm just not used to it." Then he leans back a bit and shifts himself comfortable. "So here's how it goes," he says, shoving his chin back on the top of my head. "Nobody really knows where Dexter Black came from or where he got his money. He was in his late sixties and thick-jowled. They said he was so fat that when they built the doors on his house here, they had to make them double size for him to fit inside. He just showed up one hot August day of 1865 with this beautiful young woman half his age and a leather suitcase full of Union money. Some say he got that money robbing trains bound across the United States with government payroll for the armies. Others, they said he found gold in California. No one really knew, but the one thing they did know was that he was the answer to all their problems. Money was scarce here then, people were barely surviving off the land. There weren't any jobs and the town that sat on this hillside was burned to the ground during a battle. So the people of this town lived in shacks and in the caves here and a child was said to starve for each day that passed. When Dexter Black offered them Union money to work for him and he'd give it all in cash, they came from all around to work in his mines."

Ben slows the horse at a creek with a tiny puddle of water and lets her drink. He leans hard around me and pats her neck. "He paid the men as he said," he goes on. "The money was flying and a town was started named after the mine, Black Jack. It grew and thrived. Special walkways were made along the muddy streets for the beautiful dark haired woman to walk so her boots would not get muddy. Everyone waited with bated breath each day for the beautiful young woman, who lived with Dexter Black, to take her usual walk from home to the mining company and drop off Dexter's lunch for him to eat. It was said she was so incredibly gorgeous that men would stop in their tracks unable to move until she passed—"

"She has a lover, doesn't she?"

"You are worse than a five year old. Just listen." Ben pokes me in the side. "So it happened on a rainy night, what they used to call the Nights of the Weeping Wind. It's when the moon is full and a summer storm is blowing through. Big winds bringing drizzle and the storm clouds are bulky and floating fast in the sky so that every now and then, they let the moonshine through. The young woman had a lover whose name is lost to time. He was young and handsome, though, and a worker in her husband's coal mines. She was to meet with him at the top of the waterfalls where we were this afternoon. There, they were planning a daring escape from Dexter Black. The lover would sneak into the company office where Dexter Black kept a carpet bag full of Liberty Silver Half Dollars and steal them for their flight. But that night, the young woman saw a figure at her window only moments before she was supposed to leave to meet the young man. She told a servant and she ran outside. She, too, saw a strange stick-like shadow and told the young woman she would call her husband. But the young woman stopped her, fearing her husband would stay so she couldn't leave. So she told the servant it was just her imagination. Perhaps, she thought, also, it was her husband who had found out about her plan." He stops and takes in a long, deep breath.

"She stood still and did not peer out the window until nearly an hour had passed. Then, believing she was safe, the young woman ran up to the top of Dark Piney Waterfall to wait for her lover. But she realized by the sight of the full moon on the horizon, she was hours too late. It wasn't long until she saw a brown carpet bag laying precariously close to the edge of the waterfall. She quickly picked it up, saw her lover's clothing inside along with a modest wedding band and the silver half dollars. While she peered over the ledge, she knew he must have thought she had forsaken him and jumped to his death. Then in a fit of grief knowing he was dead, she jumped into the waterfall below—"

"Please do not tell me he was still alive. I'm begging you, Ben Landowski. I hate sad endings."

"I'm sorry, Piper, but that's where the name of the waterfalls came from and then, later, the town. Dark Piney Falls isn't from the pines that cover the hills, it is for the pining and the dark desire the two had for each other. It is for the lover who returned after walking the trail to see if the young woman had gotten lost on her way to the waterfall. He found her bag beside his own and jumped to his death to the waters below to be with her. It is said you can still hear each of them pining for each other, the sounds of their tears flowing with the water over the ledge."

"Damn you, Landowski."

"Payback, Piper, for leaving me stranded."

"I came back for you."

He ignores me, shakes his head. "We get treasure hunters up here all the time looking for the carpet bag of half dollars. The rumor's always been that the lover hid the bags before he jumped."

"That's a good story, Ben." I look up and smile. He's still a little raw about me leaving him. He doesn't smile back.

Chapter 10
Kissing the Boy. Taking the Curse.

She's small town beautiful. That in no way implies all the other girls in town are just mediocre and she stands out among them because she's, by far, the cutest of their tiny pack. No, she's just plain, damn pretty and sweet and everything that implies the girl next door that people imagine, well, in a small town girl. In other words, she'd stand out even on a busy sidewalk in New York at lunchtime.

"Holy cow, I can see why you're terrified to kiss that girl." I lean in to Ben Landowski when we step into the Mount Laurel Unity Church. He's still mad at me. He barely has eye contact and when he does, he just gives me this long, faraway look like he's checked me out and I just don't rate. It's a horrible reminder of high school and looking at the boys that never looked at scrawny, frizzy-haired, size 32A boob me. Jenny Young is standing just within the short hallway leading to the sanctuary waving at us to come inside. She has sandy-colored hair, big brown eyes and is wearing a conservative knee-length skirt, blouse and pumps. She bounces when she walks to meet us halfway like a cheerleader stepping out on to a football field enticing a crowd into a lively chant. And she smiles with these gorgeous, pearly white teeth when she walks into the room. Ben just turns to me, eyes wide like he's going to bunny-bolt out the front door.

"Yeah, uh huh," he mumbles.

I look at her, realize she's got the same facial features as Ben's friend, Bucky. "Is she Bucky's sister?"

"Yeah, so what? She grew up."

Grew up? What does that mean? Thank goodness

Josif is right behind us like a broom sweeping me and Ben forward.

"Hey, Ben," Jenny says in a soft, sexy baby-voice and she kind of curls up her arms in front of her cute-shy-like and bounces her gaze from floor to Ben and back again. "You haven't been in for singles coffee break in a few days. I missed you. I mean, I missed seeing you." His face is red, her face is red. They kind of do this funny dance when they come face to face.

"Jenny, I'm Piper LaRue," I finally interrupt the sixth grade sexual tension between the two. I hold out my hand and she hesitates, stares at my fingers for about ten breaths. I'm ready to pull away thinking she's got a germ phobia. Then she giggles into her palm before she reaches out, snatches my fingers from the first knuckles to tip and gives me a limp wag.

"And I'm Jenny Young," she pipes up. "That's cute. You shake hands."

I blink at her. I know my head is twisting sideways. *It's cute?* I shake it off. I think I'm getting grumpy. This is the eighth in a long line of businesses I am stopping in to get permission to take pictures. Everybody's talking about sprucing up their shops. I keep telling them I want real pictures of a real small town and not a tidied up version of an afternoon women's made-for-TV inspirational drama. I tell them my primary concern is about advertising a clothing line and secondary, people seeing the areas where the clothing line is used. Nobody listens. I get a list of things they are going to do to make their little store stick out so I'll come and take the pictures.

They don't realize while I'm walking around with my camera, I'm already getting the views I need—them in their typical jeans and blouses, a messy stack of boxes freshly delivered from the post office and still sitting on their counters, and people acting like real people and not posing like models with a fake smile and facing the camera head-on. Then about four minutes before I leave, they ask me about the dead girl. Each time, I tell them I can't discuss her. They are still investigating the case.

Jenny isn't any different. "I'll go get my daddy," she tells me while she turns to bounce away. "He probably wants to talk to you."

"Her dad's the preacher?" I ask Ben and try not to smile while I watch his eyes follow her until she fades into a door to the left of the sanctuary.

"Uh huh," Ben answers and he's still in stupid mode so I give him a hard elbow when I see Jenny returning with a man in front of her. Ben grunts and I see Jenny twist her head around to look at us trying to figure out where the strange sound came from echoing in the silent air in the empty church.

"Piper, what the heck?" he says after stupid-grinning at her while she breaks the barrier from sanctuary to foyer.

"Then quit acting like an idiot."

"Huh? She sings in the choir," Ben whispers just out of the blue. I don't know where that came from.

"I suppose she sings like an angel?"

"Yeah, pretty much."

"I assumed your family was Jewish. How do you know she sings in this church?"

"Yeah, Grandpa is Jewish, but Grandma isn't."

"How does that work?"

"I don't know." He turns to me like it's a stupid thing to ask. I feel like he's all smiling and happy when he was looking at his white angel, then he turns to me and sees the dark monstrosity that might suck the pretty out of her at any second. "I go with my grandma sometimes." He's just staring at me with this odd twist to his lips and too long before he blinks and snaps his attention back to the father and daughter stopping in front of us.

"Oh." I'm still nodding when I shove out my hand for Jenny's dad and introduce myself. He smiles at the three of us, makes a point of getting good eye contact with Josif, doesn't quite latch on to mine. He's stoic almost to the point of boredom. He's bald and clean-cut straight down to the white collar on his shirt. He looks at my hand, too. Do people not shake hands here? And his grasp is as limp as his daughter's.

"Before you ask, Miss LaRue, we don't allow pictures inside the church unless it is a wedding or baptism, of course. I talked with my parishioners and they decided it would be best to keep advertising out of the church."

"What about outside of the church?" I ask and then this is always where it gets dicey with me. I see him getting ready to shake his head. I'm a bit on the irritated side right this moment, considering they've got a big sign with two hands holding a tiny baby out on the highway that broadcasts: ABORTION IS MURDER.

"Before you answer, I just think it is good business practice no matter what line of work you're in to have your company represented if it has a chance," I tell him, holding up my hand. "I'm not saying Spitfire will use any specific picture or business image. However, J.D.'s Corner Bar down the street is letting me take pictures."

"Aw, come on, Dad." The voice drags from behind us where the front door to the church is located. We all turn to see Bucky pushing through the door, shaking his head. "Give her a break. She's not some California crazy that's going to exploit the church."

We all give him a nod or a smile while he walks up to us. He stops short of his dad who sighs deeply and grants me permission. He and Josif make polite small talk for a few minutes. Then while I think I'm making a cool move for Ben, kind of being his wingman, I ask Jenny and Bucky if they want to go get an ice cream down the street with us. All three of them look at me like I just tugged on the cork of a champagne bottle in the middle of the sanctuary and it exploded.

The two bumble around—Ben is looking everywhere but at Jenny. Jenny is curling her fingers at her waist and staring at her arms. I look back and forth between the two. "I'll treat you all," I pipe up. Bucky just laughs and rolls his eyes while he points the way to the front door.

"So how do you get a name like Bucky?" I ask him while we walk down the street. Ben and Jenny are three steps behind us.

"Yeah, tell her how you got the nickname," Ben says slyly. I turn my head, take him in and then turn back to Bucky.

"Well?"

"Well, when you're a city boy and you move to the country, the first thing jokers like Ben here do is take you out hunting," he divulges, turning so he is walking backward and facing me. He's cute, keeps swinging his head to the right to swish the hair from his eyes. "So it was about twelve years ago and we're fifteen, he takes me out and mounts this old boar mount in the woods, nails it to a tree. We go out about four in the morning and it's pitch black. He sets me up three feet from it and I don't see it, nothing. About an hour later, the sun's starting to rise and he's been hiding behind this boar the whole time. He gives it a good whack and—"

"He screamed like a ten year old girl at a boy band concert," Ben laughs and knuckle's Bucky's shoulder.

"That doesn't tell me how he got the name—Bucky."

"He thought the thing was a deer. He was screaming: Buck—buck—!" Ben actually laughs a little. "Hence, we like to remind him with his nickname."

"My real name's Vince. You can call me that."

"No, really? I think I'll stick with Bucky," I say giving him a shove with my hand. He shoves me back, then like two little kids, he chases me around Jenny and Ben.

"Bucky! Stop! You are so embarrassing me," Jenny kept saying over and over. But she's laughing and I don't see anything wrong with it. However, I'm not Ben—

"I was trying to get your foot past the door, Ben," I mutter twenty excruciating minutes of watching those two bumble around and then walking her back to the parsonage next to the church an hour later. Not to mention Josif and Pastor Young stumbling through a conversation about car sales at the local car dealership and something about the good old days and how the National Anthem used to play at midnight on TV before the whole thing shut off. Surely, they are joking, right? TV never goes off.

"Mind your own business," he tells me. Then he reaches out with the napkin he's still holding and swipes it on my face. "You're like two years-old, I think. You've got ice-cream on your cheek."

"She's really pretty," I tell him, snatching the napkin because he's wiping too hard.

"Yeah, I know that, Piper," he gruffs. "Now, can you give me some space?"

"Okay." I nod and slide back behind him so he comes up beside his grandpa.

He just got Piper'd. That's what my family called it when I got hell-bent on something and screwed things up diving in headfirst. I don't tell them this. I think they've figured it out on their own. I suppose it won't be long before they want to spit me out as fast as they can too.

We don't really talk until a few hours later. The ride back is quiet. Josif is driving his truck and I'm smooshed in the middle between them. It's another thing that makes me homesick. I used to do this with my daddy and my brothers. Such, I'm quiet. I check on Tessa and Marcus when we get back. They are watching TV in Tessa's cabin and playing some board games. They don't seem to want me around.

It isn't until about seven and I'm stuffing a frozen Anderson Homestyle Chicken and Beans into the microwave for supper that there's a knock on the door.

"Grandma sent me over with something to eat," Ben tells me while he juggles a plate in one hand and a big glass of chocolate milk in the other. "She got one look at all the frozen meal containers in the recycling bin—" He jabs a finger toward the bin by the barn. "—and she freaked out. She says they aren't good for you to eat all the time. You need home cooked meals." He squints his eyes. "Nice glasses."

I reach up and poke the frame just above the bridge of my nose. I wrapped white water pipe tape I found under the cabin sink around it to keep them from breaking the rest of the way after our basketball game. "You broke them. I should make you buy me another pair." I don't look at him, just nod when I take the plate and glass. The meal looks good. It's meatloaf and gravy and mashed potatoes. "Thanks. I'll wash the plate and bring it back." I start to close the door.

"You want some company?"

"Do I look like I need company?" I ask him. It comes out snider than I mean it to sound. His eyes are soft and not so angry now. They seem to be getting less bitter the more I get to know Ben. Now they are just this sad blue with old smile lines at the corners.

"I didn't mean it that way. You just look—lonely. I don't know how you do it all the time, travel by yourself, eat dried out hotdogs at gas stations."

That, of course, doesn't make me feel better. "It's my job. It's what I do."

"Do you want me to come in or not?"

"I don't want you to get Piper'd again," I say. "The farther away you stay from me, the better chances are that you get out of this strangely, not-awkward friendship we have in one piece."

"Piper'd?"

"It's when I rip through people's lives and eradicate whatever sanity they once had. You know, like embarrassing you while I played tag with Bucky downtown," I tell him.

"You could have stopped after a block or two. And that cackle-yowl, what the hell is that?"

"It's my laugh, dork. My daddy used to say it every time I screwed up—*you just got Piper'd*. I'm like the person who walks into a room where twenty people have been spending an entire afternoon setting up dominoes and I manage to accidently stub my toe on one in the long, long line of dominoes and send them all falling."

"Let me in, goofball."

So I let him in. And that's when the Pipering began again. I warned him. I think it was only fair—

About ten minutes pass. I get a text from Detective Phillips. It says: *FYI just back from investigation unit.*

Roommate of victim, Kayla Delray, says she had a stalker. Male, tall, looking through her window two nights before found dead. Black Cat was tattooed within two days of death.

Ben's right next to me smooshed up against my side. It's casual and comfortable. I'm on the couch with my feet propped up on the log coffee table and my computer on my lap. He's looking over my shoulder at the pictures I was sorting through, then he turned his attention to the TV. Now, he's looking at the text.

"So are you and that cop hanging out?"

"No." I shrug. "He's just keeping me updated, I guess, on the girl they found dead."

"Is that weird? Do they usually do that?"

"Well, yeah, sometimes. It depends on the case and the detectives working on them," I tell him. "It's like I become a part of this team, trying to figure out why a victim died, who was the murderer. Some cops are stingy with giving out information. They want to solve it all by themselves and don't recognize the talents of everybody around them. I guess everybody looks at me to fine tone details of what I see through the camera. If the cop lets me in, I try to give them that."

"Cool." That's all he says. He goes back to watching the TV again.

He's quiet. It's a comfortable quiet, not awkward. I look up and smile at him. He smiles back and pokes my glasses where they're broken. I shove him with my shoulder and ask him if he is okay.

"Yeah, I'm just thinking about—stuff."

"Stuff like Jenny? You need to ask her out, Possum," I tell him. I know what he's thinking about. "You just need to walk up to her and ask her to go to dinner with you or something."

"Yeah, I guess. It's just not that easy."

"Okay, so I'm going to make this easy for you," I say. That's when I sigh and let my laptop slide to the left on to the couch cushion. Then I take off my glasses and lay them on top. I just dig my right knee into the couch, pivot, and slip my left leg overtop Ben's lap so I'm sitting on his knees. He's just blinking at me, his hands held out at my waist, but not quite touching.

"What are you doing?"

"I'm taking the curse for her," I tell him. "And I'm breaking the barrier of whatever stops you from going out with her, your phobia." Then I reach my hands upward, slip them along his jawline and give him a gentle, but slightly-longer-than-I mean-to kiss.

I'm expecting him to push me away. Yeah, he doesn't even when I pull back after the kiss. He's just looking at me with these scared-sad eyes, a buck staring down the barrel end of a gun. I know he's stunned at first, but he reaches out his hands and just slides them around my neck and pulls me forward. And oh, holy hell, we're kissing again.

It wasn't my intention four minutes ago to have a Rated PG make-out session with a guy I find I'm irritatingly attracted to in an oddly comforting sort of way. I don't even know if we're friends yet. And it certainly wasn't my plan to have his grandpa catch me doing it. But it's like one second, all's I can think of is this perfect, perfect kiss and how it's making my tummy jump and rattle and bang. I never should have initiated it, didn't really care until two seconds before I hear the bang of boots to floor like someone's trying to get the attention of another person.

I jump-slide off Ben. I think my face is so hot right then, the flesh is going to peel off the bone. He's got that wide-eyed, blinking thing going and he pushes himself to his feet and scrubs a hand through his hair. I'm snatching up my glasses to hide behind and shoving them up the bridge of my nose.

"Yeah, what'd you need, Grandpa?" Ben stutters.

"Detective Phillips called from the station, wanted Piper to call him. He couldn't reach her on her phone."

I cringe, nod.

"And I just put on some fresh coffee," he says, turning his attention to Ben. "I thought you'd want to come over and have a cup."

I get it. That must be code-words for get the hell out of the cabin with the girl.

"Yeah, right," Ben mumbles. He doesn't even look at me. "I'm right behind you."

Chapter 11

So, the Thing is, I Know How to Drive a Tractor—

"I can't do anything because it won't stop raining." That's what I'm telling Abe the next morning. It's a muddy mess from one end of the state to the other.

"Okay, just keep me posted."

"Really?" I ask. It doesn't sound like him. He's usually freaking out if he's losing money. And he's losing money on these two sedentary models who have done nothing but watch TV for the last four days. "You want me to reschedule?" I, personally, would like nothing more than to hightail it out of this God-forsaken town. I miss my morning coffee shop coffees. I miss shopping at the mall.

"Naw, it's cheaper to keep them there than pay their flight back and forth. They knew it was a two week job."

Two weeks in small town Kentucky. I groan, then set my sights on Josif Landowski's long lost brother. There's one nice thing about being a photographer under Abe Starling and it's the contacts I make. It isn't the places I travel or the people I meet, it is that he's such an idiot most of the time, I have to dig up his contacts and find out exactly what his clients actually want in comparison with what Abe has actually told me they need.

Sometimes, it involves translators. Whereas Abe will bumble through a conversation and wheedle out what he wants to hear from a customer from Germany or Mexico or France stumbling through broken English, I've learned to hire college translators in whatever area I'm in. They are cheap and know the slang. Although Abe's got money to waste, I don't. They save me tons of time and a second trip just by interpreting correctly and letting me know the client's real requirements.

I meet with a man named David Davies, a German translator, near Flat Lick, Kentucky an hour and a half away. It takes some legwork to find him. But when I started pulling up information online from the family history sites about Josif Landowski's family while the rain poured on the cabin roof, I just couldn't stop and for God's sakes, I couldn't understand anything. It's all in German—old newspapers, old articles, old World War II Holocaust records. I can see the names clearly, but all the information tucked into the story about them was completely lost to my eyes. I sit with the translator for six hours and chuck out two-hundred and fifty dollars of my own savings to have him weave me a path through the unknown world of the Warsaw Ghetto and Josif's family, giving me bits and pieces of their lives. It offers more questions than answers.

I get back to the cabin, tired and wanting no more than to watch some TV when there's a knock at the door. I am listening to Abe talking about some project he's working on in northern Florida while I walk over and open it wide to a clap of thunder working across the sky.

"Piper?" It's Missus Landowski. "Josif's not home and—" She's standing on the porch holding a raincoat over her head while I beckon her in with my free hand. She stops talking when she sees me on the phone. I hold up a finger, tell Abe I'll call him back. She looks kind of frantic while the water from the raincoat dribbles on to the floor.

"Our neighbor just called on our home phone and told me our pasture fence got knocked down by a tree uprooted from the creek," she says. "Our cows are out on the old highway. Before he could finish, our phones went down. Can I use your cell phone to call Josif?"

"Of course."

"He's halfway to Lexington. He and Ben went to pick up a hay bin for the barn."

"You just want me to get them in?" I ask her. "I can drive a tractor."

"You—you can drive a tractor? You're not afraid of cows?"

I sniff a laugh. "What is it about me that screams *city?*" I ask her looking at myself up and down. "Your grandson even calls me City Girl. No, I grew up on a farm. I showed cattle at fair. My sister was a prissy brat so Daddy had me helping in the fields with my brothers. If you've got the wire and a tractor and some hay, I can get them back inside and fix the fence."

I had to cut the tree away with a chainsaw, drag it away from the creek, and rewire an entire corner section of fence that got stretched six or seven feet. Missus Landowski told me she was a subdivision girl growing up. She left the farming to Josif so she had no clue what to do. However, she stood in the rain with me most of the time, following me around and chattering away about church stuff and her old cat and something about the mailman always delivering the wrong packages. I tell her how to use a post hole digger to make a hole, build a corner brace in the fence, and how ticked off I was that Tessa and Marcus are sitting in the dry truck right now doing nothing more than watching us and using their cell phones. I suppose it is the job I gave them, shining my car lights at the project so I could see.

My only problem is tightening the corner section of fence. I needed to be on the tractor pulling the fence section and tightening the wire at the same time. So I'd pull the tractor up and have Missus Landowski sit on it and let it jerk forward in little steps while the rain pelts us hard. She laughs like a hyena every time she hits it too hard, the tires spin, and the mud comes splattering into my face.

"I'm so sorry!" she keeps yowling back at me between breaks of laughter. I know I'm covered in mud head to borrowed barn boots. "I'm going to call you—sludge puppy!" She's like an eight year-old gleefully driving an ATV for the first time. I need ten of me, though, my little one-hundred and some odd pounds just don't cut it holding the fence while the tractor slips in and out of gear. I'm about to have her shut the tractor off so I can scratch my head and figure out another way to heave the fence post upright so I can tighten the brace when I see lights grinding on to the gravely edge of the roadway.

I bring up my hand, tell her to try it again. I'd turned my head, prepared for the spray and when nothing happens, I stand up straight and crane my neck. Another round of mud in my face and another round of laughter resounds in the air. "I'm sorry, I'm sorry—"

"She's not very convincing when she's laughing like that," a familiar deep voice tells me. I look up just as Ben leans over and helps me give a big push to the post. He's wearing a nice shirt and it's got spatters of mud all over it now.

"You saw that right?" I ask him while I grunt against the weight. "I mean she set me up. Your grandma's a bully."

"Hey, get this—Piper's even tattling on Grandma," Ben huffs while Josif snatches up the wire and tightens it while we hold it steady. Five minutes later, the fence is all finished.

"How'd you know to do that, City Girl? It looks good, really good," Ben tells me, standing back. I roll my eyes while I rub the mud off my face.

"I looked it up online," I tell him.

"I think the bigger question is how she got Lisette up on a tractor," Josif wipes his hands with a white kerchief.

"No, Josif," I giggle while she waves a big hand at us like she just built a skyscraper in New York City all by herself. "The bigger question is how are you going to get her off that thing? She's having the time of her life."

Chapter 12

Black Kitten of Death, a Twin Sister on My Step and Getting the Stick Man Curse

I sniff the air. It still smells like death to me. I'm not sure if it is all in my mind or there really is a bit of upturned soil still reeking of the old decay I smelled when I took pictures here last week. Maybe there's just a dead opossum killed on the road. It reminds me of my mama's kitchen. Every now and then, I remember Daddy moving the refrigerator across our old linoleum kitchen floor, wiggling it back and forth to Mama sniffing the air and announcing there was a dead mouse somewhere. It had to be under the refrigerator. It usually was, a little almost-mummified rodent that was nothing but stiff gray skin with patches of fur falling off.

Oh, I'm standing on the road where Kayla Delray was found dead. It is one in the morning and a full, circular moon has finally settled into the clear sky above me, wiping away the clouds. No need for a flashlight. I can see from one end of Dark Pine Hollow to the other while the fog settles like a blanket high above me. There's something eerily fascinating about this place. I can almost imagine a little town with buildings, shacks, and a couple mines poking out of the misty after-rain fog.

I ran here. Under any other circumstances I'd just be shooting baskets over and over with my music blaring in my ears. Not tonight. It's another no-sleeper. It has nothing, really, to do with dead girls at all. In fact, I blame this one on Josif Landowski and well, my sister, Peyton.

It all started when Abe texted me three days ago. The text he sent stated the clothing line the models are supposed to wear were being shipped next day air. I haven't seen anything yet and we're almost to Day 4 of the two models roaming around their cabins claiming they are going to leave because they are so bored. I'm hiding from the Landowskis, avoiding them like one of them has the chicken pox and it is three days short of Christmas.

Of course, I'm not bored. I'm taking pictures in town and outside town and everything between for Spitfire because when I call their contact at the company, a man by the name of Jimmy Bean, he tells me they want images of small town America. This is the complete flipside of what Abe told me to take. Mister Bean doesn't care if there is mud on the ground and rain on the rooftops. He wants the real deal—small town America. It's the opposite of what Abe has been telling me to do.

With my intermittent breaks, I began to dig up stuff on the internet for Josif Landowski's search for his brother including buying twelve old elementary school yearbooks from Louisville in 1943 to scan for a little boy that looks like Josif's brother. And I haven't told Josif yet that I found the sequence of pictures at the historical society of the boy he thinks is his brother. I'm torn. I listened to the detective. I can't decide if it is better to tell Josif or not. However, the longer I wait, the deeper I'm getting into this mystery of the little boy in the picture who was supposed to have died during the Holocaust.

Then, I switch gears just because I feel guilty for not telling Josif that I'm chasing miracles or ghosts. I found an old map of the mining town of Dark Pines online and in the farthest section, I can see a small slice of land that is marked with a tiny square and then cuts through the property as if to show it was not a part of the mining town. It says: Wilhelmina Patterson.

I had just made a copy of the map on my portable

printer at about six that evening when there's a knock on the door. Now, I'll admit I'm superstitious. However, I try to keep my little irrational behaviors at a minimum. Earlier, I go outside to find Ben chasing around a little black kitten that he says somebody must have dumped at the farm. He finally gets ahold of it after it crosses my path three times and he brings it over for me to pet. "It's soft, Piper," he whispers. "Touch its paw." I'm just staring at it thinking—*if a black cat crosses your path in the afternoon, turn three times or it means doom.* I'm mentally trying to talk myself down, not turning three times to ward the dang thing off. But I reach out, tap my finger on its nose and BAM, it bites the heck out of my forefinger. I'm doomed today.

I'm hardly prepared to answer the knock on the door later. And when I do, I realize that little black kitten is slowly sealing my fate when I see the mirror image of myself staring back at me. Well, I'm wearing a dress and she's wearing a pair of jeans, a flannel shirt and tennis shoes. But I open it wide, see both Josif and his surly grandson standing there. Then, the two part like they are opening a curtain to a theatrical play and I'm staring at my twin sister standing there.

"Piper," she says. Her words are a hiss. I find it mildly amusing considering it is the same tone I got when we last saw each other eight years ago.

"Peyton."

I blink at Ben who has a silly grin on his face like he's a leprechaun sitting on a pot of gold. It's not bad enough that every time I pass him now, coming and going, he raises his voice and sings this silly bit of song that sounds like *my baby drives a tractor.* We're standing there staring face to face like two old west gunfighters ready to start shooting any minute.

"Yeah," I grunt to Ben. "There's two of me."

"Holy hell, Grampa, it's good versus evil." He smiles at me, stifles a laugh. "You never told me there was like a good side to you. Is this the good twin from an alternative universe come to save us all?"

"I've known you a few weeks," I grouse at him before I turn to his grandpa. "Josif, make him stop."

"I can see you're still a tattletale." That's my sister. Her face is deadpan, but she's eyeing Ben with a strange tilt to her head. Yeah, she's my twin, but I got to say from the first day, I've never been able to know what she's thinking or what she's going to do like I've heard other twins do. We're like this strange anomaly, a weird glitch in the norm of twins. Opposites, that's what we are. We might as well be two people from opposite ends of the earth.

"Don't even say it, smartass." I turn to Ben. Because I can see his eyes widen. I know he's going to say something snarky. He just bursts out laughing.

"What do you want, Peyton?" I don't ask how she found me. I fold my arms across my chest, stare expressionless at her.

"I don't know why you're acting so snide," she replies.

"I don't know, why do you think?" I counter. "Because you all turned on me like a pack of wild dogs?"

"What you did was wrong."

"I'm not going to stand here and fight about things long gone that should be forgotten and in front of— strangers."

I look over at Ben and he's leaning against the railing, his hands folded across his chest, too. He's taking us in like we're a cup of hot chocolate on a cold winter's day.

"That kind of hurts my feelings, Piper," he tosses at me. "I thought we were on a friendly basis."

"Again, I haven't known you that long. And you called me the *evil* twin, Ben. If this was a superhero movie, I would have blasted you from here to Mars with that remark."

"You need to make amends with Daddy. It's been eight years," Peyton ignores my conversation with Ben. "Mama misses you."

"Is he dying or something?" I say blandly.

"I can't believe you said that, Piper, you are still the same old b—" she stops, looks at Josif, and then clamps her mouth shut. "No, he is fine. Mama is fine. Everybody is fine. And you would know that if you would just tell daddy you're sorry and pay him back the money."

"I'm not paying back money I don't owe to a person it didn't belong to."

"It was four thousand dollars and it was all Aunt Tammy had in this world when she died. She didn't get a gravestone because of you. And obviously you can afford it now."

I step forward until I stop just short of Peyton's right foot. She's got her arms akimbo and she's staring hard at me. "Aunt Tammy told me she'd rather see me go to college than be dead and have a stone that wasn't doing anybody any good, not even her. So there." I reach out, snatch a tiny section of her arm and give her a hard pinch.

"Stop it!" she squeals just like she used to when we were six and I'd pinch the crap out of her for being such a prissy witch. "She never told you that at all. It's a big lie." And she is prissy. If ever there could be a more opposite of me, my twin sister is just that. She sang in the choir in school, I played basketball. She liked English, I liked Algebra. If I said black, she said white. The only thing we had in common was one boy and he was one of the reasons I left.

"You're still a big baby," I tell her and wiggle my shoulders. Then I lower my voice, lean in and give her a smug grin. "So'd *he* marry you? Did he take *second* best?" I'm not expecting her to lunge on me. That's usually my classic move. But Peyton takes a prissy hop-skip with her right leg. Her arms fling out and she dives right on top of me, swinging with her left arm and shoving her fist right into my ribs. I'm caught off-guard, fall straight on my butt. It's a gasp and yelp later before I grab a good chunk of her hair and drag her head sideways and let my fist pump hard into her cheek.

I don't know how long Josif and Ben stood there in complete stunned silence while my sister and I wrestle our way down the porch steps and to the damp ground. I'm giving a knee in her belly when I feel harsh fingers snap hard on my right forearm and my sleeve at my left shoulder, dragging me up and back. I'm doing a little walk-dance step backward trying to tug down my dress and watching Peyton's fist beat the air with Josif's arm around her shoulder and neck, dragging her away.

"Oh, wow, I didn't see that coming," Ben has the guts to say while he turns to face me, still clinging to my left arm with his left hand and his right hand held between us like he's holding me at bay. I'm growling, taking steps forward while he kind of comes up and holds me back with his body like he did when we were tossing the basketball around at two in the morning. I see Peyton twisting from Josif's fingers while he soft-talks her.

"I'm leaving," she grunts at him. "Let me go."

"Don't do it." I hear Ben's voice right above me. He's so close, I can feel the heat from his body. He knows I'm getting ready to spat out something. "Piper, don't do it. Just let it go."

I see his gaze work upward and a little to the left.

Marcus is standing on the porch of the cabin next to us, staring at me curiously. I just feel my professional credibility drop to an all-time low right then. I push Ben away, step back. I stand still, fold my arms. I watch my sister stare at me for maybe ten seconds. Then she gets the old Peyton holier-than-thou, righteous tip to her chin while she holds up her right hand. "I wouldn't call me seconds, Piper," she tells me smugly. "You got this—" she holds up her middle finger. "But, baby, I got the ring." Now she brings up her left hand, wiggles her fingers and waggles her shoulders back and forth haughtily.

The ring, it has a huge diamond. It sparkles while she lets her hand drop waiting to see how badly she aroused me. I'm surprised at the size, not surprised she married him. I nibble my lip. "If I wanted the ring, Peyton, I could have gotten it." I reply in a low breath. "I'd rather had this with that stupid boy. He's not worth anything more." This time, I'm holding up the middle finger. "And I had it a lot. Over and over and—" She bursts into tears and runs to an old gray truck sitting in the drive.

"Sweetie, why don't you come over for some cool lemonade," Josif tries to coddle me with a drink while the grind of gears sends the truck spitting gravel out of the drive. I'm embarrassed he had to hear me say that. It's not true. But I know what sticks into my sister's craw.

I push my fingers to my temples, a death grip forcing back tears I haven't cried in as many years as I haven't been home. "Not right now, Josif."

"It will make you—"

"No, dammit, it won't!" I yell at him and instantly feel embarrassed and ashamed. I simply turn on my feet, make my way back up the steps and slam the door behind me.

Six hours later, I come out of hiding and take my run.

That's where I'm sitting now, on the gritty brim of the road on my rear with my arms resting on my knees and staring out into the valley. I'd taken out the map I'd tucked into my shorts to compare and see where Wilhelmina Patterson lived. I think, but I don't know for sure, that she is the witch behind all of the urban legends that are now being murmured from mouth to ear all around Whispering Hollow leading up to the murder of the girl. I also believe her house was located on the same spot where the old Dark Pines Church now stands.

"So when you took off—" the voice booms behind me and I literally snap left to right with an alarmed jolt. "—like a bat out of hell, did you think for one second that it might not be safe?"

My heart is slamming around in my chest while I watch the shadow of Ben Landowski creep over my bare legs and the toes of my tennis shoes. "What the hell?" I gasp. "Are you stalking me?"

"Me?" he asks. He's leaning over with his hands on his knees, catching his breath. I swear he's softly singing that stupid tune about his baby driving a tractor. He's like this baby doll I got for Christmas when I was four that would just belt out *I love you, Mama* whenever it got bumped, which in a family of seventeen, was often. I think the last time it did it in the middle of the night and nearly gave my Papaw a heart attack, Daddy tossed it in the garbage. Honestly, I spent more time trying to keep that doll from getting booted by my brothers, I was relieved when it disappeared. I'm getting that same feeling about Ben and his song. "Did you not see the car following you? You might want to turn down those earphones once in a while so you know what's going on around you."

I did see a car. I didn't think anything of it.

"Will you shut off the song?"

"It's stuck in my head since I saw you park the tractor."

"Well, unstick it."

"C'mon," Ben wags a thumb behind him. "I hate this section of the road. I don't want to be here."

"You can go." I wave the map at him. "I'm trying to find something."

"At one in the morning? What?"

I sigh. "The witch's house from the Stick Man story."

"The Stick Man? You're looking for a ghost?" The moon is catching on Ben's face. It's pretty even with early morning beard scrub on his cheeks. "Really?" He shakes his head. "Are you like twelve years-old?"

"It's more like a curse." I'm nibbling on my lip. "The girl I took pictures of had a black cat tattooed on her leg."

"I think you're digging your fingers into a box of marbles and you're going to pick one to match whatever mood you're in. You understand what I mean? Lots of girls have tattoos."

"Oh, you make it picture perfect," I say a little too brightly. "You're saying my deduction is farfetched. I'm not a detective, stick to taking pictures. Why are you fighting me on this?" I push myself up with hands on knees. "I think the saying is *grasping for straws*. And you should know that being an English major."

"You get offended so easily."

I glare at him, lock eyes and expect him to turn his gaze away. He doesn't. "Okay, Ben, say it. It's probably in my blood."

"Huh?" He shakes his head, then nods his head up and down. "So you got more redneck in you than city girl. I mean, you were afraid of a teeny tiny black kitty that wouldn't hurt a fly."

"It bit my finger." I hold up my hand, expose the Band-Aid I placed there to cover up the tiny fang marks. "That ought to give you hay to feed on for a while, dig your elbows into me a little harder."

"I don't do that."

"You've laughed at me since the day I got here."

"You're funny." He reaches out pokes at my arm. "I mean that in a good way. You got my grandma on a frigging tractor and she can't stop talking about it like she's got some kind of super power. She thought you were hilarious when you'd look up at her after the tires sprayed mud on you. Piper, you just need to open up. You should take that little kitten home with you, prove it isn't going to hex you or something."

"It wouldn't make a difference. I can't have a pet, Ben, I'm never home." I breathe a sigh, turn my gaze away to the valley. "My family, they didn't get that I wanted to go to college, wanted to leave all the farm stuff behind. I mean, you saw my sister. She's hillbilly or redneck or whatever you want to call it."

"Nobody's parents understand their kids. If they did, it would just be weird because we'd be hanging around with them."

I look up, smile. He smiles back. "My Aunt Tammy did. She lived with us, had to move in when she got too old she couldn't afford her rent, couldn't take care of herself. She told me to get the hell out of there or I'd be stuck there forever, married with kids and an old trailer and wishing I'd taken a different road."

"So you got out. Yay," Ben says. "Where were you from? It can't be that far away if your sister found out you were here."

I hesitate. Yeah, because everybody knows where Copperhead Creek is. This is where I lose friends. So here goes because I'm going in a week or so and it won't matter anyway. "I'm from Copperhead Creek."

Ah, silence. Just Ben looking at me with a suddenly and incredibly fascinated face. "Copperhead Creek. I should have known. You've got *that* swagger. I guess you can take the girl out of Kentucky, but you can't take the Kentucky out of the girl," he whispers it like he's tasting it on his tongue, waiting for it to leave a bitter tang. The swagger? What's he mean by that? I start to open my mouth. He shakes his head. "I—" he starts. I see him look over his shoulder toward the road. I follow his gaze. There are lights showing along the tree line far off like a car is climbing over the hillside and hasn't crested yet. "Listen, let's go down there until the car passes." He nods toward the old, buckle-walled cabin, gives me a nudge with his hand. "I've got a bad feeling and it isn't just because I hate it here."

Chapter 13
Stick Man Curse and Sealing My Doom

"I'm guessing this is a bejeebas moment."

I'm crammed up against Ben in the shadows of the cabin. That's his voice whispering just above my ear. It's more like four weather-beaten, clapboard walls and a caved -in floor.

"Yeah, in the grand scheme of things, it is." I see bits and pieces of an old table and broken wood chairs. He's shoved himself against the wall and is holding me around my shoulders with one arm so I can keep my balance. My legs are slightly splayed. One tiny step in any direction and I am going to fall into the hole in the dirt floor that used to be a cellar.

"You okay?" His voice is barely a warm whisper in my ear. I blink, realizing my eyes are wide trying to peer sideways toward the road where the car stopped and the door slammed. He slid down the hillside quite gracefully like he was riding a wave on a surfboard. I, on the other hand, fell on my butt and then did three muddy somersaults only stopped by hitting an old well pump.

"Hush, I'm fine."

"You're so badass."

I crane my neck to make out his face. I can't tell if he's making fun of me or not. We hurried into the cabin, two little rats running from a cat. Again, he crept nimbly through an opening in the wall and when he noted there was a hole in the floor leading to a cellar, he made a fluid, almost elegant veer to the right. Me, I stepped right into it and the only thing saving me was I tripped at the same time over an old whiskey bottle so my belly slapped on the right edge of an old heating stove. While my legs dangled over the edge, I latched on to the wrought iron foot and, more terrified of what was down in the depths below, I whipped my leg around and clambered out.

He's got just a hint of a smile that drops as soon as we hear the footsteps slip-sliding down the muddy hillside. Surely, he feels my heart pumping wildly beneath his wrist and feels my chest rising and falling in heavy breaths. Oh, and the fingers of my right hand have come up to clasp his own in a scaredy-cat death grip. I'm about as badass as a panicked kitten in a bucket of water.

Then, there is silence between us. Only the slap of shoes against mucky ground slides around just behind us, followed by the heavy glint of a cell phone flashlight skimming through the cracks in the cabin walls. I know twice, it stops within inches of the toes of my two-hundred dollar muddy Gina Danes Olympic Running Shoes. A hand, I see it slip through the wood slats, pause like it is going to tug back a section of the wall. Then it stops.

Who the hell is out there? We couldn't make out the car in the hazy air. I can only catch a faint scent of something bitter and smoky. It is not unlike the scent of the little propane heaters my daddy used to put in the living room in winter to help keep the house warm. And Ben's scent, something like a sweet musk aftershave and sweat, not a bad blend at all.

"Do you smell that?" Ben sniffs the air softly.

"Yeah, maybe it's the car," I answer. Then, I can hear the sound of another car far off. Whoever is wandering around outside the cabin must hear it too. The sound of the footsteps slop away before slip-sliding up the hill. The second vehicle is probably a garbage truck. It blares on a horn while the driver of the car makes a quick entry into the driver door and fishtails for a few feet in front of the truck and down the road. The garbage truck slows, then trundles on by with the scent of diesel crawling down the hill behind.

I feel my shoulders relax. "You know," Ben says quickly. "We need to get out of here in case whoever that was, comes back."

"Assuming he is coming back." I look up, feel his arm fall away from my shoulder. Just as I do, I see a flash of moonlight streaming through the slats of wood. "Look, look, look." I wheedle my way around him like a dancer performing a pirouette with a partner, our fingers still held together. I release his grasp and slide my feet so I don't fall down into the cellar. I can see it. There's something in the space where the hand had slipped through the wood. Ben's steps are longer and stop before my last one. I watch him reach down, his fingers dangling over what looks like a tangled mess of moss and sticks.

"Stop!" I whisper-yell. I've got just enough time to smack his arm and he whips it up, gives me a questioning furrow of brow. "It's a—" I almost wish I didn't have to say it. My redneck roots will show. Screw it. "It's a death charm, Ben. My mamaw told me about them." I kneel down and so does he on the glass and dirt encrusted floor. Before us is a palm-size stick figure made by crossing twigs for arms and legs and glued together with wax. The head, it has a swatch of white cloth, like a bed sheet.

"Is that—real hair?" Ben asks, looking closely at the white cloth at the head. "Oh, that's so gross. It's mixed in the wax too."

"It's made from beeswax and twigs. And the hair, it is cut from whoever's head they are cursing. Mamaw said if you throw one in a fire, it will kill the person." I take out my phone, snap a couple shots of the figure. He reaches out again and I juggle my phone, push his hand away again. "I said don't, Ben. If you do something to deflect the curse or try to break it the wrong way, you bear the burden of it."

"By touching it? You don't believe that do you?" He looks over at me and sees the hesitation in my eyes.

"My mamaw didn't lie and yes, I know that sounds silly, but I just can't discredit my own mamaw, you know?"

"Okay, I get it." He leans back a bit. "Grandpa tells me stories of how the Golem was made from clay to protect the Jews. Who knows where to draw the line, right? So, whose hair do you think it is?"

"I dunno. I can't quite tell what color it is. Does it really matter? It's not getting burned—"

I snap my head up at Ben at the same time he snaps his eyes down to me. "Oh, Piper— he whispers, his eyes wide and wild while we both take in a breath of the bitter scent of fuel. He's got the reflexes of a dang coyote, I think, because one second he's staring at me, the next, he's snatched me up by my shoulder and he's towing me like a sack of potatoes out through the closest opening in the wood while I do a sideways clown dance to try to keep up.

So my eyes veer to the right to a gnarled pile of wood next to the cabin. There's a portable propane torch sitting upright and it is lit and spewing out a three inch fire. Next to it is some kind of a cardboard box. I have no clue what it is. I just know while we're reeling backward in our strange dance along the mud-covered hillside, one corner of the box catches fire. It is slow because of the damp air, but I see a fizzle of light just like the tiny gold-wire sparklers we would light and hold up on July Fourth as kids. Ben must see it too, because he just kind of keels over sideways and drags me with him, shoves my head into his chest by wrapping his arms around my neck.

It's a horribly loud blast. There's rotting wood flying buckling and banging in the air and against the hillside. Dirt and little beads pop like balls of snot against my bare arms and legs. I feel Ben's hands release after maybe two minutes, my ears are ringing and I'm giving him the wild-eyed stare right then while the scent of burned wood singes my nostrils and smoke fills the valley floor.

"Well, whoever was getting the curse is crap out of luck," he tells me shaking his head like a dog trying to get water off its head. He reaches out, snatches my hand and helps me to my feet. "What? You okay?"

"I don't know. Yeah, I guess. Thanks. But they've got nothing to worry about," I say softly and holding up the little stick figure between us. "I—I just got this horrible feeling the moment we realized what was happening, it was your hair or your grandpa's hair or who knows, another innocent girl's hair. I didn't think. I just grabbed it up. It's on me, Ben."

Chapter 14

Running From the Law and All's I Can Think About is Holding Ben's Hand

"You don't believe that stuff about Stick Man, do you? It's just urban legend or folklore or something." Ben has spent the last half hour of our slow walk back to his grandpa's trying to convince me I'm just being superstitious. Twice, we've ducked into the woods while one firetruck and one police cruiser sped past. Neither of us feels comfortable with going to the cops right then. I know he's right. But there's still a bit of doubt in the back of my mind. I'm sure that's why I'm coddling the stupid wax doll in my hand. He gives me a shove on my head and sends me two steps to the right. I elbow him in return. Then we both look behind us to make sure nothing's following us.

"No, don't be an idiot." Still, I eye him carefully. "Did you ask Jenny out yet?"

"I didn't. But—Grandma invited her and her dad over for dinner. That's a start, right? What'd you think of her?"

"Sure. And I think she's pretty."

"She's pretty? That's all?"

Yeah. That was all. She was as dumb as a rock and doofy. I don't tell him that, though. "No, I mean, I just really didn't get to talk to her much. She seems sweet."

"Sweet. Yeah, she's sweet. That's it?"

"If you're being a smartass and you're trying to get me to tell you she has a nice set of tits or a cute butt, let me remind you I'm a girl—a girl and one who likes boys so it isn't happening."

"You're a girl?" Yeah, he's being smartass. "No,

really, I respect your honest opinion."

"You want me to judge a girl you've had a major crush on for probably a year, so much so, you can't even ask her out?" I shake my head back and forth. "So in the same way you respect my opinion, I'll ask you to let me value our friendship for what it is and not criticize or appraise her."

"So you think there's room for criticism?"

"Wow, I thought you'd skip right past that and have a snarky remark about me calling our relationship a friendship."

"It isn't? I didn't think there was a conflict there."

We are probably still two miles from his grandpa's farm. The only way I know of to shut this boy up and change the topic of conversation is to do something girly. "Okay, so you obviously know how to kiss. You're not going to have a problem with that," I say and give him a lop-sided grin and a jog of my eyebrows up and down. "So let's say after dinner while you're all sitting around the table, what are you going to do?"

"I don't know, talk?"

"I'm assuming her dad's there and your grandpa," I tell him. "That's hardly romantic. I would suggest you lean in and ask if she wants to go for a walk, check out that little kitten in the barn or a bird's nest in the tree, I don't know, something interesting to get her away and with just you."

"You act like I've never been alone with a girl before, never done this before. I'm not a virgin, you know."

I take two steps so I'm in front of Ben and try to get him to come to a stop. He doesn't, so I walk backwards with my hands wagging. "You're an enigma to me, Benyamin Landowski," I say, making a silly face at him. "The guys I know, they are either all over a girl or not. I mean, I get it every guy's different. Some guys like girls with round faces, some guys like girls with big butts. I don't get it. You could have any girl you wanted—smart ones, pretty ones, smart and pretty ones, for that matter. What gives? Jenny, she's cute and maybe she's popular because her daddy's the preacher, but she's—" He reaches out, gives me a little nudge before I step off the roadway where it turns.

"She's easy. Not easy to get into bed, but easy to like, easy to have around because everybody likes her," he answers. "She's pretty and sweet," he says. "Is that what you want to hear?"

"She can't be that easy if you've crushed on her this long and you're not married with at least two kids."

He's silent. I'm thinking I ticked him off so I sidestep and come up beside him, walk forward for a change. "You want to hold hands?" he utters and I snap my head up at him. Did I hear him correctly?

"Yeah, sure," I answer and hold out my left hand, wait for him to take it.

"No, I mean, that's what I'd say to her if I was walking with her, showing her a kitten or bird nest."

"Oh." I'm embarrassed, drop my hand. But he reaches out and takes it. "I guess that would work. It did for me." I try to toss it off, but his hand, he twines his fingers with mine. Damn, I'm getting that feeling again. I haven't felt this since I was in high school. He's quiet and I look up. Ben is looking down at me. I'm not sure what that means. He doesn't smile or anything. But I smile at him and he breaks out into a grin, rolls his eyes, and gives me two squeezes of his hand. "Ha, I was getting ready to say something. Then I realized I can't call you City Girl anymore. I got to call you Redneck Girl from Copperhead Creek."

"You know that insults me."

"Yep." He's quiet a minute. "Everybody asks about Jody. You didn't."

"Jody?"

"My fiancé."

"She was in a car wreck, right?" I ask. "What more is there to know?"

"That I think she was dead before the wreck and nobody believes me and nobody's ever looked into her death."

"Are you saying you think it might have something to do with Kayla Delray's body being found there?" I ask. "Detective Phillips didn't say anything about it, didn't even insinuate they had anything in common except they occurred in the same place. There's a curve in the road. I could see where folks hit the guardrail all the time."

"Forget it," he says and shakes my hand away. I realize now, the more he talked, the tighter his grip would get.

"No, not *forget it*," I utter and hold out my hand. "Dammit, Ben, you give up like I won't believe you. Give me a chance. I'm just trying to wrap my head around this." I'm surprised he takes it. "I told you I'm a photographer."

"You took classes in forensics, right?" There is a moment when we're walking side by side, holding hands that I question the reason we're doing this. Trust? Or is there more?

"I did. But I'm a photographer first. I look at everything through my eyes, not always my brain like a detective or a cop does. I have to assimilate it—chew it up and digest what you're saying." I realize we're close to the farm when I recognize the long line of maples on both sides of the road.

"Piper, I think you look at things differently than

everybody else. I don't know if it is because you have learned to focus because of your photography or that you just have learned to use your instincts to figure out how to see things from other people's point of views. But I see something—I don't know what, that makes me believe you can figure out and do things I can't do."

"What makes you think there are grounds to your fiancé being murdered, Ben? I guess that's what I'm asking you. Nobody's told me anything about her." I stop, tug on his hand. "Don't take this as me being crappy, but was she being stalked? Did she sell drugs or—"

"I think she was seeing somebody else."

"Did the cops know this?"

"Listen, I'm telling you this. I'm trusting you with this. I mean, I don't even know if it could come back to kick me in the butt that I never said anything. I've never said anything to anybody, would you? It's a small town. When the cops came in and asked me questions, I was standing in the hospital waiting room with her family. I was still digesting the situation and not just the wreck. There were rumors. I heard them. Would you bring that up while her daddy's standing there sobbing into a tissue? Then, I figured it was too late."

"You had an alibi, I'm assuming."

"Yeah, of course. I was in class at the community college. My professor, my friends—they vouched for me." He's glaring at me. "You still think I did it."

"No, I don't. Don't look at me like that," I spit back at him. "Do you want me to pursue this if the finger's going to point at you?" I honestly don't believe a guy who wraps his arms around a girl like Ben had done to me so I didn't get blown to smithereens could murder a fiancé because she was going out on him. He'd just break up with her, walk away. I nod toward the driveway. I'm tired and sore and slightly freaked out. I just want to go to bed, wake up tomorrow and put this behind me. "What man was she seeing?"

"Um, it's not just *man*. It's *men*."

"Oh."

"She worked at J.D.'s Corner Bar. She was a bartender. She went to the community college to learn bartending. That's kind of where we started hanging out together. But J.D., it stands for John David Reynolds. There's a J.D. senior and a J.D. junior who everybody calls Junior. She was supposedly seeing Junior." Ben looks up at the moon, then shakes his head. "And Tommy Pinkerton at the hardware store. She was seeing him and—"

"Whoa, whoa, whoa," I push out a hand. "I don't get it. You knew she was seeing these men and she was your fiancé. I mean, I've been in some screwed up relationships, but—"

"She broke up with me three weeks earlier," Ben tells me in a huff of breath. "We were still kind of hanging out. She just made it clear she wasn't sure about the relationship, but didn't want to cut it off completely. You got to understand, Piper, she was this shy, quiet girl in school, never dated. Her parents were so over-protective and churchy. I remembered her. She sat in the back of the room, never talked to anybody. When she started pushing her parents away and working at the bar, she was kind of forced to talk to guys and she came out of her shell, you know? She told me she wanted to date other guys before we got married, just to make sure I was the one for her. She didn't want to look back—"

"Okay, stop there." I am shaking my head. I feel rain spattering on my arms. It is starting to rain again. I can see this is excruciatingly humiliating for him. "I get the picture."

"I know you think I'm an idiot. Everybody does. Some stupid, small town goof that can't let go of a girl who didn't even like him. And I knew she was just putting off completely breaking up because she told people that I was just too nice and she didn't want to hurt me. Imagine hearing that from your grandma because she overheard it during choir practice at church. I just—she was the only girl I'd ever felt this way about. We had plans—"

"Ben—" I have to stop and tug on his arm, make him look down at me. His face is sad, he keeps looking away. "Look at me. I will say three words: Harley Joseph McCarthy."

"What?" He does look at me.

"He's the guy who played me like an idiot, told me I was the only one in the world for him while he was doing other girls and telling other girls the same thing. I loved him. I don't know if it was truly or madly, but it was deep. And even after I found out about the other girls, I made excuses for him. So don't be so hard on yourself. We all get kicked in the teeth."

"Yeah."

"So I'll play you a game of basketball—"

"And if you win, you'll buy me an ice cream."

"That doesn't sound quite fair," I tell him. "If I win, you have to hold my hand again. I liked it."

He gives me this funny look, then a grin. He doesn't answer, though, just bumps me with his hip and walks toward his grandpa's house.

Chapter 15

Abe's Lie and I Can't Run From My Past

The rain stops the next morning. It's thick, gray clouds and hardly pretty. The creeks are overflowing the banks, the yards are brown and mud-covered, and the second set of clothing Abe's sent for Tessa Youngblood and Marcus Keating to model, they don't fit them.

"I haven't gained any weight," Tessa has done little more than whine about nothing to do here for the last week *and* eat what she keeps telling me are o-calorie potato chips and salads with five big spoonfuls of Tennessee Farms Fat Free Ranch Dressing. "I haven't. I don't know what it is about you photographers. You think you can make those kinds of remarks and think it's okay. Well, it isn't. I've got feelings." The dressing offers about three hundred calories a teaspoon. I showed her that on the back. Tessa giggled and called me a liar. I also told her there is no such thing as potato chips without calories, she threw the bag at me and told me to shut up.

"The clothes don't fit, Tessa," I say. "You're flying back out tomorrow night. I've got one day to take shots with you and Marcus and I can see that you're five pounds heavier than you were when Sasha fitted you with the clothing." I wish I could just take the batteries out of her walking-baby-doll back and toss her in the Goodwill bin, let her be someone else's problem.

"Sasha doesn't know what she's doing," Tessa grumbles back while she does a little jump up and down to get the pants over her waist.

"Oh, God, I hate mud." That's Marcus Keating who is trying to tiptoe across the mud to the barn where I'm going to take some clothing shots. "Abe's not paying me enough for this. We need to get this job done so I can go back to the beach." He is going the opposite direction than Tessa. He found Josif's garage full of workout equipment and he's been working out for six hours a day. Guess whose biceps don't fit the shirt sleeves? Yeah, in less than two weeks, he looks like a gorilla because not only is he working out, but he's also eating Lisette Landowski's wonderful home cooked meals that are spread out on the table with more food than my mama laid out for a good Thanksgiving.

I do the best I can taking shots aimed at Tessa's tops (she can fit the camis and flannels) and the Farmer's Outlet jean and boots Marcus can still wear. According to Abe, I can also take a trip to the Farmer's Outlet store and buy another set for the big shoot tomorrow. They've had the same line of clothing for forty years.

But I've got no choice. Abe's sending one of his professional makeup artists and hairstylists in tomorrow afternoon, along with the wardrobe stylist who sets up the clothing. When I talk to him on the phone later that day, he's elusive at best.

"You need to keep them busy for another three days. That's it." Abe was about to hang up and he hesitates.

"I don't know what you mean by that, Abe. What does *keep them busy* mean?" I ask him. I don't. We usually do a shoot in one to three days. We're going on a week and a half with Tessa and Marcus here. "Remember when I asked you to do me a favor?"

"Yes," I answer warily.

"Well, the reason I've got them up there with you is because I've got Layla Hope and Zane Haskins down here with me on the coast doing a shoot for Costa Rica Clothing Company."

"Layla and Zane," I repeat more to myself than Abe.

They are new to Abe's company, not new to the business. I remember Layla being one of the babies on a diaper commercial when I was younger. "They're like sixteen, aren't they?"

"Yeah, that's the point. Delta Raines suggested we go with a younger set of models. Tessa and Marcus are on contract with my company and I'd already set them up to do this shoot, signed them on and everything. Costa Rica wants fresh faced models to market to late teens and college kids, not twenty-somethings. Tessa and Marcus are just a little over the age limit Costa Rica is looking for to run their line of clothing. If they are there with you, they can't be here. So if it comes up after, my butt's covered, you understand? They are already on an assignment."

"I'm confused. This project was set up so you didn't get sued for not utilizing two of your models?"

"Well, and so I don't lose them. They get me a lot of money—just not from teen marketing companies anymore."

"So simply tell them there was an age stipulation, Abe," I groan. "Why didn't you do that? There's a certain degree of leniency in the courts, you know that, on hiring someone of a certain age if it is a necessary part of the job. They know you're not going to hire a forty year-old to model clothing for a ten year old."

"Well, I didn't want them for this job. Two models that were perfect for the job flew into my radar. I don't want to tell them that."

"So this layout for Midwest Farmers Magazine, it's not a done deal?"

"Well, we are— I mean, I needed something quick so I grabbed up something easy. We're going to submit the photos and an article to them. I just don't have it yet."

"Crap on a stick, Abe. There isn't a contract yet? You mean, we may not have this project, we're just submitting stuff? You better not be screwing me. Tessa and Marcus are getting paid off my bank account."

"I'm not screwing you, Piper," he says. "You know I'd never do that to you."

What, toss me underneath a train to save his ass? I scrub my hand over my eyes. Yeah, that's kind of his Mode of Operation. I'm two credit cards and the last of my savings deep into this assignment.

"I can get you out of there if you want."

Get me out of there? He makes it sound like I'm on a sinking ship and he's trolling past in a WaveRunner ready to give me a rescue. No big deal if everybody else goes down with the ship. "No, Abe, I'm invested now." I can't believe I just said that. But I'm looking up from my phone and Josif and Lisette are standing outside watching me take the last of the photos. Josif waves and smiles. He paid for a gazebo that three guys are finishing up today along the lane leading to the cabins. I know for a fact he didn't have the money. The hardware store in town wouldn't loan him the money. He ended up ordering one from some store an hour away and signing up for a credit card with twenty-four percent interest rate.

"Hey, do I look alright?"

Hell, yes, he does. Ben Landowski is hovering a few feet away while I pack up my camera equipment. I've got two tripod stands and the lighting left to pack up. I look up, push my hair back from my face and adjust my glasses. He's freshly shaven, smells like the clean side of a men's shower room, and is wearing ripped jeans and a t-shirt. Hot, just plain hot.

"Why, you're purdy," I say with a thick country accent. "Darn near as purdy as that cow out yonder."

"Be serious, Piper," he says, looking over his shoulder and a bit impatiently. "Jenny and her dad are going to be here any second for supper. I got my hair cut. Is it too short?" He waves his hands over his torso. "Does this look alright? Grandma says it does, but she'd say I'd look good if I had on an—an old dishtowel or something."

Oh, I let that particular impression tiptoe around my imagination and try not to gnaw on it too long. My, yes, he would. I don't say that, though. "Well, your grandma would be correct, dumb butt. You would look good in just about anything. But yes, you look nice."

"Nice? Like nice-nice or—"

"You're starting to sound like a twelve year-old girl on her first day of school." I lean back, sigh. Then I walk over and pretend like I'm sizing him up and down. "Zip your zipper and you'll be fine."

"Huh!" He drops his head and I get a good laugh while he fumbles around. His zipper is fine.

"I'm just kidding, relax," I tell him. I think he's mad at me because of the zipper thing. He's giving me a long look. "You look like a model. She won't be able to do anything but stutter when she sees you. Work on the hand holding and then blow her away with one of those holy hell, knocked-my-socks off kisses. Try to sneak her away and maybe behind the barn, it's romantic."

"I should have practiced on you."

I had dropped my chin to fold up a tripod and I snap my attention up to him. I'm strangely hurt by his words. I know my eyes look a little wounded. My brother, Matt, used to tell me my sad eyes looked like his first doe kill when he stared down the barrel of his gun at her. I blink the expression away, force a smile. "Yeah, right?" I laugh. "I'm your test bunny."

"Test bunny?"

"You know, the bunnies they use in lab tests."

"Yeah, I like that. I think I'll call you Bunny."

"No, no nicknames, please." Enough chit-chat. The conversation is only going downhill fast. "Listen, I'm tired. I've got to get things packed up. I've got to run to Lexington and pick up some stuff for the shoot tomorrow before the stores close. Then, I have to get back and meet with the wardrobe stylist and the makeup artist."

"Lexington's two hours away."

"It's the closest store that carries the line of clothing the magazine is asking for the shoot. We've had some issues. I'm improvising." I give him a grin. "Knock her off her socks, Possum. Save the sordid details for me. I want to hear it all—from first kiss to first baby." I give him a punch on the arm and he snickers a laugh.

"Ow." He rubs his arm, gives me another funny gaze. "That was a bit hard—" He stops, gives me a tipped-chin teasing gaze. "—Bunny." He pretends to shoot me with his forefinger and starts to turn. I just shake my head and tug up the tripod. "Hey," Ben says and acts like he's going to say more, so I look up.

"What, dude, I've got to get done."

"*Dude*, that's funny." He doesn't laugh though. "You're being careful, right? I mean, safe, like you're not going anywhere by yourself or running at night."

I lie and tell him I'm not. He doesn't look so convinced. "If you want to run at night, get me. I'll go." I wag my head up and down. But no, I won't.

I think Detective Phillips has a crush on me. Or maybe he's crushing on Tessa. I can't tell. He's come by in his cruiser twice a day and sits in the car until either Josif or

I come out and talk to him. Chit-chat. "You heard the little cabin burned down where the girl's body was dumped, didn't you?" he tells me while I'm trying to get in my car to leave. He announces it like it is new information. Josif actually walked over to show me the pictures of it in the morning newspaper.

"They find anything new on the Delray girl?" I ask him. "Any updates on the cat tattoo?"

"They're still running DNA. It could take weeks for the results to come back. The family is offering a reward for anybody who will step forward. There's no leads so far, barring a church lady who called and said it was probably God who did it because the girl was vain," he answers. "Who's at the Landowski's? Is that Preacher Young's car?"

"Yes, they are having the family over for supper."

"You weren't invited?" He chuckles like he is saying something funny.

"No, why'd you say it like that?" I'm slipping myself in my driver's side door, tossing my backpack across to the passenger side.

"I don't know. Just hearsay."

"Hearsay?" I shake my head. Small towns. Boy, people talk.

"It's nothing big. Why didn't you tell me you were from Copperhead Creek?"

Arrrhh! There is silence between us while I just stare at Detective Phillips waiting for him to spout out some derogatory remark.

"I didn't think my past would play into any part of the job I'm doing here. I haven't called it home since I was seventeen."

"I ran a background check."

"So what's your point, Low Po?" I ask him. I'm

slightly off-kilter again, out of focus, out of whack. I just want out of Whispering Hollow and it can't be soon enough.

"I'm just saying. I guess you can take the girl out of Kentucky, but you can't take the Kentucky out of the girl."

"Why does everybody say that?"

"I don't know. You've got an accent, deep and drawn out. Your voice, it's hoarse like the girls I knew from Copperhead Creek. You try to hide it. But the longer you're here, the more I hear it. It's the way you walk. The way you talk. You got redneck in your blood and you strut it and hide it both at once. That's how I found out your last name wasn't always LaRue. You changed it when you were eighteen. LaRue was your middle name. You're one of the O'Sullivan kids. Your brothers have a reputation in those parts, a wild side, I suppose. There's what, twelve of them?"

"Seven." I nod toward my car. "Then there's me and my sister. Listen, do you need anything else? I've got to run to Lexington."

"Naw, just checking in. How's that Tessa doing?" He asks, situating the hat on his head. "She's a pretty little thing. She knows about the murder, right? She knows not to go walking around outside alone?"

"Yeah, she's a big girl and a city girl," I tell him. "She doesn't leave the cabin except to go eat at the Landowski's."

"Good for her. They're still trying to read that driver's license. It's been worn down with some kind of file like whoever killed the girl didn't want anyone to identify her." He plays with the radio on his shoulder. "Got to go. You tell that Tessa I said hello."

I slide into my car, watch him ease out of the driveway. He eyes me in his rearview without even blinking his eyes. And I suppose my past will haunt me no matter how hard I try to run away.

Chapter 16

Going Home and Papaw Tries to Beat the Ugly Out of Me

"Hop in, sweetie, go for a ride with us. I promise we'll get you back in plenty of time for supper." Josif is sitting in his truck and leaning around his grandson sitting in the passenger seat. I am just getting out of my car, scrubbing a hand over my tired eyes.

"I can't. I've got to pack all my gear."

I don't have time for a ride this morning. I just got back from taking Tessa and Marcus to the airport in Knoxville. It was a five hour round trip. The photo shoot was surprisingly simple yesterday. I did three different clothing changes at four different locations. As arrogant and annoying Marcus and Tessa are, they're experienced and let me get the right shot within fifteen to twenty minutes. They even chatted happily with the people in town between sets which I find can be crucial to the selling of the product. I think they are just happy to get out of here after a week and a half of rain in the country without their favorite coffee shop, mall, and bars.

"You're leaving." Ben appears surprised like he didn't expect I was going anywhere soon. And yes, he sang the stupid *my baby drives a tractor* song when I looked up. I don't even think he realizes he does it anymore.

"Well, yeah." I close the door behind me, slip out into the morning sunshine and tug down my skirt. It's short and I always feel uncomfortable around Josif like he might think it is inappropriate. "Surely I've worn out my welcome. These shoots usually only take a few days, not two weeks. I'm thinking you'd be happy to see me go. No more keeping you up with midnight basketball games," I tease Ben but he doesn't laugh. Actually I got a call from Abe this morning. I should have known I couldn't go two weeks without another job up his sleeve. "I'm heading to someplace that has snow this late in May, if you can believe that. Alberta or the Yukon in Canada. Some ballet company needs shots for a winter scene for their upcoming program."

I stop. Josif is staring at me with bored detachment. He has a look in his eyes that tells me he won't take *no* for an answer. "Alright. But you got to get me a coffee somewhere."

He agreed, but he wouldn't tell me where we were going. Stupid me. I should have seen it coming even before we hopped off the highway near Big Stone Gap. I should have gotten a hint when we passed Big Rod's Gas and Burgers to the beat of soft country music. There wasn't much chatter between us, just Ben tapping his fingers on his knee and me looking up at him once in a while and catching him looking at me. *Hey hi,* I'd say to him and he'd snicker a laugh. I asked him how supper went the other night and he gave me a sideways glance. I had stuff to talk about, but I was tired. I'd gotten five of the Louisville elementary school yearbooks in the mail yesterday, but I was keeping it a secret to myself until I had a few minutes to run through them, see if the boy in Josif's newspaper matched any of the little faces in the books.

I suppose I got this rush of adrenaline right as my eyes slipped around Ben when we passed the old, white Copperhead Creek Community Church. It didn't look any different, just a rundown, one room paint-peeling church sitting akilter on a steep-sided mountain with a little white sign in the parking lot that says: FREE MEAL THURSDAY.

"Oh, no, Josif." I feel like a bucking pony right then, while I make a panicky snap of eyes to Ben like he will help me. "What's going on?"

"You need to go home, sweetie, you need to make amends."

"What? I don't need to do anything. Stop." I can't do anything. I can't grab the steering wheel. I feel out of control while I sit there and turn my attention to Josif. "Josif, you've got no right to decide what I should or shouldn't do. You've got no right to make a decision for me. I severed those ties a long time ago. You have no idea what you're getting me into."

"I think I do, sweetie."

"Grampa, maybe this isn't a good idea," Ben starts. "I told you that you should have asked her—"

"No!" I interrupt and I think both men are surprised. "I'm not going back to Copperhead Creek. I don't know if this has to do with losing your family or not, but things are different with my family. It's different." I'm holding out my hands, turning sideways in the seat. "We don't get along. They don't understand me—"

"That's family, Piper," Josif says. "It doesn't matter."

"It matters to them. Please stop. Because if Peyton talked you into this, there is someone else who has talked her into it and has ulterior motives or she has some motive. I can guarantee it is the last thing she wants, me coming back. Please do not force me to face them again. It is not going to go well. My daddy, he told me that if I left, I could never set foot on his property again. Ever."

"He probably said it out of anger."

"Everything my daddy did was out of anger, Josif," I drop my voice, rub my forehead while I watch him making a right on Copperhead Creek Mountain Road. "You don't understand." It is gravel and bumpy and I sit back in the seat. Sweat is furrowing on my brow and I refuse to look at Josif because he isn't stopping. I refuse to look at Ben because he isn't stopping him.

Then Josif stops the truck. Right in the middle of the old, beat up road, he stops. He sighs, pats the steering wheel. "Piper, I don't know what went on in your life that makes you hate your family. I don't know. I just know that you can keep running and maybe you won't think a second thought about it. But those folks up at the top of this mountain, they want to see you. I'm asking you to do this for me. Because I will never see my family from Poland again. Never. They are gone. But this, I can give to you, to your family. You, Piper, can see them again."

"They aren't like you, Josif," I say softly. "You don't understand. You don't know the reason I left."

"It doesn't matter. They are blood. I am asking you to please go home this one time. Just once. Let them see your face, know you are alive and well and—" He just stops there. By gosh, he's got tears in his eyes. I just lean forward and take him in while he lets one tear fall down his cheek.

I sit back in the seat, roll a hand through my hair.

"Well?" Josif asks me.

"Do I have a choice?"

He shoves a sleeve to his eyes while I turn to roll my eyes at Ben. Ben just shrugs while his grandpa pushes the truck back into gear and heads on up the side of the mountain. The mountain where I grew up.

"Don't pull into the drive," I tell Josif when he pulls in front of my daddy's house. He tips his head to the side, doesn't question me. I don't look at their gazes. I know they are letting their eyes slip down the rutted, dirt path and past six or seven old trucks and cars in different sequences of deterioration. The one thing they all have in common is they have thick grass growing up along their sides where nobody can hit with the mower.

"My great-grandad and my grandad and my daddy, they all grew up here on the mountain and coal mining was all they knew. My daddy was a coal miner until the coal ran out in Copperhead Creek ten years ago. All's he had left was tobacco farming and it didn't work out too well."

Right after, there's the cluttered lawn complete with broken down riding lawn mower, what I think might be a computer printer laying sideways and an odd assortment of kid toys. And then, Daddy's house is settled into a thick copse of old maple trees with two matching mobile homes slightly to the right and left. It's big and the pale paint is peeling off the walls and there are foldup 1970s lawn chairs cluttering the old porch.

"You don't want me to pull into the driveway?"

I turn my head to Josif and shake it back and forth. There is only one other house on this entire mountain and it is right across the street from my daddy's house. It belongs to Martha Reagan and her sixteen little yappy dogs. She was constantly calling the police on my brothers for blowing up firecrackers on the holidays or practice shooting for hunting in the fall. I imagine if she is still alive, she's peering out the curtains taking in the truck and wondering what's going on.

"Nope. I'll just get out and stand at the edge of the property. I'd suggest you go and turn around at the gravel pull-off up the street in case we need to get out of here quickly. Don't—" I point to Missus Reagan's drive. "—pull into this driveway. She'll call the cops."

Ben laughs. He cuts it short when I turn my gaze to him. I'm not kidding. "My daddy is good to his word, Ben," I tell him softly. "It's what they call good and true up here on the mountain. When I left, he didn't just tell me to never come back. He told me he'd fill my butt with buckshot if I did."

"Grandpa, maybe we should leave." Ben looks a little wary when he tears his eyes away from me.

"Give it a chance, boy," Josif says. "Just give it a chance."

There's a four or five kids coming out on to the porch. One has a melty Popsicle with orange running down his arm and he turns and screams something in the screen door, then slams it shut. Josif doesn't leave when Ben slides out and stands there with his hand on the door while I scoot across the seat.

"Hey, this is kind of scaring the crap out of me." Ben leans over and nudges me with his knuckle. "I frigging think you're fearless, Piper, but right now you look—" He sighs deeply. "A bit scared."

He closes the door. I look at him, look at the truck.

"What are you doing, Ben?"

"I—I guess I'm getting your back." He forces a smile. "If your daddy starts shooting, you can go one way, I'll go the other."

It breaks the tension and I huff a half-hearted giggle.

"Are you really just standing here?"

"Uh huh." Crap, I'm shaking. I never wanted to come back here. Never. "So how'd your date go? Get a kiss?"

"I did." Ben shoves his hands in his pockets, peers out of the corner of his eyes toward the slamming of the screen door. More kids. I'm imagining Ben and Jenny kissing and I'll be damned if it doesn't make my toes curl a little in my boots.

"You were supposed to text me or tell me."

"I know. It wasn't as great as I thought it'd be."

"The kiss wasn't good or getting to that point wasn't good?" I ask. "Because this is the fun part, getting to know her. You bumble, you bump noses—"

"Yeah, that's what I did. I about knocked her out, leaning over and we hit foreheads."

"I guarantee she thinks she did it," I tell him. I see a man leaning out the doorway. I think it is my brother, Lee. He's a big dude, six feet and eight inches and chunky. I try to look over at Ben. "But she probably went to sleep thinking about how soft your lips were, how sweet your eyes were—"

"Did you?" he asks me, bumping me with his elbow and giving me a sly smile. "When I kissed you, were you thinking that?"

I see another body come out the door. I feel a dribble of sweat forming on my brow right before it scoots along my hairline. "Okay, so if we die today, I just want you to know that was the best damn kiss I've ever had. Just saying—dude."

"*Dude*? What's that mean?" he echoes. Then it's like he realizes what I just said and gets this big grin on his face. "Like better than that model guy you dated?"

"Shut up, Ben," I mutter. "I'm not going to talk about it."

I see my papaw coming out the door. It's his aluminum walker first with little cut fluorescent green tennis balls stuck to the bottom to keep Mama's linoleum floor from getting black skid marks on them. Then he shoves the door with his hip.

"What you want?" he growls across the lawn. "You sellin' something?"

I see my brother lean in and I know he's telling Papaw who it is. Because suddenly Papaw's squinting across the expanse between the porch and me. He's leaning into Lee and his eyes are dead-set on me.

"Piper?" Papaw has a little handicap accessible walkway Daddy built alongside the porch. He starts down it two steps when the door slams again and out pours a whole load of people like ants flowing from an anthill that just got stepped on including the biggest man I've ever known—my daddy who is six feet and something like ten inches and four -hundred pounds of farm-boy meets hard-ass biker.

"He's got a shotgun," Ben grunts at me. He slips his arm over and catches his fingers on my wrist. I'm not sure if he's scared or he's getting ready to drag me back to the truck. I can hear Daddy yowling at Papaw, telling him to turn around like he's a traitor. Then Daddy just stops and the only sound you can hear is the *poo-plaw, poo-plaw* of the tennis balls on Papaw's walker getting smooshed while he's patting down the wooden ramp.

"I'm scared, Ben," I say that before I can stop the words.

"I won't let him hurt you," he mutters.

"I don't want you to protect me, butthead," I mutter. "I just don't want to do this." He's looking at me as earnestly as a loyal dog waiting for me to tell him to sit. I hear the door to the truck open and Josif is getting out. "This is a bad idea," I whisper to Ben. "I want to leave."

"Grampa, we're leaving," Ben says and just as I feel relief by Ben's nudge, I hear my papaw calling out my name again. He's down the ramp and four walker steps across the lawn. He stops long enough to give a good beating to a tricycle to his right so he can get around it.

"Go on, sweetie," Josif goads me on from the front of

the truck. "Just go."

"No way. I'm not crossing the line." I am looking at Josif and I nod toward my daddy. "You have no clue."

"This is not time for pride, sweetie." Josif nods toward Papaw. "Go to him."

He just doesn't understand it's not a matter of pride for me. I tell Ben that: "This is crazy. Will you please tell your grandpa to get back into the truck, Ben, we're leaving." And it is right then my eyes cross over the little porch and I see the reason I left. His name's Harley Joseph McCarthy and he's standing with my sister, Peyton, and his eyes have not left me since I looked away three times and then slipped back to him again each time. Tall, red-haired, and with a fiery temper that's like a tiny wick just waiting to reach for the flame coming from a lighter. The entire time, I can hear my daddy yelling at Papaw, telling him to turn around or else.

"Grandpa, we should go," Ben says, turning his neck while he wags an arm at his grandpa.

It's thirty of my papaw's steps later that things go from bad to worse. Because just as my papaw comes within an arms-length of me, I hear the click-click of my daddy's shotgun. Then right after, Papaw's deep and resounding voice fills the air cussing daddy up and down and the next thing I know, he's got his fingers latched in my hair and he's trying to balance on his walker and waggle my head as if he can wiggle it hard enough, snap it from my neck.

"What the hell do you think you been doing, girl? Are you stupid? You steal your aunty's money. You walk out on this family and think you can just work your scrawny little butt back and—" He's dragged me over to hold me between elbow and ribs and he's banging my head with his palm like I'm six years-old and he just caught me getting into the cookie jar before supper. "Piper, I'm going to beat the ugly right out of you!" I'm screaming for him to *stop, dammit, Papaw, you're hurting me!*

Just then, a couple of my freckle-faced brothers come careening down the driveway like they're out to watch a third grade fight. They are followed by the rest of the pack coming out of an old barn, a shed and the garage. I can hear Josif trying to talk Papaw out of scalping me and then I hear my mama's sweet voice start howling in the air and Lee's trying to peel Papaw off my head. I got a good two-footed kick into my cousin, Jerod and a head butt into my second cousin, Maggie who poked me in the eye. They must have been having a family supper because there's thirty people out there in all manner of a riot, either trying to get in the middle of the fight or trying to break it up.

Right at the moment I'm feeling Lee give me an accidental elbow in the ribs, I just happen to peer upward through the slit between Papaw's flannel-shirted elbow and his belt buckled hip. I see Ben wheeling back his right arm and he's getting ready to punch Lee right in the face. And, oh, nobody ever hits Lee. He's a frigging giant and as mean as a bear if he doesn't know you. I feel his arm tuck around me and it skewers my view in half. I feel Lee's belly jerk when Ben's fist makes a solid thwack right on his right cheek. It's like everything stops when Lee makes the quietest of grunts. And the only thing I know to do two seconds after I get view again and see my sister, Peyton, with her hands over her mouth in quiet terror is to open my mouth and chomp down hard on the tender flesh of Lee's inner forearm. It always worked for me when I was little.

My teeth latch on hard. Lee throws back his head, wags it side to side like a furious bull lets loose before he charges at a fence. The curse-bellow that comes from his lips is loud. I cringe even as I feel his fingers peeling back my lips and I relax my jaw and release his skin.

"She frigging bit me! She drew blood!"

I push myself back through a wall of chests and stand to face him one arms-length away. Somebody's grabbing my arms and I see Johnny, my second oldest brother, latching on to Ben's arms and dragging him backward.

"Daddy, Lee's trying to kill me!"

There's screaming and hollering and then I hear a blast that's louder than a box of firecrackers in a steel drum. I know Daddy shot into the air above our heads, but everybody's grabbing their heads and doing this funny bent-over, duck-and-cover stance.

The only sound, though, I'm hearing above the roar is the screaming siren of a police car tearing up the old gravel road.

"Trouble!" Papaw yells at me. "Piper LaRue O'Sullivan, you are and always will be nothing but trouble!"

Chapter 17
Jail Time

The jail cell for the Copperhead Creek Police Department is a small room in the local, two-story community building that was a brick school up until the 1960s. It now houses the police department, the township offices, the school administration, and the local court when it is in session once a month. On Sundays, a non-denominational church service is offered in the front foyer. I know this because as I was walking up the concrete steps to enter the building with Officer Walker, who detained me with handcuffs, the twenty or so odd members of the congregation of God's Holy Hands Church were silently leaving and staring me down with curious eyes and whispers behind palms.

All that said, I'm in the tiny jail cell that isn't much bigger than the average house bathroom. There's one metal foldup chair and I'm sitting on it and one rickety table where my elbows are resting. I'm dabbing a piece of toilet paper from the bathroom under my nose and hard-staring a cop who is pacing back in forth in front of the door.

"Listen, I've got a flight to catch." I try to convince him there's urgency to this situation. "I'm already a bucket load of my savings deep into being in Kentucky. I want out of here. I didn't do anything. I didn't want to come back."

"You're not going anywhere until I find out where we stand with this situation." Officer Walker is a chubby, no-nonsense cop. It doesn't occur to me until five minutes ago he never read me my rights. I'm not going to remind him of this minor infraction, he's a bit on the spicy side already. Officer Walker's been on his cell phone for the last hour and a half trying to contact the chief of police. From what I'm understanding, the chief of police job position is part-time. Big John Edwards, who has the elected office is also the only plumber in a fifty mile radius of Copperhead Creek. Such, he is working an emergency contracting job on Coal Hill where some pipes busted in the grocery store and flooded the canned good section. There's no cell phone service there so the assistant chief, who is the only other paid police officer in Copperhead Creek cannot get ahold of him. There are plenty of volunteer firemen in the county, though. Six of them showed up at Daddy's to break up the fight and three helped escort me into the church. Two are still guarding me along with Officer Walker.

Now I've got one wrist cuffed to the metal leg of a table. I've got a bloody nose. It is probably a good thing or my wrists would still have the steel chain handcuffs binding them behind my back. I would probably have to say the highlight of this day, barring getting whooped by Papaw, was getting handcuffed and tossed up against the hood of a police cruiser in front of Josif and Ben who were being held at bay by an officer wielding a stun gun.

"Listen, I'm only five and a half feet tall and a hundred and something pounds. What can I do to convince you I'm not going to run?" I ask Officer Walker who is waving his cell phone over his head as if it will help him get better service. "The big dude over there could tackle me in two seconds." I point to the buffest fireman. He grins at me.

"She is kind of small, Pokey." Pokey. It must be Officer Walker's nickname. He doesn't seem to like it, rolls his eyes and gets a cocky twist to his neck. I think I remember him from high school. He was three years older than me, always had his nose up teacher's butts.

"Don't underestimate her, Goodwin, she's an O'Sullivan."

My family's reputation precedes me. At least I have one hand free. I can't swipe the long chain of toilet paper underneath my bloody nose if I don't. I'm not sure how I got it. I remember my nose getting bumped somewhere between the time the police officer showed up with his army of firemen and when they dragged me off to my daddy screaming it was all my fault. I was nothing but a good-for-nothing thief who stole his sister's only savings and ran off with it eight years ago.

I think if it was any of my brothers, he'd just kick their butt and move on. Bygones. Not us girls. Or at least, not me. He never really knew what to do with us. So Peyton got away with everything, sat in her little chair like a princess crying and daddy coddled her with a candy bar even the time she almost caught the house on fire. But me, I'm different. I didn't sniffle and cry, I'd get mad and go hide in the woods. And I was different than them. I never fit into their mold even when I tried like heck to do it. I got good grades in school. I wanted to leave the mountain, see what was beyond the little brick schoolhouse down the road. I didn't haul off and punch somebody and ask questions later. But daddy and the rest of my family, they were always in some huge battle with the world. I got towed in. Because there's always got to be somebody to take the explosives and toss it over into the enemy territory. When it comes down to it, I'm the one daddy was always handing the lighter and box of dynamite and thought it was okay to sacrifice me for the good of all.

So when Officer Pokey says I'm an O'Sullivan, he's only partly right. "I'm not an O'Sullivan anymore," I mutter. "I left the mountain, changed my last name."

"Oh, you're the one who got out." This is someone new coming through the little doorway and pushing past Officer Pokey. *Got out?* Whoever he is, dressed in tan khakis and a white button-up shirt, makes it sound like I'd jumped from the cold and dingy confines of a foxhole surrounded by the enemy and hightailed it past the foe's lines to freedom. He's clean cut and scrubbing a bit of beard at his chin, looks a little too city for someone hanging around Copperhead Creek when it isn't hunting season and the city boys come down to shoot at the donkeys and the wind.

"Got out?" I question him.

"Yeah, you know. It's not like it's a secret your family's a bit redneck. And once an O'Sullivan, always an O'Sullivan, isn't that right boys?"

"A bit?" one of the firemen laughs. "Didn't anybody ever tell you that you can take the girl out of redneck country, but you can't take the redneck out of the girl? How many times have we pulled one of their ATVs out off the cliff up on Copperhead Mountain? Or called in half the county to put out one of their bonfires?"

The two are looking at me like they are waiting for me to gobble up the insults to my family, laugh it up with them. I stop and think about that a moment. Maybe he's right. I kind of escaped marrying at seventeen and settling down with six kids in a dumpy house with a husband hunting most of the time. Believe it or not, it irks me the way they say redneck. Because if they aren't a redneck, my daddy always used to say, they got no right calling me a redneck. And that is my family he's suggesting is lesser than himself.

"I would recommend you two stop the banter before you say something that I would consider offensive. They are my family." I stare at them deadpan. "Who are you?"

"I'm the township's attorney, Jimmy Price. I was just getting out of church and heard Officer Walker talking to a

Mister Landowski, explaining the situation. I went up the road where I could get cell phone service and contacted Big Bob. We've come to a conclusion that might work for everyone involved."

I had no clue where Ben and Josif went from the time I got dragged backwards into the police cruiser until right then. I rub my temples. "And what would that be?"

"If you can come up with the money to repay your father—I think your sister said it was five-thousand—"

"Well, last I heard it was four-thousand," I counter with a sigh. "But when Aunt Tammy offered it to me, it was actually only three-thousand."

He simply ignores my last statement, bobs his head up and down. "So I'll drive up to your parent's house today. I'll tell them you've offered to come up with five-thousand dollars in repayment for the money stolen. In return, they'll drop the charges. All's forgiven." He drops his voice, leans forward and suddenly, he's got a deep Southern drawl. "You all can spend the next hundred years of Christmas whooping it up and waling on each other on the hillside. No harm, no foul." He reverts back, stuffs his hands in his pockets. "And I've got to be honest, Big Bob doesn't want to leave his worksite. If he does, it won't just be you down here in the hot seat. He'll drag your daddy down here and your grandpa and start asking questions. We know how that's going to work out, don't we?"

I do. I imagine there isn't enough room in the county jail for everyone of my family members once the pack lays on me and kills me dead. I bite down hard on my lower lip. I'm insulted to the point my cheeks are red. I breathe in, breathe out. All four men are staring at me curiously disgusted like I'm the little girl with the chocolate ice cream cone leaking brown rivulets down my forearm.

"Yeah, you know what?" I finally let a long puff of air blow from my lips. "I'll figure out a way to come up with it. If I can fly back tonight, I can go to the bank—"

"You're not leaving until you have that money in your fingers," Officer Walker says, holding up a hand like he's warding off some evil. "And handing it off to your daddy."

I whip my head up to Jimmy Price while he scoots the hair from his eyes. "He can't do that, can he?" I ask him.

"Well, if that's what you agree on," Jimmy says with a shrug. "I suppose he can. If not, I'd probably be prepared for sacking down here for the night. Big Bob's not in a hurry to get here. If you don't return with the money, we will get a warrant for your arrest."

Chapter 18

Chocolate Chip Cookies Do Not Make Up for Leading a Lamb to Slaughter

There's a soft knuckle-knock on the cabin door. I'm back at Josif Landowski's recovering from the longest, completely awkward and silent truck drive I have ever ridden. I told them to shut up the moment Ben stepped away from the truck and walked to the stairway I was trudging down. I shoved on my earphones and turned on my music. They respected my instruction, kept peering out of their eyes at me while I swiped the blood away from my nose.

I'm staring at fifteen elementary school yearbooks. Eight are from 1943, seven from 1944. They are stacked up in two piles by year. I'm not motivated right now, don't feel like sorting through them looking for some little boy that might have existed, but maybe not. And especially, right now, for someone who dropped me in the snake pit at Copperhead Creek.

Still, I get up and pad across the wood floor in my stocking feet, open the door.

"What?" I ask, peering out of the four inch crack at Ben's face. He's nibbling on his bottom lip, forcing up a guilty smile. In his right hand, he has a plate of chocolate chip cookies. In the cleft of his left arm, he's got a basketball.

"Please don't be mad at us. I made cookies. Chocolate chip, your favorite."

Chocolate chip is not my favorite, but I don't tell Ben that. "I am mad. I'm mad at you. I'm mad at my family." I stare at him with a deadpan face. "Go away. I don't feel like hanging out. I don't feel like doing anything but hopping on the first flight out of here. And I can't. The bank isn't open today. And if I take off without paying, they are going to get a warrant for my arrest."

"I brought the basketball." He reaches up, holds a basketball out in his left hand between us. "Want to shoot some baskets? I mean you're stuck here for a few days, right?"

"Yes, I am stuck here like a fly in a spider's web until the bank can release and wire the cash. No, I don't want to play basketball with you." I start to close the door. "Is that all you want? Because I've got stuff to do."

"Mom said you got a bunch of stuff from the post office." Ben is looking over my shoulder. He can probably see the yearbooks sitting there.

"I did."

"Oh. You sure you don't want to hang out?"

"Yes."

"Leave her alone. Let her cool down."

I didn't see Josif standing at the bottom of the stairway. My eyes veer out and land on his face. I'm not sure Ben knew he was there either. He kind of stiffens like he's just realized the man must have been, unknowingly, a few steps behind him. "Josif, I don't need to cool down. Don't imply that I'm hot-headed. My family brings out the worst in me and that is just one of the many reasons I don't go back there. Nor do I ever want to return again."

He ignores me, wiggles his fingers at his grandson. "Benyamin, leave it rest for a few. Everything will feel better tomorrow morning. We'll sit down together and figure out how we can come up with the money. Then everything will be alright."

"*We* don't have to come up with a five thousand

dollar payoff, *I* do, Josif." I fold my arms across my chest. "And I shouldn't even have to do it."

"We all make mistakes when we're young, sweetheart," Josif says softly like he's trying to console a sniveling four year-old who just spilled a glass of milk. "You've got a chance to make things right. You're a busy girl with lots of jobs. I know it seems like a lot of money right now, but you'll be able to start a clean slate. A clean slate for five-thousand. Do you know how many people in jail would give a million dollars to start over? That's a—"

"Stop!" I hold my hand out. "I'm not a thief. And it is difficult to earn money when your credibility is shot because you've been arrested."

"They said you weren't formally arrested." He seems to think he's said enough and wiggles his fingers at Ben. "But for now, Benyamin, Jenny's father called again and wondered when you're picking her up. You're late. The movie starts in an hour. She's been dressed and ready for hours. He's concerned."

"Yeah, alright." He takes a step back, takes on a straight-lipped frown. "I guess I got better things to do. Remind me of that before I take a punch for you again from your gargantuan brother."

"I didn't ask you to protect me."

"I wasn't protecting you. I was covering your back. You know, because friends do that. It wasn't because you were a—a stupid girl or a prissy one that wouldn't fight back. I know that would insult you because you come off like some tough redneck tomboy, right? Is that—"

"Screw off! You don't know me! You don't know anything about me, Benyamin Landowski, nor does your grandpa. So stay out of my life!" I slam the door in his face. I know the door hit his plate because I could hear the *ker-*

thunk and then the dribble of cookies hitting the deck.

I stop, bang my forehead to the door, then open it up to see both men grumbling while they pick them up.

"I'm sorry." I start to kneel down to help them out. Josif just grunts and waves a hand at me. "We'll get this. We'll leave you alone."

I kneel there just a second to their cold shoulders, then stand up. Home. I want to go home. But as I waver there and mentally whine about it, I realize, I really don't have a home.

It's not a half hour later and after I hear the sound of Ben's truck leaving the driveway, I get a call from Detective Phillips. I'm ankle deep in old elementary school yearbooks, looking from one picture to the next trying to find any resemblance to the picture of the boys in the Louisville parade. I've got a pad of sticky notes marking any page where a boy has any semblance of light-colored hair, a pug nose and a little crooked smile.

"Hey, LaRue, heard you stuck my girlfriend on a flight back to Toronto. What's up with that? You jealous or something?"

I sigh. "Yeah, too much competition. However, she sent her love."

"Did she, now," he grunts a chuckle. I imagine he's sitting in a chair in the police station with his feet kicked up on his desk. "Don't I wish? She's one sweet-looking woman. But that's not why I'm calling. We've got another body over in Dark Pines."

"You're kidding me, right?" I ask him. "Are you sitting with your feet on your desk?"

"Yeah, how'd you know?

"I don't know. Just thinking that's the pose you'd

take, laid back."

"LaRue, you're a funny one, a regular detective." He sniffs. "This corpse is older. Not as old as the ones on the hillside, but pretty decayed. I only got a look-see from a cell phone image. It's like somebody's digging up bodies or something over there." His chair squeals and I can hear him humph while he kicks his legs off the desk. "What are the odds you'll come down and do some of your picture magic for us? I'll supply the coffee."

"I'm not getting paid for this, am I?" I grunt.

"No, probably not. Maybe I can take you out for supper sometime."

"Tessa would be jealous."

"Would she, now?"

"Yeah, I would suppose." I feel strangely like I'm keeping a secret when I look through and past the bedroom door and see the little wax stick man laying on top of a shoebox. I never did tell Detective Phillips about being in the barn during the explosion. I suppose I've got trust issues, a big long and yellow swatch of caution tape around my soul.

"So does that mean you're coming or not?"

I blink past the secret. It's too late to divulge Ben and I were there the night of the fire. It would only appear suspicious. Still, I can't help but wonder if whoever left the stick man was responsible for Kayla Delray's death. Or maybe, I'm hoping, just some superstitious local trying to remove whatever hex left her there.

"Yeah, I'll be there. I need an address."

Chapter 19
Another Dead Body at Dark Pines

"You can't have too many more dead bodies, Low Po," I say while I lean over and plop a marker next to a ring laying by the body. Detective Phillips is kneeling two steps away trying to do a balancing act on his heels while he holds a respirator over his face to guard his nose from the foul smell. "I am almost out of protective gear."

"Low Po," he repeats, sighs, and shakes his head. "You're a real comedian, LaRue. Considering I had to call you Miss LaRue the first two days after we met."

"I'm a lady who demands respect."

"So I've heard."

I snap my eyes up at him.

"Marcus told Tessa that you were slugging it out on the front porch of the cabin with your body double."

"You're kidding me, right? I can't yawn without somebody knowing in this state. She gave you her cell phone number to chat it up?"

"Yeah. She likes cops. Of course, she also said I reminded her of her dad. And it's a small town. People talk. From what I heard, it wasn't a yawn, more like a brawl."

"Um. Her dad. That's funny." I'm trying not to gag, gnashing my teeth together. I'm pushing my wrist to my nose right now and I see Detective Phillips chuckling.

"Yeah, real funny," he answers. "It made me feel ninety-five."

"If it makes you feel any better, she told me she's supposed to wear glasses and won't because they leave a red line above the bridge of her nose," I tell him. "She's almost blind."

"I'm back to feeling like I'm forty again."

"Good. You're killing me with these dead bodies, Detective."

"I see your eyes watering. Don't you dare retch, LaRue, once you start we're all going to be vomiting all over the evidence." Even the mentholated chest rub isn't cutting it on this one. It just smells like the blue bottles of salve my mamaw would rub on my chest when I had a cold, and death mixed together. It's a female with brown hair matted to the skull. She's laying on the grass off Jenkin's Junction Road and next to a parallel set of old railroad tracks about two city blocks from where Kayla's body was dumped. The ties and the tracks themselves have long been pulled. It looks almost like she was rolled out of an old sheet or a piece of canvas the way she's laying like she's sleeping on her side.

"She's wearing clothes from 2008, maybe 2009." I finally push out the words. "She's either been dead a while or she's got really outdated clothing tastes."

"Now, how would you know that, LaRue?"

"Her perfume is not of my same tastes, but her clothing is. I had an outfit like this. Jean jacket, short dress with stripes by Tracy Designs. I see the tag on the dress. The heels are high and arched, typical for that time period." I look up. "Assuming it's not something she got from the second hand store."

"Interesting. Do you smell—chemicals?" Detective Phillips tips his head forward, takes in the face. It's nothing but this dry skin like a dead fish left out a day on the bank of a creek, kind of gray and minus a bit of puffy flesh, quite intact.

"Yeah, like formaldehyde. You notice the eyes are closed."

"I see that."

"She's been dead a long time," he says. "I mean, I'm not a mortician or a coroner. I'm just guessing. From what you've said and from what I can see, she's either been in some creep's living room for ten years or she's been dug up from the ground."

"You think that's the chemical smell? Embalming fluid?"

"It's a thought."

"You ready to roll her?" I ask him. "See if she has a black kitty cat on her thigh?"

"I was just waiting for you to ask me that, my love."

"We've got to stop meeting like this," I mumble, shaking my head. "I've got two-hundred plus pictures of this one. I'm thinking if I have to look at her five more minutes, I'm going to throw up."

And so, we do, scoot her body over with the help of several police with gloves and who are gagging up a storm. I'm on the side of the body being raised and Detective Phillips is on the other.

"Talk dirty to me, LaRue, what's the verdict?"

I'm just staring at the thigh. There's something clear and black sprayed on to the leather-like flesh on one thigh. And, there is a plastic card, gritty and worn, a driver's license that I'm taking shots of even before I look up.

"Detective Phillips, you need to come look at this," I wave him over with one gloved hand and he rises, tugging his suit pants down before he eyes me carefully. "Please."

Chapter 20

A Snake in My Car

It was a black cat. It was painted on with a black indelible marker. It looked just like the cat on Kayla Delray's thigh. The driver's license was obscured. I could see it in the plastic evidence bag. It had been marked out. Black cats, ghostly driver's licenses that had been maimed, and dead girls.

But that isn't the only thing I call Detective Phillips to see. There's a snake curled up on the floor of my car right underneath the accelerator pedal. I was never one who was opposed to the little beasts until I was eleven. I used to catch them—black rats, little queen snakes and lots of corn snakes. I'd rub them on my cheeks, feel their smooth skin. I'd even put them in my shirt to feel them tickle my chest and belly. It made me giggle. Then one day, my little brother, Will, caught six big black rat snake s and put them in my bed. I climbed in and didn't notice them all tucked into the sheets until I was awakened from a dead sleep with one curled up next to my head.

Will got the paddling of his life. I got ophidiophobia, a phobia of snakes. Mama told me later that's how phobias start, being traumatized by something like waking up to a snake wiggling in your face. Every time she caught one in her garden, she would bring it over and coax me to touch it so I wasn't afraid. I couldn't. But even if I wasn't terrified by the sight of those little buggers now, I'd be wary of the one in my car. I can see it is as burnt orange as my eyes and has little hour glass shapes all over its back.

"It's a copperhead," Detective Phillips announces just like he had called out the answer to a song title we were trying to figure out in the drive over. "He's kind of pretty."

"He's kind of poisonous."

"You're afraid of snakes, LaRue? Wow, you're as pale as a piece of paper. That's funny. You stare dead people in the face and you're afraid of a snake."

"I'm afraid of poisonous ones."

He grunts and gets a long stick. "You'd think you'd done this a thousand times. These are all over the mountain, LaRue."

"Well, my papaw would take an ax to their head."

He shakes his own head. "Well, I don't." Then he wiggles it under the snakes belly and lifts it out, takes it up the road and tosses it into the bushes.

I'm still getting the shudders later when I stare at pictures on my computer. I keep looking at my feet to see if there are any more in my personal space. One stupid snake and it tips me off, makes my usually straight-focused, level-headed mind go left of center. I can't shake it off. For hours, I look at Kayla Delray's photos, then this new decomposed body. What's the same? I keep asking myself these questions and I don't understand why I don't just leave this up to Detective Phillips and his officers to figure it out. Back and forth, back and forth. It's like I'm missing something. Two dead girls. Two cats on two thighs. Two driver's licenses. And me, I'm stuck in Whispering Hollow with nothing better to do than look at pictures of dead girls and a little boy who has a ninety-nine percent chance, as far as I'm concerned, of being buried in some mass grave in Treblinka Extermination Camp.

I text Detective Phillips. *Do you have the images of Jody Mills for me to look at?* He doesn't return my text right away. Then, about forty images start coming through my e-mail. I sigh and begin pulling them up. They aren't the best pictures, probably taken with a cheap camera by a police officer. There's not much left of her body. I can't help but think it looks like a hotdog that fell off the stick that was holding it and into the bonfire that was cooking it. There's nothing that would identify the charred remains baked into the front seat of the car as a male or female. Still, I think of her eyes that I can't see and think those eyes once looked at Ben and her mama and daddy.

So there I am again, running like a crazy woman and then, bouncing the basketball in the graveled lot at the old barn at midnight. *Boom-boom-boom-pop.* I make the basket. Again. *Boom-boom-boom-pop.* I miss. *Boom-boom-boom-pop.* The ball bangs off the backboard. Two hands grab it. They aren't mine.

"Around the world. Here's the rules even if you know them. You shoot twice at one spot. If you make it, you move on to the next shot. If you miss two in a row, you start over. The first player all the way around wins."

"I know how to play the game."

"And the loser has to go on a date with Bucky."

I stop, stand up straight. "What? You're kidding me, right? Bucky? I'm leaving as soon as I get my family paid which I'm hoping is tomorrow morning. Not that I'd lose, anyway. So, you think Bucky'll go out with *you*?"

"I'm not losing. Even if I did, he probably would. I'm fun."

"You're weird."

"Just come back for a date."

"Dude, I live a half hour from North Cascades."

"How far is that?"

"It's in Washington State two-thousand miles away. It's maybe 30 hours by car. I don't know. I flew and I worked the entire time I was on the flight."

"Oh." He'd been working the ball in his hands, kind of twirling it and he stops, gives it a bounce. He looks letdown and I feel guilty like I let him down. "Really? I was thinking you lived in Ohio or something."

"Why do you want me to go on a date with Bucky?"

"A double date with me and Jenny so it's not so excruciating trying to come up with conversation." He goes straight in front of the basket and makes a shot. "It was horrible tonight, worse than awkward. We just both stared at the movie screen. Then a sexy part comes on and I about died. She excused herself to the bathroom and didn't come back for twenty minutes. Don't laugh." I laugh and he gives me a stink-eye glare. The ball flies through the hoop. I catch it, give him a shove so he moves out of the way. He's with the wrong girl. I can see that. She may sing like an angel and look like an angel, but there's something not clicking between them. I take a shot. Thank God, it went in.

"You guys are trying too hard." He takes a shot, hits it dead on. "I think you'd have been good friends by now considering you're friends with Bucky."

"Her mom left about three years ago. The same year Jody wrecked. Jenny went with her. She just came back to Whispering Hollow this past year."

I dribble the ball a second. Then, strangely, my phone rings. I toss the ball to Ben, take a couple steps to the brick wall where I laid it next to my glasses.

"Hey, Low Po, what's up at—" I look at the time on the phone. "—midnight? You do realize it is midnight." I answer it, see Detective Phillips's phone number.

"You sound wide awake. Or did I miss up the end of a late date?"

"No date and not one in the near future," I say. "I just

had a messy split up. You know, I liked him. He liked somebody else—"

"Okay, Kayla Delray just showed up alive and well at her mom's house."

"Huh?" I know I tilt my head like I'm in a stupor. My eyes work upward and Ben is squinting at me with a furrowed brow. "That's not possible. I smelled her. She was dead."

"Well, those were Kayla's clothes. It wasn't her body. Her mom identified the clothing and a bracelet, refused to go into the room and see her dead. They were waiting for her stepdad to come fully identify her. He was driving down from New York and was just about through Ohio and Kayla walked in the front door."

"No way."

"Yes, way, LaRue. I guess they were renovating some of the apartments where she lived, had a bunch of different contractors there—builders, plumbers. One of them kept telling her she'd better repent her ways or she was going to hell. He kept looking at her clothes and the beer bottles on the sink when he came in to her apartment to work, had a little bumper sticker that said: *Proud Christian Construction Worker*. She told her friend about it and the friend told her to come stay with her. Then a water pipe broke and there wasn't going to be water for a few days. On a whim, they decided to go camping in the Smokey Mountains until the renovations were done because the contractor creeped her out. Then, she scared the pants right off her mom. The local police have checked on most of the contractors. They've just got a bunch coming and going."

"Alive," I whisper. "What does that mean?"

"Well, here's the kicker. That body we looked at this afternoon, that *was* embalming fluid we smelled. The Jane

Doe, Jane Doe Two, had been professionally embalmed. We think it's about ten years-old. We're not sure if it has been dug up from a proper burial or we've got some crazy mortician out there. So the coroner is taking a look at the body that we believed was Kayla's, now we're calling her Jane Doe One, and I'm checking to see if there have been any desecrated graves anywhere. It was Kayla's clothing, Kayla's driver's license. They've got the girl on 24-hour patrol. I guess somebody'd been stalking her, broke into her house, stole her license and some clothes. That's what the corpse was wearing straight down to the underwear."

"Oh, that's freaky." I'm stunned. What a weird twist. "Have you checked the driver's license that was sticking to the other dead girl?"

"That's in process now." He sighs deeply when there's a lull. "I hear you're shipping out, LaRue. I'll miss watching you talk to dead people."

"Ha ha," I fake a bad laugh. "The guy who owns the company that sets me up with those jobs says I creep people out when I do that."

"I've seen worse. I'll keep you updated. Have a safe trip back."

I hang up before I take my phone over and lay it back where it was on the bricks. Ben is taking shots, the sound of ball to basketball rim making an echoing twang each time.

"Everything alright?"

"Yeah," I answer. I've got a bottled water and I reach over, pick it up and twist off the top. "So the girl they thought was dead, isn't dead."

"Kayla—?"

"Kayla Delray, yeah. She showed up at her mom's, didn't have a clue everybody thought she was dead, I guess."

"So who's the dead girl?"

"Dunno. There's two. There was another one this afternoon. This one was ten years dead."

"You know, stuff like this didn't happen here until you started hanging around Whispering Hollow." Ben snickers and pretends to toss the ball at me. I'm in mid-sip and jump, put out a hand to stop the ball. He stops, rolls it around his hands.

"I can't quite pinpoint what annoys me so much about you, Possum. Then you do something like that and it all comes together. Can I ask you something?" I think about his remark, take another swig. "About your girlfriend, the one who died in the wreck."

He drops the impish grin, nods his head up and down and I feel like I've just told a four year-old his favorite blanket got lost. "Yeah, go ahead."

"Did they do any DNA testing on her?"

"DNA testing? I wouldn't think so. Just the normal stuff. From what I understand, she was pretty burned and all the way—um, to her bones. Why do you ask?" He bounces the ball, then sends it over to me. "I mean, I don't know why they'd do it. It was her car, her clothes. She'd just left work."

"Yeah, you're right," I say. But I'm not so sure. What if it wasn't really her body? "You still think about her a lot?"

"I don't know. Not really," he tells me. I stand facing the hoop and take a shot. It sinks right in. "I mean, sometimes late at night when I can't sleep, I think about her." He catches the ball, stands on the far right side, shoots and misses.

"Yeah, I've got one like that too," I nod. "An old boyfriend that caused me pain. He didn't die, though."

"Then I realize she left me a long time even before she died. Maybe she was never mine at all."

"Yeah, same here." He misses again. I take the ball.

"So who were all the people in her circle, Ben?"

"What do you mean? Like the people she was around?"

"Yeah. Anybody. Just name the people in her life."

"Well, obviously me," he says slowly, focusing on the dark ground like he's thinking it out. "Junior at J.D.'s Corner Bar. I don't know what they had going. I just know the mail lady saw my truck at his house one Friday night. She asked me if we'd gone fishing or something. Of course, I told the mail lady I didn't know what she was talking about. I didn't. I let Jody borrow the truck because her car was a piece of crap and it was always breaking down. It needed a new fuel pump that time. I think that's when I finally broke down and asked her what was going on. She said it was just one time. I doubt it."

I'm trying to be casual about this conversation. It isn't awkward, but it is uncomfortable to watch him tell me this. I hurt for him, I suppose. "Okay, so we've got J.D.—"

"Eddy Schmidt," Ben interrupts with the name tossed into the air. "He's the guy at the Whispering Hollow Quick Stop and Carry Out. You bought your hot dog from him."

"Are you sure? You're talking about the guy with greasy black hair to his shoulders and smells like cigarettes and B.O.?" I'm looking at Ben. I'm thinking this idiot girl had this beautiful man standing in front of me and she's screwing around with a guy who works at a gas station with greasy hair and a crappy attitude and creepy, ogling eyes?

"Yeah, Piper. We used to call him Weird Eddy."

"Well, I can see why your confidence is shattered," I mutter. "Was she ugly or something?"

"Why would you ask that?"

"I don't know. Because he's gross." And because you're hot. "I just don't see the attraction."

"So, moving on," Ben is eyeing me with a flat-line gaze. He's got pouty, heart-shaped lips and I can't help but notice them like it's the first time.

"Wait. One second. How long has Weird Eddy been living in Whispering Hollow? I mean, did he get the nickname Weird Eddy in high school?"

"Tenth grade. He's really not that bad." Ben wipes the sweat from his forehead with his arm. "It was stupid high school stuff. He used to carry around this big video camera to the ball games and dances and stuff. He'd act like he was taking pictures of the game or whatever, and he was always aiming it at the girls."

"Not the murdering type?"

"You're kidding me, right?" He watches me shrug, then goes on. "Nobody I knew that was around her would be suspect of anything like that, Piper. The cops checked out everybody, everything. The only others I know of are her mom and dad. They're really religious—you know the Sunday, Wednesday and Friday church people. They're really judgmental, made her go to these bible study classes and I think she was getting counseled by Jenny's dad, Preacher Young."

"Who else?" I try to tuck all these images in my mind while we shoot the ball back and forth. I can't. I stop with the ball tucked between ribs and arm. I tell him to hold on, walk over to my phone and turn it on. Then I snatch up my glasses sitting next to them and shove them on with a flick of my wrist. Now Ben's giving me this silly grin while I poke the names into my notes on the cell phone. "What?"

"You've got that librarian-sexy thing going right now with your dorky glasses—"

"They aren't dorky." I look up, snap back. I set the ball down and sit on it while I type. "These were three-hundred bucks."

"Okay, whatever." He shrugs, but he's still looking at me with that stupid grin. "But I was wondering if I could check out a book and you could find it for me in the back section of the library, maybe show me a thing or two—"

"I'm trying to help you out and you're making fun of me." I pause, shake my head, and sigh.

"Helping me out? The case is closed on Jody."

"You told me nobody looked into it very well, Ben," I say. "Nobody believed you when you said she was dead before she wrecked. So here's how I see it. There's been three bodies found in the area around Dark Pines. One was burnt beyond recognition. The second has not been identified and was wearing another girl's clothing. The third, is also a Jane Doe, and has been dead for probably ten years."

"What are you saying? That Jody isn't dead? That the burned body wasn't her?"

"I'm not making a conclusion on anything, I'm tossing this out to you because I'm not sure." I put down my phone, snatch a hair tie from my wrist and make a messy bun of my hair on top. "Did Jody have a black cat tattooed on her thigh?"

"No, but she could have done anything from the time she left me to three months later when she wrecked." He reaches down, flicks the bun on my head with his forefinger.

"You know, really," I grunt, pushing his hand away. "I'm going to miss you when I leave."

"Yeah, like hives after a bee bite."

"Yeah, right." I point a gun finger at him and pull my thumb trigger. "You do get on my nerves."

He's quiet. I'm expecting Ben to retort with some sarcastic remark. He doesn't, just takes a step like he's going to kick the ball out from under me. Instead, he sits down next to me with his back resting against the barn wall and snatches up my water for a swig.

"You already shared spit with me. You mind?" he asks me while he downs the entire bottle. He gives me a grin while I'm staring at him and he tries to hand me the empty bottle. We tussle over who is going to take it for thirty seconds, then I finally sit up and toss it over his head. It makes a muffled clatter while his eyes follow it into the shadows.

"Go fetch. I'm done. I'm going inside."

"We never finished our game."

"I won. You missed twice. I got the basket." I stand up, give the ball a gentle kick into the grass. Then I reach out an arm, extend my hand to help him up.

"Oh, yeah." Ben grabs my hand and stands, dusts off his shorts with both hands. "So this is it? You go to the bank tomorrow, drop off the money, and take off?"

"Yes." I start to turn. He reaches out does a little hand swipe on my back like he's pushing away whatever little pieces of grass or dirt must be sticking to my shirt. Then he does two long swishes to my bottom like he's swishing off the grass there too. I turn, thinking he's joking, playing a game because of the offhand remark I made about my ex-boyfriend not caring enough, nor desiring me enough to slap the sand off my bikini bottom at the beach.

He stops, holds his hands out in front of him like he's backing off. Ben's got this funny twist to his lips. "He didn't. I just—did, I guess," he says and walks around me. *I did?* What's that mean? "Did what?" I ask him while I follow his back toward the house. I don't understand. He doesn't answer.

Chapter 21

I See Stick Man

It is one-thirty in the morning. I can see the time on my phone in my hand before I shove it back on the nightstand. I heard a bang and my eyes popped wide open. The wind is blowing, a tree limb banging on the roof of the cabin. I blink just as a shadow crosses the foot of my bed. I snap my gaze upward and to my left where a dim security light from Josif's house illuminates the grassy lawn from cabin to home. Was it on earlier? No. It only goes on when something large like a human passes nearby. Someone's outside my window blocking the light.

My eyes catch on the window and the filmy curtain blowing with the gentle breeze. I think I hear the gritty skid of shoes on the mix of gravel and grass surrounding the cabin. Knowing that someone might be outside my window and the feeling I'm being watched while I sleep sends a chill along my arms ending in a full-blown, convulsive shudder. *Someone just walked over your grave.* I can almost hear my mamaw saying those words, rolling her forefinger along the cleft of my elbow when I used to get chill bumps along my arms. It was one of her sayings in a long line of deep Kentucky old wives tales.

I don't feel safe. There isn't often I get this heavy feeling of anxiety in my chest and shoulders my mamaw called the heebie-jeebies. Traveling alone for the last eight years, I've had my share of creeps standing outside my hotel room door, following me around a midnight grocery store candy bar run. So I'm not jumpy, just always ready. I got my Deep Hills Hiker Bear Spray, a tiny orange stun gun that matches my eyes, and a pistol. All of which, I groan, are in my backpack and I can't remember where I left it.

In the light of having no protection and being unable to see it anywhere in my vicinity, I stand still worrying I didn't lock the door. Did I hear the knob turn?

I slide off the bed, slip across the floor in my bare feet. It is darker in the cabin than it is outside. So I carefully peer out the window.

HOLY SHIT! I feel dizzy with fear. I see him. It is a man in the shadows of the tree on the porch and next to the window. He's not two feet away from me. My eyes are wide, my heart pounding, grinding in my chest. I don't breathe. I just stare, stare, and stare. STICK MAN. He's there. He's wearing a black suitcoat and black pants. He smells like bitter ginger.

I stand there unable to move. One breath. Two breaths. My hands are shaking. I'm trying hard not to think of the little wax figure made of twigs. Does it call to the shadow figure? Maybe he keeps coming back until he can find a way to seal my death. Silly. I'm being silly, right? There's a person out there. Oh, hell, that could be even scarier. I blink. I hear a shift of boards as if a weight is being carried across them. Whoever or whatever is standing there, is moving.

I realize I have to face my fears. I have to know what is out there. I look to the table. There's an emergency flashlight sitting there, big and silver. I take it in my hand and tiptoe to the door. I slide my fingers on the knob, turn it and take a deep breath before I step outside.

I scan the perimeter. Shadows. There's so many of them beneath the almost-full moon and the security light. I shift and nearly trip over a broom laying across the doorway. The splintery handle digs into my bare, big toe and a shock of pain slips through it. "Shit." I curse and clamp my mouth shut before I take a step over the broom. I look to the place where the figure had been standing. I walk slowly and carefully to the exact place it had been. There's something on the wooden deck. I kneel down. I feel my heart drop knowing what it is even before I feel my fingers scrape across the cold wax, the little pine needles sticking from the makeshift doll. I stare at it just as I see the shadow creeping along the porch again behind me this time, slowly covering my own silhouette draping across the wooden porch floor. I scream at the exact moment the hand touches my shoulder. Then I jump up, heart pounding and brace myself for whatever pummeling I would receive. But not without a fight.

"Cripes!" A deep voice shouts. Oh. I blink. It's Ben making this funny jaggedy-walk backward like a string puppet dancing. "What are you doing?" he demands.

"There was somebody out here!" I was inches from hitting him in the head with the flashlight. "Was it you?"

"No, the security light went on. Grampa sent me out."

I am shaking. I wouldn't mind beating Ben Landowski with the flashlight right now just for scaring the bejeebas out of me. "Did you do this?" I hold up my left hand with the doll. "Did you leave this doll as a joke or something?"

"Another one? No. Of course not."

My heart pounding is slowing. I feel drained, wide awake at the same time. "I've had enough of this," I hiss-whisper. "This better not be some kind of joke you and your friends are playing on me. It's not funny." I pull my foot up, rub my toe where it banged into the broom. I know why it's there. Putting a broom in front of a door stops a witch from entering. Or leaving. "It's not funny at all."

Chapter 22
Face to Face with My First Love

I'm knee deep in close up shots at seven the next morning when the knock on the door jolts me from the computer screen. I close the laptop cover, blink away from the grisly photos. I'm still in my pajama shorts and silk pink camo camisole Romeo got me. I feel guilty wearing them since we're not going out. They don't show anything above a Rated PG, but when I get to the door, Ben blinks and his face turns at least three shades of orange-red.

"Hey, there's a guy in a truck that keeps driving up and down the road." He's standing on the front porch jabbing a thumb toward the end of the driveway. He's got a plate of food in his other hand. "And this is for you. Grandma said you should have one more nice hot meal before you leave." I'm not sure if it's an excuse to come over and tell me that or his grandma really fixed me a plate. "Regardless, I think it might be somebody from your family. Oh, there it is again."

There's a truck pulling in the driveway. It's light green, old and beat up. I'd heard it drive past twice, rolls of thunder growling from the muffler. Finally, on this third pass, the vehicle stops just short of Josif's driveway with a black cloud spewing out of the exhaust. I can hear gears grind while the truck goes into reverse to back up. I know who the driver is long before he slings gravel all over the driveway with his over-sized tires. Harley Joseph McCarthy.

Ben's starting to turn. I push out a hand to stop him. "This is for me. Can you put the food on the counter?"

"Yeah. You think you should put some clothes on? Is he—?"

"My sister's husband," I interrupt. It sounds strange on my lips. I suppose I always knew she'd be the one to get married. I just didn't want to believe it would be Harley. I look down at my outfit. It really isn't that bad. "It's just pajamas. Daddy probably sent him to pick up the money, make sure I didn't cut out of town. The banks aren't even open yet."

"I'll come out."

"No, please don't," I tell him with pleading eyes. "I can do this one all by myself. He's—he looks wilder than he really is."

That's not quite true. Harley McCarthy's as wild as the bucks he hunts on the mountain. He's the kind of boy a girl dreams of taming, of gentle-breaking like a pretty, young pony. Oh yeah, he's pretty with his sweet smile and green eyes. And homegrown. He's also the kind of boy a girl can never tame, won't ever break. He'd just as soon make her feel like she fit right into his easy gait, then buck her off as far away from the barn as he could if he saw some young filly that's cuter or easier to sugar up for a hook up.

I ease out the door, see Harley in his truck. He's alone and he sees me. He just nods his head up and down as if he knew all along some secret that he now has evidence to back up.

"Hey, Piper," he says, making a smooth shove of his door open and steps out with his chin up high and cocky.

"Hey, Harley, what you need?" I cringe inwardly, knowing I've suddenly reverted to my old talk, my old drawl. "Did Peyton send you? Because I don't have the money yet. I've got to call the bank and get it wired."

"Money? I'm not worried about that. Peyton, she don't know I'm here." He's four steps from the porch. Fresh t-shirt, old blue jeans, cowboy boots. "Nobody knows I'm here." I'm standing with my elbows resting on the deck railing. I can almost feel him, feel his hands slipping along my shoulders like they used to do. *Baby, you're so sweet, so sweet. Peyton, she don't got nothing on you.*

"Why'd you come back, Piper?" He just asks that and stops, shoves his hands in his pockets. "I thought I'd died and gone to heaven when you pulled into the house the other day. Dammit, girl, I miss you."

"Well, you married her. It's about the same." I'm uncomfortable. I know Ben's within earshot. This conversation isn't one I'd like to share with anybody.

"It ain't the same. You know that. Baby, she's not you. She looks like you, but inside, she's—she's different. It—it could have been you. You know, I wanted it to be you."

"She got the ring," I offer. "That's enough proof for me. It's not on my finger. Where'd you get that kind of money for a ring?"

"I've got my ways. I sold some stuff."

"Sold some stuff or *stole* some stuff, Harley?" I smooth back my hair just like I used to do, grab it in both hands and pretend I'm tying it back. Why am I flirting? I'm not sure. He always thought it was sexy, me playing with my hair. I always thought my little brother, Will, took the money. He was always stealing stuff from everybody else, tucking dollar bills, treasures, and toys into a shoebox under his bed. Maybe not.

"Holy shit, Piper." He says that and takes two steps up the stairway. "I'd trade her off in a second if you said for me to do it."

"How many kids do you and Peyton have?"

"Three. Two boys and a girl. Tessie, she's just like you, all tomboy and trouble. Every time she lobs one of the boys with a baseball, I think of you."

"You're still playing us both, aren't you, Harley? You

got kids. You're not leaving her." I take a step back. "Two for the price of one? You walk around with her on your arm and put the ring on her finger. You sneak around with me behind the barn." I was fifteen when he tugged my hand, drew me behind the barn the first time. He'd been dating Peyton since I swear, they were eight. It was always me who had the crush on him. I never said anything, just watched from afar. She was always following him around and teasing him with little dresses on. I was more into punching his arm and wrestling around with him in old blue jean shorts and t-shirts. He was always ignoring her.

Then, it was like they were a couple about the time we all turned fourteen. One soft, sultry summer night, we were all out sitting around a fire at the creek and I started across the pasture for home. He caught up with me in the backyard, whispered something soft and sweet in my ear. The next thing I know, he's hard-kissing me and it was my first man-kiss. He told me it was me he wanted to be with but didn't want Daddy mad at him if he left Peyton. And so, he never did.

"I'll leave her, you know that. You just say the word and I'll forget I was ever married to her. Let's leave. Let's just jump in my truck and go. Dammit, girl, I miss you."

"And it'd be her you'd be looking in the face every day." I laugh. And there'd be some excuse after we drove off, stopped and made out in the truck. He had to go home and tell her. Then, he'd be gone a couple days, come back and say he never could tell Peyton, couldn't quite look her in the eyes just yet. *Please give me more time.* Oh, I've been there before. Now he's up at the top of the steps in one bound and I'm staring at him knowing I could make this happen. I'm not some little girl who's afraid of her daddy anymore.

"It was you I bought the ring for," he says softly,

trying to slip his hand to my waist. "You know that. I've waited so long. The day you left, I died inside. Come home. You can get a job at the grocery store. Forget all this." He waves a finger in the air. I almost laugh. Sure, I was going to give up my career I'd worked so hard for and work at Copperhead Creek Grocery. I knew Harley was backwards even when I was fifteen. I suppose a cute butt in blue jeans mattered more then. But I've been waiting a long time for this, too, for him to profess his love so I could tell him to screw off. I'm just not so prepared. Because although I thought it up in my mind all these years, I never thought it'd happen. Because there is one small problem, he's Harley. And like my mama used to say, he could talk a dog off a meat truck.

I let him poke at my waist. I let him tickle me under the chin and I give a little grin. "You stole that money, didn't you, Harley?" I ask him in a throaty whisper. "That's how you got the ring."

"Naw, maybe. What's it matter? Aunt Tammy's dead and gone. She don't need it where she's at. Did somebody say something?"

Naw. Maybe. What's that mean? And who would say something to me about the money? With Harley, it is a full confession. I shake my head, give his hand a little push back. "You're a crap, you know that, right?"

"Aw, come on, Piper, baby—" He's grinning and chuckling like I'm playing with him. Because this is how we used to play. He'd touch me, I'd push him away. He'd kiss me, I'd turn my face.

"I'm not playing anymore, idiot," I say, giving him one final and good shove with both hands. "Because of you my daddy hates me. He thinks I took the money."

"I didn't say I took it."

"Yeah, you kind of did."

"So what, Piper? Nobody's going to believe you. Your mama loves me, your daddy loves me. I'm the golden boy with a job at the gravel pit. I make good money. They all think I'm sent straight from heaven. They ain't ever going to believe you and get mad at me. You're not going to tell Peyton because she'll know you came on to me. Imagine what that'd do to my kids. You're trouble and have always been trouble. You paved your own path. So I just led them to it and did what I had to do. Like I said, it could have been your finger that ring sat on. Could still be. I'm not opposed to leaving her."

"Get out." I step back with my foot hard on the wooden porch floor. I start to turn, feel Harley reach out and snatch at my shirt. I smack his hand away, cock my chin and hold out both hands. "I'm not doing it. I'll get that stupid five-thousand dollars and bail your ass out. But don't ever come around me again. I'm not stupid and fifteen anymore Harley McCarthy. And I carry a gun."

I hear the screen door to the cabin squeak open. I turn my head slightly, wonder how long Ben's been standing there listening. He just pushes his way through the door. "Get and go," Ben says in a deep tone. He looks different, not wearing his silly grin. He's stoic and carrying himself like he's ready to fight if he needs to. "Just in case you can't understand her northern accent, I'll translate. She's telling you she doesn't want you around."

For maybe ten seconds, there's silence. Harley's gazing Ben up and down. Ben's unblinking looking down at him. Size to size, there's maybe a five inch difference, Ben being the taller of the two. I'm thinking there's going to be a knockdown, drag out fight right here. Harley rubs his chin, gets this self-satisfied tip to his lips. He shakes his head. "Your loss, girl," he tells me. "But you ain't worth a fight."

Chapter 23
Another Round of Flirting. Another Kiss.

"Is he always such a jerk?"

"Yeah, Ben, he's always a jerk." My bags are all packed and sitting next to the front door. Well, all but the dress I'm wearing for the flight home flopped on top and a few things I'm leaving with Josif. I've got it down to a science, this never-ending meander from one job to the next. A bag of clothes, a carry-on bag with my laptop and camera and odds and ends that never seem to get done.

"So what are all of these?" Ben ignores that when he follows me back inside. He is poking a finger on the elementary school yearbooks. He opens one with his forefinger while I watch him. He's so pretty, he reminds me of my ex-boyfriend, the one who models jeans. Not the one that just left in a good dose of gravel aimed toward me.

"They are yearbooks. I felt like I was leaving your grandpa high and dry not finishing what I started for him. I got caught up in dead girls and photographing spoiled models. So last night, I stayed up all night searching for little boys in Louisville during the 1940s matching your grandpa's little brother. I figured I'd sleep on the plane. I found a few who look like him. Can I take your picture?"

"Huh?" He turns around. He's got on an old t-shirt and basketball shorts. He looks down, shakes his head. "Naw. I look like crap. Why do you want a picture?"

"You don't look like crap. I was thinking that if I can find some pictures of your grandpa's brother when he's a little older, he might look like you."

"What are the odds of that?" He rolls his eyes sarcastically.

"Okay, I'm lying. I wanted something to remember you by. You remind me of Romeo."

"From Shakespeare?"

"No, my ex-boyfriend. He's really Zen, you know, easy going. You are too. I mean, you have your moments."

"The model. His name is Romeo? You've got to be kidding me, right?"

"No, I'm not. You want to hear something funny?" I ask him, leaning up against the table next to him. "My real name was Piper Juliet LaRue O'Sullivan. Mama and Daddy couldn't come to a compromise on which middle name to use. They always said it was either two middle names or they were going to end up divorced."

"Romeo. Juliet. Wow, you two were probably never meant to be, right?" Ben pokes me with his forefinger in the ribs and I chuckle.

"Yeah, now he's with—I think the dude's name is Robert." I feel kind of bad right then. He was excited sending me the text with the picture of him and his new boyfriend and I blew him off. "Romeo and Robert. It just doesn't have the same—kind of passion."

"The story's not so romantic to me. I teach high school English. I think I've read it to my classes a thousand times. Once you break it down sentence by sentence so they understand the gist of the storyline, it's incredibly—boring. I think a storyline with Romeo and Robert would stir things up a bit. If not with the kids in a small town like this, but also with their parents."

"My Romeo was definitely not boring."

"I bet. I got to go. I've got stuff to do in the morning. Grandpa's got some cabin guests coming in." He slaps the table with his palm, does a little drumbeat. "Have a safe trip home."

"Oh." I'm caught off-guard again. "Okay. You're mad?" I reach out and poke him in the belly. Ben grunts, holds a hand to the place I just jabbed.

"No, not really. Not until you did that."

"You mean this?" I reach out and knuckle him in the ribs and he stands back.

"You're annoying, Piper." His eyes are irritated. He starts to reach a hand out and I step back. He tips his chin, gives me a bold look. "Yes, that."

"And this." I give him another pop in the tummy.

"What the hell? Stop."

"No," I give him a smug grin. "You like it."

"I don't like it."

"You liked it when I kissed you."

He's standing there blinking at me like I'm an idiot. It's like he's letting the words sink in, waiting for the punch line to his joke. My face turns a deep shade of red and he pats the table and acts like he's going to leave.

"I think *you* liked it when you kissed me." He's got that snarky look on his face. I roll my eyes. I can't help to see the stubble on his cheeks, remember what it felt like on my own cheeks. He watches me walk over toward the bedroom. I stop, lean against the wall and bump my butt on it a couple times, rocking back and forth.

"But who does that without a reason?" He belts out suddenly. "Is that kind of your thing? You hop from place to place, flirting it up with guys who already have girlfriends or are married because they're easy to leave—? One day here, two days there. No love, just fooling around. Then boom, you're gone. There's no paper trail, just a short line of Post-it Notes that stop at the nearest airport and some poor idiot staring up at the sky wondering where you went. Like your sister's husband and probably your Romeo who's still hung up on you so he's sending you pictures of him with his new boyfriend in a vain attempt to make you jealous."

"That's a bunch of crap."

"No, it's not. So—you think it's okay to leave me standing there holding a little piece of yellow paper and wondering what the hell that kiss was all about?"

"First of all, I've never slept with a married man. Second of all, if you thought I was going to leave a trail of Post-It Notes, why didn't you go buy a couple hundred stacks and hand them to me so I knew you might be wondering where I went? Or better yet, just ask me to stay a couple more days." I feel my heart beating hard. I didn't see this one coming. But if he's feeling something right now, I am too. "Do you want me to leave you a paper trail, Ben? Because one kiss does not make us close enough for me to assume—"

"Okay, so, let's make it two. No guesses."

He caught me off-guard. Ben seems to be good at that. He's four steps away. I'm still against the wall next to the bedroom. He hesitates and I'm thinking he might just be too shy to make the move. Then he kind of throws his head back, wags it back and forth, and rolls his eyes like he's being forced to do this. He walks right over to me and stands three inches from my chest. "Here's the first box of notes, Piper," he says softly. He takes his hands and runs his forefingers along my arms and down to my wrists. He leans into me, takes my hands and brings them up so I'm gently pinned to the wall. That's when he kisses me. It's true, deep and incredibly tender. I close my eyes, fall into it.

"Piper, you've got the most beautiful eyes. And your lips. I've never seen a girl with heart shaped lips like yours." It's followed by a peck on each eyebrow before he kisses my lips and pulls back just enough I feel a coolness between us where our bodies had been so close. "So here's another box.

Stay one more day." I feel his fingers twining into my own. "Let me look into your beautiful eyes just a little longer. Let me kiss your lips one more day." Holy shit. I've never had a guy talk to me like this, so romantic, so—sensual. It's like he's telling me a love story with the soft breaths he leaves on my cheeks. They tickle. He kisses me again. My heart is pumping.

"Okay, one day," I whisper.

"So you like this? You like it when I talk to you like this? Some girls do. Some girls don't."

"I do." I almost question why this same man can't hardly walk when he's around Jenny. How he seems so shy and now, he's got this game going between us, soft words caressing my mind. Then he kisses me again and again until I don't know how much time has passed and he stops, looks back and forth between my eyes. My burnt orange and his deep blue. I feel one hand release and he drops it to my side. His fingers alight next to my ribs. Goosebumps roll along my bare arms. He has to see it. He laughs softly.

"So I can whisper sweet things in your ear all day. That's easy for me," he tells me hoarsely, softly. "I know you are big city. I'm small town, Piper. But when it gets to this, I'm not so—sure. I probably don't know—"

"If you're not sure, I can show you—"

"I've been kind of putting it off, waiting—"

"—for someone special?" I ask him. I can see where he's going. He's not sure about it. Small town boys have few choices, especially ones who are still stuck with baggage everybody knows about. I'm not a one-night-stander either. He's waiting for Jenny to take this next step. My own voice is husky. "We can stop. I understand. Someone special."

"You. I've been waiting for you, Piper."

Chapter 24
Pillow Talk

"Where was the step between insulting each other and doing this?" I ask, untangling myself from Ben and finding a place in the cleft of his left arm when he rolls to his side. "Because I think I blinked and missed it."

"Yeah, right?" Ben's voice is low and husky. We made it to the bedroom, almost missed the bed. We bumped foreheads, tripped over sheets. I kneed him in the belly, he elbowed me in the chest. And we laughed. "I didn't see it coming. So tell me about this Harley."

"Oh, no, we're doing pillow talk." I furrow my brow, give him a curious glare-stare. He's so warm against my belly and thigh. My tummy's still making funny jumps, forcing a happiness mixed with a melancholy ache.

"We're kind of in that place." He's right. This is about as intimate as it gets, shoved up next to each other half-dressed and nestled together. He's got his right arm wrapped around my shoulders. He's tickling me with the fingers of his left hand. They are soft and gentle when they reach up and cup my chin. He lifts my head slightly and kisses my forehead. I giggle. It tickles.

"Okay, he was my first, you know." I shrug, look up shyly. Shy? It's just not me. With Ben, maybe I am. I don't know why. "You know on the outside, he's like an old tough piece of leather, kind of snarky."

"Kind of?"

"Let me finish." I poke Ben softly with my forefinger in the chest. He grunts. "Every girl wants to tame the wild pony-boy. I thought I could too. I thought he'd just drop Peyton and come to me because I was holding out the little treat in my palm. I don't know why it sounds so naïve when it comes out of my mouth. But when you're fifteen, the reality of the idea kind of floats off into the air like a misty dream. You don't see beyond. Anyways, he was a good kisser and it was fun sneaking off, I guess."

"When you're fifteen."

"Why do you say that?"

"You didn't leave with him at—what was it, eighteen or nineteen?" Ben says. "You didn't leave with him today."

"Yeah, it was seventeen. Why would I?" I scoot in closer, feel the beat of Ben's heart and wonder if I really want to do this, get so close to somebody.

"Because you knew he was using you and your sister?"

"Well, no," I sniff. "When I was younger and stupider, I was enjoying it for what it was. You know what it was, Ben, which made me leave."

"The fight with your family?"

"Yeah, and you know the truth. You heard."

"He took the money. Why didn't you say anything?"

"And have everybody know we were screwing around? You think my parents hate me now, imagine if they knew that. It would have gotten blamed on me, the skank. Imagine what it would do to Peyton. She loves him."

"Look what it did anyway. She's married to some guy that would leave her in a heartbeat if something better comes along."

"Yeah, well, I'm not better. That in itself is scary," I mutter. "And it wasn't even getting blamed for stealing or Daddy kicking me out. I suppose I just needed the push. I wanted out of there. I am different than them." I stop, push a finger on Ben's lips because he's getting ready to interrupt me. "No, I'm redneck. I don't mind that. I just don't see eye to eye with my family. I wanted to see the world, get out of there. Aunt Tammy, she said I had a gift for taking pictures. She got me a camera when I was eight. I cherished the thing, took it everywhere with me. Before she went blind, we looked through my pictures every day because she couldn't leave the house, she couldn't walk anymore. Then, when she went blind, I described all of them to her, told her stories about them. She said she could see the world through my eyes."

"That's nice."

"When I was sixteen, she told me about this old antique tobacco tin she kept on her shelf. It was her daddy's old tobacco tin and when he was done with it, she used to take it to school as a lunch box pail. It had these pretty red flowers on it and little handles. She kept all her savings in that box." I sigh. "The problem was, sometimes me and Harley would sneak into the house when nobody was there. Aunt Tammy, she would sit out on the front porch for hours. She never knew we were sneaking into my room. One afternoon, she came in for some sweet tea and would have caught me and Harley if she could see. He hid around the side of the kitchen. That's the day she told me about the money, said she'd been saving it up for something her whole life and didn't know what to do with it. She said she wanted to give it to me so I'd go to college and do something with my gift. Two days after she passed on, it disappeared."

"Why'd they assume you took it?"

I shrug.

"Tell me."

"Because I was the one who always got caught doing the stupid stuff. When I was little, they all called me a tattletale when I told Mama and Daddy the truth that Lee let me try the cigarette or Chad was driving Papaw's ATV and not me. After a while, they got cold to me and it was hard. So I started covering for them. I took the blame."

"Yeah, what you're doing for that jerk, Harley."

"Yeah." I tap my fingers on his chest, work them to his belly. "Now I think a part of me is cursed and not just from the little wax doll." I nod to my luggage where it is carefully tucked into a plastic bag and stuffed inside. "Do you think whoever had the doll and followed us that night knew it was me in the shack at Dark Pines?"

"Why would someone try to kill you?"

"I don't know. I thought maybe someone was mad at me for not picking their farm. What if it's you they are trying to kill?"

"Why?" he asks me. "I just figured they didn't know we were in that shack."

"Yeah, you're right," I sigh, smile up at him. He smiles back. "I've got another hour to kill before the banks open. You want to look at some pictures? See what I do?"

"Dead people pictures?"

"No, silly," I laugh. "I usually only get called in for high profile crimes. Mostly I just do advertisements, models, and backgrounds for Abe Starling who's my boss. I've got animals and just about everything. Maybe that's boring for you."

"No, actually, it's not."

It isn't an hour into sitting on the bed and rolling through the images on my computer that there's a knock on the door. I'm careful about keeping the stored photos of crime scenes separated on travel drives I keep in my bags so I'm not worried we would accidently bump into the body of Ben's ex-fiancé. Ben jumps up, looks like a cat with his tail caught in the door.

"That's probably Grandpa."

Chapter 25
Josif's Story

Warsaw, Poland. I couldn't even point to it on a map until five days ago. It's between Germany and Russia. The weather year around isn't much different than Kentucky.

It's just hard to imagine that eighty years ago, in October of 1940 all the Jewish people living there were shoved into a community sealed off by walls and hatred. Sometime between 1940 and 1941, within those walls, Rysiek and Irena Landowski moved with their family into the brick-walled ghetto and found a tiny room they shared with at least six others families on Bielanska Street.

I am relating this to Josif Landowski while he stands inside the doorway to his cabin eyeing Ben and me cautiously like we're two twelve year-olds he's caught in the barn sneaking a kiss and a smoke. Then, I see his eyes veer down to my suitcases. It's like he hasn't heard a word I said while his gaze comes to my own.

"Are you leaving without paying your father back?"

"No, I was waiting for the bank to open to see if I can have the money transferred. I'm just getting packed for my flight."

"Back to—?"

"To Canada for some cold weather pictures. Abe has another job for me."

He stares at me hard for a good five seconds, then takes in a long and deep breath. "That's my family. My father was Rysiek."

"Yes, do you know that your father wasn't Jewish at all?"

"What? No."

"He was Catholic, Josif, and a pharmacist who refused to live without his wife and three children—one of them being you. There are several newspapers before 1940 that show advertisements for Rysiek's pharmacy. Rysiek received permission to continue his pharmacy within the Warsaw Ghetto. Along with Rysiek and Irena, was Rysiek's mother, Malka, two little boys—Josif age 8 and Aleksander age 6 and two girls—Lila, age 3 and Chaja, age 5. Chaja was a niece of your father."

"My cousin," Josif is rubbing his face with his palm. "When Chaja came to live with us, she cried all the time. I tried to play with her and we drew pictures on the walls of our apartment with chalk. It made her happy."

"Yes, her mother died of starvation in 1942. I found a notation in a Holocaust article that I collected noting her death. I also found a newspaper which a man translated for me stating: *Zysla Licht, wife and mother, died. Age 26.* Chaja's father was shot by police. Malka was hit by a tram and died in 1942. On May 22, 1941, Lila died during a cholera epidemic."

"I remember." That's all Josif says. He is pale now. Maybe it isn't good he remembers. I look over at Ben and he is eyeing his grandpa with the same unsure gaze.

"Josif, I can stop. Do you want—?"

"No, go on." He's working his hands, wrinkled hands. His eyes are staring at his hands. Eyes that have seen dead eyes like I have seen. Only his, they were people he loved.

"Okay," I feel a bead of sweat form at my temple. I push my hair behind my ear nervously and look to Ben who nods his head. "In January of 1942, Irena and Chaja were rounded up during a Gestapo raid and sent to the Treblinka I labor camp where Irena most likely worked on the labor camp farm."

"She just did not come home from visiting a friend."

Josif is staring at the ground. His breaths are puffs.

"There is one record of her making it to the camp when they brought her in. Sadly, your father probably never knew where she went. There was a short plea for her in the Warsaw Ghetto newspaper like a missing person's advertisement."

"Yes. He would pace the floor at night after she came up missing. He was never the same again."

"There is no record of her death or Chaja's death. They just didn't keep very good records and so many were burned when the war was ending."

"What about my father and my brother, did you find anything?"

"Okay, so it is like this," I say softly. "He went to Treblinka thinking he would find your mother. There is a diary note from a cousin who lived with your family. The entire diary was saved in an archive. It has a couple entries of how your father searched for your mother. When it all failed and his health began to fade, he boarded the train on one of the roundups to find her. Instead of Treblinka I, the work camp, he was taken to Treblinka II, the death camp. He was, most likely, murdered within hours of getting off the train."

I'm uneasy standing there. Josif looks one-hundred and ten years-old standing there staring at the floor. He's pale and I see Ben looking back and forth between me and his grandpa.

"And my brother?"

"That is what I want you to see," I say. "You know the orphans were taken to Treblinka, the death camp."

"Yes."

"There are no records of the children. There were supposedly rumors that the children were all taken to safety. But it was just wishful thinking. They all died."

"I know."

"Okay, so that is where I am."

"We don't know then. You tell me things I already know and some things I don't. But you aren't telling me what I asked. Is the boy in the photograph my brother?"

"Show him." Ben says.

My eyes snap up to Ben's questioningly. "Show him the yearbooks."

I shake my head. "I don't know. They're a longshot."

"Let me decide." Josif heaves a sigh.

So I dig out the images I got at the historical society, lay them out in sequential order for Josif to see. I tell him about the war bond parade and how I found the images of the two boys sitting on the curb and the boy from the newspaper article sitting on the stool with the soldier. He's staring at them, gaping at them. His finger touches one, then the others one by one.

"These—these are the actual pictures?"

"Copies from the newspaper archives," I tell him. "Did Aleksander have any identifying marks, Josif, which would make you believe this is him?"

"He had a little cut on his bottom lip. He bit an electrical cord when he was two or three." Josif has the pictures in his hands. He's touching the faces, looking closely at them. "It was burned. My father had some medicine he put on it and it healed, but not all the way."

"Okay, then you need to see these," I tell him, tugging the pictures from his hand. I take one of the yearbooks with the little yellow Post-it Notes and hand it to him. "The photos are too far away to see small identifying marks. Maybe most people would overlook them. But my mind is hard wired to watch for specific details at a crime scene. You know, a tiny mark, bugs on the body. In this case—" I sift through the yearbooks. On the front of each, I had made small notes on identifying marks on each boy's face—freckles, a birthmark, a cut, dimples or anything that stuck out to set him apart from the others. I pull the one that has a listing with the small boy by the name of Timothy Nicholson with a cut on his lip and one on his forehead. I open the yearbook wide to the yellow note and poke my finger on Timothy's picture.

"Oh, my." Josif leans forward. I watch him lose his balance, nearly keel completely over. Ben grabs him by the shoulders, moves in and slides his arm beneath his grandpa's arm.

"Grandpa, what?" he asks. "Is that him?"

"Aleksander. It is him. It has—to be him. The cut on his forehead, I did that with a tin can playing kick the can in the streets. Malka was so mad—"

Shay Lawless
Chapter 26
Mean Girl and Stolen Wallets

"What do you mean I have to wait three days to withdraw my money?" I am screaming those very words into the phone while I am sitting in Detective Phillips's cruiser outside the Mount Laurel Unity Church. "You didn't question it when I deposited it now, did you?"

"Miss, calm down. You're not listening," is the message the croaky-voiced woman on the other end is telling me. I can tell she's gritting her teeth against my wrath. "Three full business days is the minimum time it could take. Any withdrawal over three-thousand dollars requires a review. And it may be delayed because you are trying to transfer it from a bank in Washington—"

"You have a mean face on today." Detective Phillips is sitting next to me texting somebody on his phone. He looks up, crosses his eyes. "And you're using your outside voice inside my car."

"Sorry," I mumble, hanging up. "This is just getting drawn out. I've got nothing to do but stare at the walls and I can't get ahold of my boss who needs to reimburse me for every last penny in my account he's drained on this one." I rub my hand against my face, pinch my temples. I've got just enough money in my bank savings account to fly home and eat one meal. I'm getting the feeling Abe had ulterior motives to this shoot. It's like as soon as Tessa and Marcus left, he has been invisible. So earlier this morning, I pulled up his social network page. Wonder of wonders, he was doing the same shoot I was doing here, but at some rich ranching community along the coast of Florida. He's got these two really young models on all of his pics. They are decked out in fancy clothing compared to mine in flannels and jeans. It looks more like a New York runway photo shoot.

"Well, you can be the girl on my arm and help me with some of these interviews, how's that?" Detective Phillips tucks his phone into his pocket.

"The girl on your arm, really?" I hesitate to push the issue too far. "That's insulting. Are we in the 1950s?"

"No," he says. "But these people cling to those type of values. So I'm asking you to play the part. It's kind of like good cop, bad cop. Except you need to ask questions, play dumb. Can you act?"

"I was the lead turkey in the Thanksgiving play in third grade, does that count?"

"I can see how this is going to go."

I almost laugh at him while he hands me a blank notebook and a pen. "You'll need this." He's dressed like a 1950s detective with his gray suit and coat. He has to be hot. Me, I'm all dressed up in a baby doll dress and high heels for the flight back to Washington that obviously isn't going to happen today. Instead, Detective Phillips leads me into the church sanctuary and to the tiny room that Preacher Young uses for his office.

"I'm glad you could come, Bill," Preacher Young extends his hand to Detective Phillips, but not to me. He just gives me a suspicious glazed-eye gaze and offers us a seat.

"Well, we could do this here or down at the police station. I thought we'd stir up less gossip if we did it here."

I try not to seem too curious while Detective Phillips waits for me to sit. He nods his head at me, tells the preacher that I've worked a lot of crime scenes, including those he's investigating in Dark Pines so he wanted me along to take notes. Both of them look at me, then the paper in my hand. "Oh, yeah," I mutter, hold up the pen. Yep, this is why I'm paying back a million dollars in student loans, so I can work for free and take notes like a secretary for a small town cop.

"So, you said you had some information you wanted to remain confidential about the girls who were found on Dark Pines Road? You know and I know I've been getting a lot of pressure to solve this crime from the local tourism. They're afraid it's going to make the national papers and nobody's going to come to visit The Pines."

The preacher is still eyeing me warily. "Sir," I say. "I have taken pictures of hundreds of crime scenes. I know the ropes. It isn't my job to talk. I can't divulge anything I notice to anyone until it becomes public information, and even then, I send any questions to the local police. I just take the pictures, and in this case, the notes."

The preacher's eyes sway away from mine and both Detective Phillips and I follow his gaze to a small framed picture hanging on the wall. It is a family picture with the preacher, a woman in modest skirt and blouse and two children, about fifteen or sixteen. I recognize Bucky right off and then, I see the resemblance in the girl. It is Jenny.

"Whenever I'm making a decision that impacts others, I always look at that picture. It is my family only a year and a half before I made the stupidest decision of my life." My gaze sweeps downward and catch on the preacher's before he looks at the detective. "I had an affair with one of my parishioners. I was counseling her. Although my wife was kind enough to keep this a secret to save my profession, it still eats at me every day. It still wrecked our marriage. She left me. But we both knew divulging this affair would only make things worse for the family of the young woman I counseled and myself."

"Jody Mills?" Detective Phillips tosses the name out there and the preacher nods.

"Yes." Preacher Young scoots up in his chair, then back again. "I've got to tell you that it was nothing more than a kiss. However, emotionally, she and I became quite attached. I knew she was seeing other men and we were working past these obstacles—" He sighs deeply. "I thought you should know. I did not, nor would I have killed her. However, you should know I have never thought she died in that car wreck. I believe she was murdered. I've had no substantiation, though, other than the fact she never went that route home. It terrified her that there was a ghost at that turn in the road, the witch from the old legends that might curse her when she passed. She grew up hearing those stories and told me she wouldn't even drive that way out of town during the day. In the light of the new bodies found, I had to let you know a few things she told me. They were out of the bounds of counseling and while we met at a rest stop off the highway. I feel that if I voided my major mishandling of a situation and you did not know the entire truth—"

"Say." Detective Phillips nods to the preacher.

"She had a man following her, stalking her. Jody could be—a little over-dramatic. She staged things so she could be the center of attention."

"Like what?" Detective Phillips asks.

"She would make up some elaborate fight with a man she met and say he hit her. She'd even go to great lengths like giving herself a black eye to make it appear he had hit her."

"How do you know he didn't?"

"One of those men who she did it to was me. She came in and told me she would show everybody a bruise on her arm I'd given her if I didn't go out and get a drink with her. I don't drink. It terrified me that when I met with her outside Hazard at a dive bar, somebody would see me. Hence what seemed an affair to her, was only a blackmail for me. I feared she would tell someone I'd hurt her. It was like Jody Mills enjoyed making men uncomfortable. I could imagine she might have made some man so angry by her antics, he killed her."

"But you believed her about this stalker?"

"When she first told me about this man, I believed she was making the stories up. Jody said she caught a suit-coated man peeping in her apartment window on High Street that she shared with a couple friends. I tossed it aside, told her to contact the police if it happened again."

"You don't know who it could have been?"

"No. I only know that I read in the paper that the young lady whose clothing was found on the body dumped at Dark Pines had a stalker too. My mistake should not stop you from catching whoever killed Jody and who may be wanting to kill this other girl."

"Hey, Piper, can I talk to you a wee second?" The soft voice scoots along the foyer just as Detective Phillips and I start down the church steps outside. "Alone." It's Jenny Young and she's smiling her shy smile, twining her arms and giving the detective a soft, flirty gaze. I find her more than mildly annoying. She's like a five year-old in women's conservative 1980s clothing, wholesome and sugary sweet. I try to imagine if I was a guy, if this type of girl—chaste and naïve—would appeal to me. I suppose, I'd feel like I was raising a girlfriend, that's what I decide. Maybe that appeals to some guys. I just don't get the fascination.

She wiggles her fingers at the detective. "Hey, Bill." He nods back, smiles sweetly.

"Um, yeah," I answer, looking to the detective who looks back and forth between the two of us. I lag, he saunters forward.

"What can I do for you?" I ask. I almost feel like I need to push my hands on my knees to talk down to her. It isn't just that she's tiny, but I feel like I'm going to have a conversation with a child. I'm thinking maybe she's going to bug me about going on a double date with her brother. Or maybe, ask for advice on how to talk to Ben. I don't know. I see her looking over my shoulder until we hear the slam of the detective's car door.

"I know you like Ben," she says in the softest of tones, leaning into me. A grin spreads across her face, then it is more like a leer. I feel a little jolt of adrenaline. I don't understand the reason. I'm just getting mixed feelings about this awkward meeting. She smiles softly, nibbles her lip. "So I've got something to tell you. Stay away from him." She stands up straight, loses the bashful tip of her chin and suddenly, her voice isn't baby-talk soft. "So let's just be frank between us girls. I'm assuming you're giving out since I'm not. Because girls like you, that's the only way you can get a guy to pay attention to you. Like the whore who broke up my mom and dad. But he ain't yours. I'm willing to fight for him, unlike my spineless mom who just runs away. And he ain't never going to be yours, slut. Never." She's got a head waggle going on and her *never* sounds like *neva,* long and drawn out. "When he's done using you, he's coming back to me. And you do know, he's only using you for sex, don't you?"

I'm blinking thinking this girl's got a twin sister too or something because one second, she's all cute and cuddly like a newborn kitten and the next, she's an old bitter outside cat that doesn't get fed half the time. She reaches out, snatches my collar and leans in hard. "Don't make me bust your ass. I will. Touch Ben again and I'm going to wake you up in the middle of the night and wale on you like it's next Tuesday. Then I'm going to go around town and tell everybody you're a whore and that you've done it with all their husbands and boyfriends. And you know what? They'll believe me because, well, you know—" She wags a hand in front of her and goes back to her baby voice. "I'm little me, all cute and sweet."

"I think I just came face to face with the devil." I get in the car, blink at Detective Phillips.

"What are you talking about?"

"Jenny Young just went from this cute, baby-talking small town girl to—wow, I can't even—"

"Satan. You already said it. Did her head spin around? Maybe she needs exorcised."

I give him a muted laugh. He laughs heartily. "You've never met a *mean girl*?" he asks and I shrug.

"I don't know. Not like that."

"Maybe you've never liked a boy that a mean girl liked."

"She knew about the affair. Compared me with Jody. Did you know about it?" I ask Detective Phillips.

"Nope. Not a clue. We'll keep this to ourselves, right? It didn't sound like much of an affair. More like a blackmail."

"It's none of my business." I raise my shoulders, let them fall. "Besides, my daddy always told me: *Judge not, lest you be judged.* You know, from the bible. It's not my job to be the critic, well, when I'm making mistakes all the time too. Can I suggest something?" I ask him, patting the notebook on my knees.

"LaRue, I am guessing you're going to advise me

whether I say yes or no, am I right?"

"You asked me to come along. You don't have to be so caustic, Low Po." I wag my shoulders. He looks tired today, said he'd not been able to sleep since he got the call the night of the body showing up. "But, yes, I suppose." I scratch my head. "Ben Landowski gave me a few names of guys Jody was seeing."

"I bet he did."

"Ben's a good guy, detective," I tell him. "He comes off as a jerk, but he's alright. I think he's like—"

"Purdy and sweet and—using one of you two girls to get to the other."

"Let's not go there, off the record, it's a sore spot today," I warn him, pointing at the road so he gets the hint to put the car in gear and go. "I don't even think he has a clue she's putting on an act."

"Oh, so—"

"So don't ask questions."

"The girl's leaving. The boy doesn't want her to go?"

"No," I counter. "You're not a very good detective at all if that's what you think. It's more like—" I sigh. Here is what it is. I'm leaving out the front door, dragging my little suitcase across the bumpy gravel this morning. I'm talk-screaming at the first bank trying to get my money and I nearly run straight into the side of Bucky Young's truck. I look up and Ben's leaning against the passenger side of the truck with his elbows on the window like he's been talking to Bucky. Bucky rolls down his window and about the time I put on the brakes, he's giving me this strangely unwieldy smile like he just got caught in a lie.

"Ben says you want to go out with me."

"Huh?" I am half digging into my backpack looking for my credit card and driver's license to use at the bank to get the money to pay my daddy and half talking to Bucky. I look over Bucky's shoulder and Ben is goofy-smiling at me and nodding his head up and down.

"Ben says you want to go out with me. You know, a double date. He's going out with my sister. I go out with you."

"I—I—" I'm stuttering which isn't good. I'm caught between two conversations with predictable endings, neither to my advantage. "I'm leaving right now."

"Oh." Bucky snaps his attention to Ben. "I thought you said she wasn't leaving."

"Oh, maybe she is—leaving." Ben pats the top of the truck. I'm distracted, more interested in finding my stupid clutch wallet that doesn't appear to be in my backpack.

I jam on the brakes, stop short of the truck. "Well, no, I'm not leaving if I can't find my purse," I say to nobody in peculiar. I drop everything right there and turn back to the cabin.

I scream. It's one of those high-pitched, horror movie screams. I cut it off halfway. Mama used to get mad at me when I reacted so violently to seeing snakes. I learned to curtail it quickly. Still, there's a snake slipping under the pillow of my bed. I see its tail. My heart is doing this pitter-patter and I'm wobbling backward when I bounce right into Ben careening through the door. He's freaking out, thinks I got shot or something because I screamed, then stopped.

"It's just a little snake," he tells me in a soft voice after he and Bucky jerk the mattress off the bed, tear off the sheets and crawl under to find it. It is just a little snake he holds in his hands and allows to wiggle through his fingers, a black racer like we used to see down by Copperhead Creek. Ben eyes me cautiously. I see him take me in like he knows my weakness now.

"It's going to be a dead snake if you let it loose near me." I glower at him. He takes it outside far from the cabin and returns. Gone. Just like my little wallet from my purse. Ben and Bucky come back and help me look under the beds and under the sink and all the places the purse wouldn't be even if I had misplaced it.

"Do you remember the last time you saw it?" Bucky asks and I try not to screw up my face into a sarcastic grin. Why do people always ask such a stupid question?

"If she knew that," Ben mutters for me. "She'd be able to find it, dumbass."

"True that." Bucky throws out his arms to his sides. He grins anyway. I don't think that boy ever stops grinning.

"I hope this isn't some stupid ploy to keep me here so I'll go out with your friend," I spat. I wish I hadn't said it. It sounded really stupid like I think I'm worth a bribe to go out with. "It's got to be here somewhere." I drop my head.

"You don't think whoever it was out here last night took it, do you?" Ben is looking at me, his gaze secure on mine.

"Maybe they traded the snake for the purse," Bucky offers with a laugh.

"Not funny," I gripe.

"I'm sorry. Why are girls afraid of snakes?"

His remark irks me a little. It's like now I'm a girl. And I have a weakness. "I don't think all girls are afraid of snakes," I sniff back.

"I'm sorry." He gives me that silly grin again and I can't help but grin back. "My mom is. My sister is. I shouldn't assume it's girls. Maybe it is just a genetic trait in my family. I just missed out."

"I wasn't scared of them until my stupid little brother

turned on me and got mad. He put a bunch in my bed when I was a kid," I divulge. "You know why he was mad at me?" I reach out with both hands, grab Bucky's arm with my fists and twist in opposite directions. "I gave him an Indian rug burn, also known as —"

"Ow. A snake bite," Bucky mumbles, swiping my hands away. "I can see where your brother got the idea for his payback." He grabs up my wrist in one hand, my fingers in the other and pulls me up to him. "I got one of those to repay you with. A noogie." He takes his knuckle, rubs it on the top of my head. We tussle around laughing.

"Hey! Are we going to look for the purse or not."

We stop, look up at Ben. He's snapping his eyes back and forth between us. Bucky releases me, kind of gets a curious tip to his chin. I pull away. Funny thing, Ben scowls at him, then just looks at me like a whipped pup. What does that mean?

"I don't think whoever it was came inside. I mean, I don't know. Snakes slip in through windows and doors all the time," I say really fast. I feel like Ben just caught me and Bucky wrestling it out on a bed or something. "And—and I'm always losing my stuff. Even you know that. It's got to be here." I pause look at the cabin door, walk up to it and bend down at the threshold. There's mud there. I suppose anybody's boots could leave mud, but we've been really careful about taking off our shoes just outside, then walking with stocking feet across the floor.

"It wasn't locked." I'm pinching my temples. "Yeah, you know what?" I toss out. "Somebody could have come in here, stolen my purse." Honestly, I think the two clowns in there with me snuck in there and took it. I don't know why. I just get the feeling. I mean, they just show up right when I'm leaving. Ben shows up last night two inches from the porch at the exact time the shadowy figure disappears. Because that's where my driver's license is and that's the first thing the girls see before the figure comes to their window. "I need to make a few phone calls, Ben. I can't leave without a driver's license and my identification and passports. I'm screwed. I need to think this out."

I called Detective Phillips. I did it at first right next to Ben and Bucky just to see if they would squirm. They didn't. Then I feel like an idiot while Detective Phillips joins the search because I get this awful feeling he's going to find my purse under the bed or sitting on my car seat. However, another forty-five minutes later, my purse is still not found.

"Let's go for a ride, LaRue, we need to talk anyway," Detective Phillips finally eyes the two younger men carefully, then he jabs a thumb to a black car he drove today.

"I got a flight to catch."

"And you're not without your purse. You need to take a break."

I reluctantly agreed. And that's where the conversation arose about the boy not wanting the girl to leave. I think he thinks Ben might have taken it. He just doesn't understand because he missed the conversation while he was helping Ben lift up the bed in the cabin to look underneath.

Bucky comes sauntering out. "Did you just not want to go out with me or do you really have to leave tonight?" Bucky catches me squatting inside the door of my car, driver's side. I'm patting underneath the seats for the tenth time.

"This would be a pretty elaborate scheme to turn down a date, don't you think?" I ask him. I'm grumpy. I look up and he's still smiling away like I just didn't spat out something sarcastic.

"Yeah, you're right. I'm sorry," he says.

"No, I'm sorry." I pat the seat, smile back. "I'm just a little stressed."

"Well, if it helps. I'd rather he wasn't seeing my sister anyway. He's a player. I'm his friend and I recognize it. There isn't a girl in this town he hasn't done once. Once. Then he's out of there. My sister's an easy target."

I stare at Bucky. Is he kidding me? "Ben Landowski? He told me he—" hadn't been with any girls. Crud. I heard the same thing from Harley and I fell for it like a stupid fish rushing toward a worm on a hook. "He seems shy, I guess."

Bucky laughs out loud. "I don't know what he told you. But I'm sure it is what he's told Kylee Lane, Janie Harper and Lauren Hill, just to name a few I know. Don't tell me he's done it to you. You're not even close to his type."

"His type?"

"You've got a head on your shoulders. Those other girls are dingbats like my sister. Gullible. The kind of girls who sit around waiting for him to call back even when they see him with another girl."

"I guess I'm dumber and more naïve than you think. He's in a long line of guys who've emotionally dumped me in a manure pile."

So while I stare at Detective Phillips an hour and a half later in his car, I just shake my head. "Okay, so skip all that. No, the boy does not care if the girl leaves. And the girl, she doesn't care either." I pat my bare knee with my finger. "Has it ever crossed your mind that the body burned up in that car wasn't Jody Mills at all?"

"Why wouldn't it be?"

"I don't know that answer. I just know that Ben told

me they didn't do DNA testing to see. She was burned beyond recognition. There are two more bodies in Dark Pines that were possibly dug up. It's a guess, I'm sure—"

"If you are suggesting that I have Jody Mills dug up, exhumed, for testing, LaRue, that's just not happening. We don't have the resources nor do I want to put her mama and daddy through that."

"Okay."

"Well, I can see in your eyes it's not okay. Yet, there's just nothing to support your theory. I mean, I know there's reasons people would want themselves to look dead. But that girl, I just don't think she'd go through all that trouble. She just wasn't that bright, came from a poor family—"

"Like mine."

"Why do you say that?"

"I don't know. Maybe it wasn't Jody who was playing dead. Maybe her family did it."

"Now you're shooting at stars."

"I don't think the body was hers."

"What could possibly give you any evidence beyond two dead bodies of girls—" The detective's phone beeps and he holds up a finger. I nod and he twists around to wiggle his phone from his pocket. He makes about ten *uh huhs*. Then Detective Phillips knuckles his nose and points at me.

"Yeah, we'll be right over. Give us about forty minutes."

"There's a desecrated grave in a cemetery ten miles from Hazard." He turns off the phone, looks at me. "It's an old coal mining town cemetery, but a couple local churches still use the church there and the cemetery for burials. I figured you'd like to ride along. Can you grab your camera?"

I open my backpack, point inside. "My purse isn't here. But they didn't take the camera I keep in there."

Chapter 27

Two Graves. No Bodies.

"Twenty-five bucks says this is one of our Jane Doe graves." Detective Phillips has this stance. He kind of leans over like the investigators did on the old black and white detective shows. He did that when he made the bet. I didn't agree or disagree considering I don't have twenty-five bucks to my name right now.

We can't drive all the way to the cemetery. We have to stop at the ancient white clapboard church that says: HOLY TRINITY on a board above the door and park in the gravel lot. The road from there is too rutted and muddy for his car. He tried. There's brown sludge from bumper to bumper and we were almost sideways only thirty feet from the church.

"Are you coming, LaRue?"

I have to walk up the less muddy grass on the side of the old cemetery drive. The heels of my shoes keep digging deep until the backs of my feet are parallel with the toes.

"I'm wearing heels, dude."

"Next time, you'll grab a flannel and those funky looking running pants you had on the other day when you were getting gas, now, won't you?"

"I was taking pictures in a pasture. And there isn't going to be a next time, detective." I heave a groan, look up to the top of the hill which is only a quarter way up a mountain. When we finally crest the hill, it opens up to a small, but well kept, cemetery with some graves boasting fresh flowers.

"Over here." There's a man in blue coveralls waving us across the cemetery. He's chubby and balding and swiping a hand over his head.

"Hey, Pete, long time no see." Detective Phillips greets the man with a handshake. "Last time I saw you, you were digging a grave in Whispering Hollow."

"They got me working all the old church cemeteries now. Mowing. Cleaning. More pay, I guess. Lots of driving."

Detective Phillips hunkers down on one knee to peer into a concave indentation in the ground in front of a newer grave. It is a few feet deep, more sunk in than properly covered, with chunks of grass tossed back on fresh dirt.

"They did a messy job of it," Pete says. "There's mud everywhere—" He waves a hand. "We found the casket shoved over the edge of the little embankment over there. They probably filled the grave pretty well, but didn't pack it down. The rain turned the dirt to mud and it made a hollow here. If it hadn't stormed and Judy Montgomery hadn't come up here to make sure no trees had fallen on the graves, we wouldn't have seen it for some time."

"Alexis Potts." Detective Phillips looks up at the stone. "She just passed a month ago. She was what, twenty-two?" He comes to a standing position, looks at Pete.

"Committed suicide, she did," Pete adds. "I remember when it happened. I was down at the fire station dropping off some chairs. They got the call. The family was all wrought up. Me and my aunt stayed up with them."

"Did she hang herself?" I ask, remembering the rope marks on the first Jane Doe's neck.

"Yeah, tied a belt around her neck and stood on a chair in her bedroom," Pete says. "Then she stepped off."

"Did they embalm her?" the detective asks.

"I doubt it," Pete says. "They don't have to in Kentucky, I know that. They had a home funeral just for the family, you know, because she killed herself. They kept it quiet. I don't think most folks know she'd even passed."

"Have we had any other suicides this side of the big highway?" Detective Phillips kicks the dirt with his foot.

"Not that I recall."

"Well, I'm going to have this girl take some photos, then we'll get out of your hair. We've got those two Jane Does down at the funeral home on ice. I'll see what we can do about checking if one of them is Alexis."

"Hey, now wait a minute." I'm about a half hour into taking pictures and almost done. Pete comes lumbering over. He's pointing to a picture on his phone. We both look up. There's an image of a younger girl, seventeen or so with dark hair and eyes. "Raeanna Simms. She's Junior Simms's daughter. She hung herself back eight or ten years ago. I thought there was somebody else. I just called my mama and she said she remembered little Raeanna kilt herself way back when."

Raeanna Simms has a grave at Potter's Church Cemetery. Like the one we were just in, this cemetery is located on the side of a mountain above a white church.

"Holy hell," Detective Phillips is swiping the sweat off his head with a white kerchief while he stands over Raeanna's grave. "I'll bet another twenty-five this is Jane Doe Two. You're going to be poor by the time we're done with this investigation."

"*We're* done?" I ask him absently. There isn't a vault around her grave. Detective Phillips says this high on the mountain and in these poorer communities, it isn't required. Already, I've got ten shots of the open grave. "I don't know where you got *we*."

"Yeah." He's staring down at the open grave, a huge hollow all the way to the casket which is open until the dirt stops it. "You can pay me back the fifty dollars by climbing down in there and seeing if there's a body in there."

"Not on your life, Low Po, ain't' no way—"

"This sucks," I grumble. "If this is what *we* means." Ten minutes later, he's talked me into it and is lowering me down by one hand. "I get to crawl down into a grave. Our relationship is a bit lopsided. Remind me to discuss this at our next couples therapy session."

Detective Phillips has his knees crammed into the mud and I watch as he cranes his neck suddenly. "You're funny, LaRue. Oh, crapola. Be right back."

"Crapola?" I ask while I try to balance on a hillside of mud and the dirty casket edge in my heels. I'm covered. I think I look like a gingerbread cookie. "What does that mean, *be right back*?" He suddenly lets go and I watch him walk off. "Low Po, really?"

"—well, hello, good ladies."

"Great." I grumble. That's all I need is a bunch of church ladies finding me crawling into a casket to take pictures. I'm balancing my camera in one hand and trying not to get mud under my fingernails. The coffin is open about twelve inches. I try to lean, peer inside. It's like straight-up walls. I sigh, hunker down and slide my foot just within the coffin. There isn't much room. Whoever dug this one out was in a hurry and didn't care too much more than to get into the casket and get the corpse out. But I can just barely peer into the coffin so I reach down, wiggle the lid against a good ten or twelve shovels of dirt that has fallen on it. There.

"Oh—shit." I don't know why I tried to open the casket farther than halfway. There's too much weight. As soon as I get the lid up and shove my shoulder underneath and keel sideways to look inside, both of my high heels I had locked into the edge of the casket just slide like sharp skates over ice right along the edge and out from under me. My knees buckle, I fall on my left side and slide about three quarters of the way into the casket.

I don't scream. I'm too busy forcing my right arm upward to stop the lid that is slamming down toward me falling into the casket devoid of anything but pillows. I curse instead, wiggle-freak left to right. I've got nothing to hold on to. My feet are slipping and sliding around everywhere.

"—Ma'am, I really don't think that's a good—" Detective Phillips's voice is the last thing I hear before the screaming. I look up while I'm wiggling out and see two ladies, mouth agape and hands slapping cheeks. They are screaming and screaming and one just faints dead right there above me.

Detective Phillips tells me later that they were two of the women from the Yates Holy Redemption Woman's Society. They come once a week to check the graves, add new flowers. One of them walked right past him because they didn't see the police cruiser, thought he was trying to bury somebody up there without the county coroner knowing. They saw me climbing out and thought the dead were rising.

"Son of a bitch. That was not what I wanted." I shiver it off in the car. Detective Phillips has the impudence to grab three garbage bags out of the trunk of the car to sit on. "That is the freaking most awkward and humiliating situation I've ever been in."

"The look on your face while we are all looking down and you're climbing out, I'd give a million dollars to have a picture of it."

"Oh, really." I sniff. I roll through the pictures until I get to the ones where I'm holding the camera and falling into the casket. Sure enough, there's my contorted face right before I went inside. "Here, let me make your day."

He starts laughing two seconds out of the parking lot. He doesn't stop until we're a mile from the Landowski's.

"So now will you think about exhuming Jody Mills?" I ask him.

"No," he answers and pushes a finger in the air. "Let me tell you why. I'm just questioning your ability to make simple deductions, considering you can't even figure out that those two boys, the Landowski one and the preacher's son, are fighting it out to see which one of them can get you on a date."

"You've got to be kidding me," I retort. "Ben likes Jenny. I'm just in his radar and he knows I'm leaving."

"I'm not so sure about that. Are you sticking around another day?"

"I can't get my money. I suppose I am." I turn to Detective Phillips. "So here's my question. Do I tell the boy about the devil-girl or just let him figure it out himself."

"Are you going to stick around Whispering Hollow to pick up the pieces of his broken heart and the little bits of feathers when he sees his angel get shot out of the sky?"

"Ow, that hurts," I mumble. "I'm not the wicked one here, you realize that, don't you?"

"I didn't say you were wicked. And I didn't say Jenny was the angel, now, did I?" The detective grunts. "Because if there is any doubt you're moving on, let him have something or someone as back up when you're gone. She may not help him pick up the feathers, but she'll be a generic brand Band-Aid for his heart." He shakes his head back and forth. "Come on, LaRue, I saw it the day we drove to Louisville to pick up the models, the silly-in-love grin on your face when Ben texted you at the gas pumps. I backed off right then. I can't compete with that. Nobody can."

Chapter 28
Fired

I don't see anyone at the Landowski's home when I get back at six. I call Abe to wire me the money. He picks up on the first ring.

"Thanks for covering for me, Piper," he says. "You can just toss all those pics. I don't want them."

"What are you talking about?"

"The shoot you just did. We're not going to use the pictures. I got them all while I was here in Florida. It seems we got some better backgrounds here and the models I had with me were more what Spitfire was looking for. They are looking for high end mall kind of stuff people will buy online and not necessarily what's in the outlet stores. I sent my files to Jimmy Bean and he liked them. He's only got a few other companies competing for the job—"

"What job?"

"It's for the Midwest Farmers Magazine, Piper, I told you this. It's an ongoing project."

"You didn't tell me that."

"Well, it doesn't matter. I got Delta Raines down here with me. She can handle it."

Delta Raines. Not her again. "So this is how it's going to be, is it, Abe?" I ask. I know my voice is angry-squeaky. "You're scooting me out, working her in?"

"I didn't say that, Piper."

"Where's my next job, then? You still got me lined up in Canada?"

"I don't know. I've been busy down here in Florida. This is a huge, huge contract and I've stuffed all my energy into it. I just didn't think you could handle it, alright? You just don't have the—background like Delta has. She just blows me away. She can come in, pick the models, set it up and tear it down like an army general winning a battle. You understand me? We got two separate shoots done in one place and in the same amount of time it took for you to just bumble around with one."

"You used me, Abe." I just say it right at the moment it hits me. "Do you know how unethical this is, what you did to me?" He was never really setting up a photo shoot here in the boondocks of Kentucky. He was just putting me and Tessa and Marcus a million miles away so we'd be out of the way. But he also doesn't like to be told he's wrong. He doesn't like to have his transgressions pointed out.

"You know what?" Abe's voice is deep, gruff. "Piper, you can go find your own jobs from now on. We've worn out our working relationship, don't you think? I'll send over the paperwork to end your contract. Just sign it and send it back along with any images you have while you were on assignment."

Chapter 29

Cursed and Hanging Out at Rest Haven Hotel with the Prostitutes and Druggies

I'm staring at the little wax dolls on the table next to the couch. It's not the cozy leather couch at Josif Landowski's. It is the dingy, red couch that I fumigated with an entire can of disinfectant spray at Rest Haven Hotel. Yes, it is the dingy one off the highway with the pool filled with two feet of green slimy water, six semi-trucks in the parking lot, and four girls who keep coming and going with new boyfriends about every two hours and fifteen minutes.

I wish I could call my mamaw and ask her how to break whatever curse someone's left for me. Because I'm feeling superstitious tonight. Things aren't getting any better. One curse, two empty graves and three dead girls. I'm out of a job, I owe a bunch of money and I've got not much more than a nickel to my name. And I think somebody might be trying to scare me to death with snakes. And Ben and Josif, they're not my friends anymore. It happened pretty fast. The detective dropped me off. I got out of the shower at my cabin and there was a knock on the door.

"So—what's going on? Are you coming? Are you going?" Ben's got this strange twist of his lips. It's like he knows some secret that I have yet to learn. "Because I was feeding the horses this morning and there was a little snake—"

"Shut up, *Possum*," I spit angrily.

"No, no," he holds up his hand. "I'm not teasing you. Not at all. It's really small and I thought maybe we could work on getting you so you're not afraid of snakes, that's all.

You could touch it or I can just stand in the room—"

"No, my mama tried it a hundred times. It doesn't work with me." I pat my legs. "Anyways, there's been a change of plans," I start out slowly. "The shoot is cancelled."

"I don't know what you mean." Boom! It's like all of a sudden, he's taking a step back and he's a different person. I should have known. I'm just not very good at this. I figure maybe people like me and it isn't just because I'm taking pictures of them or holding out a twenty dollar bill for them to take. Then when the pictures stop or the hand is empty, I realize they used me in the first place.

"It's cancelled. They aren't doing the photo shoot, the event?" he asks defensively. "I don't get it. What's cancelled?"

"Everything. There isn't a photo shoot. There isn't a festival at the end. They are doing it all in Florida."

"I mean, I know we're right there on the edge of Midwest and South but I thought this was for a Midwestern magazine, not the deep South."

"I don't know what to tell you, Ben. Maybe they moved the regions. I don't make the rules. I just follow the orders. Somebody thinks Florida embodies Midwestern farms better than Kentucky, I guess."

"We invested our last dollar into that gazebo, into putting new gravel on the drive and a couple thousand dollar's worth of—"

"Well, you shouldn't have banked it all on this shoot, alright? It's in the contract. I'm sorry. You signed it. Your grandpa signed it. Everybody in this town signed a waiver and a contract. There was no guarantee."

"So do we get paid for putting you up in the cabins for the last two weeks, for the meals and the models staying?"

"I don't know. Probably not. At this point, I don't know."

"You're a real piece of work, Piper. You know, I believed all that crap about you not stealing that money from your dad. Now I get it. That's what you do. That's your thing. You come in and get free room and board, then take off again."

"That's not how it works, Ben, I—" I'm standing there watching Josif walk across the expanse of gravel driveway. I know he can hear the conversation. He's got this angry blackness to his eyes, arms folded across his chest.

"What's going on, buddy?"

"They aren't doing the shoot. We've been screwed by that company, by Piper."

I think the correct term my daddy used was *getting Piper'd*. I don't say that, though.

"Is that true, Piper?"

"I don't have a choice—"

"Well, we all have choices," he says. I see him eye the suitcases inside the doorway. "So I'm assuming you're taking off without paying your father back too."

"I don't know—"

"I should have known this was too good to be true," Josif says. Ben is standing beside him, staring at his grandpa, eyeing him carefully.

"Get out," Ben says. "Pack your bags. Leave."

"I think it's time for you to leave, Piper," Josif says. "We'll pick up the pieces, move on. You aren't welcome here anymore. I think you've worn out your stay."

Hence the reason I'm at the Rest Haven Hotel with the prostitutes and druggies. I don't know if I'm coming or going. I want to leave. I found that two miles down the road, guilt and something incredibly gut-punching has stopped me from taking off down the highway and driving until the gas runs out, then walking the rest of the way to Washington State or until I can get a new copy of my credit cards. Damn you, Ben. Why am I seeing those glazed-angry-used eyes over and over again in my head?

The hotel takes checks. It is the only form of payment I have available without my credit card wallet. The only form of conscious conversation I am getting are occasional texts with witty remarks about me crawling out of the casket by none other than Detective Phillips and a knock on the door once in a while with somebody wanting to buy weed and looking for the last renter of my room. So it is me, the TV set, the bounce of the beds against walls of the girls on either side of me while their ephemeral boyfriends visit. And my computer.

Chapter 30
Calling Peyton

"Peyton, we need to talk." I found the landline phone number of Harley Joseph McCarthy online. It wasn't difficult. He answered once. I hung up. The next time, my sister picked up the phone. "Listen, I'm not sure who else I should call. I can't call Daddy. I just need somebody to tell him that I can't come up with the money this week. My credit cards and my cash got lost or stolen along with my driver's license. I need my driver's license to show identification at the bank. So until then, I'm stuck."

There's this long, long silence. "I didn't think you'd come up with it even if you could, Piper," she finally gives me a gruff, throaty whisper. "You're nothing but a trashy whore. I hate you."

"Why do you have to be like this?" I ask her. "Trust me. If I could get out of this God forsaken place, I'd be in China by now. But I don't have any cash—"

"Are you actually asking me for money?"

"No, but without my credit cards, I can't leave and go home and go to my local bank and get cash out. Without my driver's license, I can't get any cash out here. I'm kind of in this perpetual cycle of being stuck here and the longer I stay, the more I'm spending and my savings account is nearly depleted. If I take out the five-thousand, I only have a few hundred bucks left."

"You actually have five-thousand dollars?"

"It's what I'm saving up for a down payment on a house. So, yes," I say. I'd have about forty thousand more if Abe would reimburse me. I can't even hold his pictures hostage for the reimbursement. He doesn't care about the photo shoot. And write my family a check? I don't think so without being able to move that huge amount from savings to checking. If I asked them to hold it a week until I could move it over, they wouldn't. They'd cash it.

"So is that the money you stole? Or did you spend that?"

"I'm going to tell you the same thing I told everybody when it came up missing. I didn't steal it."

"You went to college."

"I got a million dollar's worth of student loans I'll be paying back until the day I die. I did not steal the money."

"So it just disappeared."

"Why don't you ask your husband where it went?"

I wished I didn't say that the second I did. But I said it and I'm pinching my temples on my side of the phone while I know my twin sister is gritting her teeth on the other end.

"Oh, okay, blame Harley." She laughs. "Right. He stole it to do what? We don't got a pot to piss in, big fat liar. He was right about you. He said you'd blame him for it because he was the only one who knew you were coming on to him when I wasn't looking. I know about you and Harley. I'm not stupid."

"Okay, I'm not fighting with you, Peyton," I say. Now I'm the one gritting my teeth. "Just tell daddy I can't get the money this week."

"I'm not telling him anything," she growls back. It is right then I hear a strange click like there was somebody listening on the phone. I cringe. I know there is a long pause on the other end and Peyton must have heard it too. "I hate you. I hate you more than anything in the world, Piper. You stay away from my husband or I swear to God, I will kill you."

Chapter 31

Committing Professional Suicide

"I heard you were staying here. I needed to drop off your bill. Are you selling weed?"

I stare at Ben Landowski outside the hotel door.

"No, of course not." He knocked and I was sure it was somebody banging on the door and looking to buy again from the last renter, so I'd screamed out: *Go get your weed someplace else! I'm busy!* I suppose I could have worded it better. There's a party going on in the parking lot, three cars of drunk boys who keep driving around the hotel trying to pick up girls. It's loud behind him. I can see he's trying to ignore the woman who's making a wolf whistle at him.

"That your girlfriend or is she steppin' in on my jobs?" she's asking from the balcony above me. "Baby, you gonna answer me? I got stuff for you." I let my eyes veer upward and for no other reason, I'm thinking she might be ready to throw something at me. She's just leaning over the railing, grabbing her chest and making a lewd hip roll.

I lower my gaze to the papers Ben's holding in his hand. There must be seven pages. I imagine he and his family sat down at the kitchen table and jotted down everything from each individual square of toilet paper to the cleaning of an eyelash from the sink. Obviously, they didn't read the fine print of the contract. If the shoot didn't go through, they don't get paid. Small print.

"I'll see what I can do. It will be a couple months."

"No, we want the money within a week. There are no offers. This is what we require. I know you're going to try to get out of paying us. I wouldn't. We're getting an attorney."

"And he'll show you in the contract that it clearly states we are not responsible for the payment if the shoot does not occur. It didn't occur."

"So you're not going to pay for anything. The meals, the cabin rentals, the gazebo—"

"I said it would be a couple months."

"You're a crook, you know that, right?"

"Is that all you needed, Ben?" I ask, easing the door closed between us. "You've had your say." I look down at the invoice. "Twenty-two thousand is a bit steep, but I'll see what I can come up with." *And by the way, your angel-girlfriend is Satan in sheep's clothing.*

I close the door wondering when it all started going downhill, why I didn't see the signs with Abe replacing me, using me like I'm the garbage can full of his trash that's easier to take to the dump and toss with the contents than just keeping around and using again. I know it was before I had those two wax, stick dolls in my grasp. Still, I can't help but think there's something to their curse. I can't quite pinpoint when his hand holding began to be a hand pushing my head deep into the garbage. To make matters worse, I've got to tell my family I can't get the money to them this week. That's not going to go over well with local police.

Later, I'm just about to shove all my pictures on a travel drive to send to Abe when I catch a glimpse of the notes I took when I had the conversation with Spitfire's spokesperson, Jimmy Bean. Yeah, that's when I should have seen it coming. It was pretty obvious Abe was making things up as he went, telling me the wrong things and leading me on a stupid wild goose chase. I poke at Jimmy's name, then pick up the paper and my cell phone, take a deep breath. It's professional suicide I'm thinking about, going around Abe Starling and competing against the biggest agency in the business. But really, what do I have to lose?

"Hey, Jimmy, this is Piper LaRue—"

Chapter 32
The Truth About Delilah Gray

The Whispering Hollow Historical Society has one muddy picture of Dexter Black with about fifty of his miners in raggedy clothing standing in front of a dilapidated wood building. It is actually a picture of a woman taking a picture of Dexter and his miners. It is strangely artistic for its time. I can clearly make out the darkly-dressed woman while I lean over the wooden railing protecting the display of a mining camp inside the renovated one-room schoolhouse that once housed a church and school for Whispering Hollow.

"If you're looking for clues to the treasure, there aren't any in the picture." I am precariously close to flipping over when I hear the woman's voice behind me. I straighten myself, pivot on my feet. A fifty-something woman in a prim suit dress is holding out her hand. "Linda Keeton Young, volunteer for the historical society and part time librarian at Whispering Oak Community Library."

"Nice to meet you. I'm Piper LaRue," I say, taking her hand. "You're related to Preacher Young, Bucky and Jenny—?"

"They are my kids."

It's not quite awkward for a moment while I adjust to the idea that the preacher's wife had returned. I guess I should have assumed that since Ben told me Jenny was back in town. "I'm not actually here for treasure, although I wouldn't mind finding some right now. I'm just trying to find some local history to tie into my submission for an article."

The article. I contacted Jimmy Bean with Spitfire. He

was quick to tell me the submission process for the magazine layout ends in three days and they weren't accepting anything other than the three agencies who had signed up for the shoot. They'd been chosen ahead of time. All were going to be used for the magazine. They were just not sure of the order they were being used.

"Would you make an exception?"

"Is this for Abe Starling's company? Because we already received all of his information."

"No, we kind of parted ways and I've got a lot of time invested in it. The folks I've been working with have a lot of time and money invested. You know, small town people like the kind that buy the outlet's stuff and the ones that buy that magazine. I'm going to lay it out on the table for you, I feel like I'm letting them down. Could you make an exception, just take a look at what I've got. That's all I ask. I truly believe what is right here in Whispering Hollow, Kentucky is what you're looking for and the people will inspire you and those who read the magazine. I—I can get it to you in three days. Please."

"Is this Piper? The one who's always taking the pictures for Starling?"

"Yeah."

"You know, we met at a birding conference in northern Ohio. It was along Lake Erie near Sandusky. I've probably seen you ten times since then. Everybody else was taking pictures of birds. You were just cracking up taking pictures of people taking pictures of the birds." He sniffs a laugh. "There was this one lady, a bigger lady, who slipped on some rocks and fell right on her rear. I remember you got the shot midway down and showed it to her, gave her a copy. She used it for her Christmas cards."

"Oh, yeah, she sent me one. She was upset everybody

saw her. I remember. Her hands were in the air. She looked like she was flying. I called her Bird Lady. She was pretty popular after her flight."

"Yeah, that was my Aunt Lucie. She's the one who likes birds. Me, I wear the binoculars and look at the horizon. I drive her wherever there are birds." He does the deep sigh before silence. "Listen, you took an awful moment for her and made it into something fun. Every conference we go to, every birding event, they still run up to see her and call her Bird Lady. Everybody thinks she's some great ornithologist. I'll tell you what, Piper. I'm not making any promises, but if you get the stuff in—and that means everything including the photos and the write-up, I'll submit it to the staff. The odds are slim, but it gives you a chance."

So I stayed up and pulled all the pictures I could find with real people in Whispering Hollow. I jotted down their stories and laid them out next to each. I got Ellie Lightfoot who owns a little souvenir shop in town and who came from Ohio ten years back. I got J.D. Junior standing above me with his arms folded and in the picture, I realize his dad had been standing in the kitchen window with his chin on his wrist listening to us. He's chuckling while his son's trying to look tough. And Dee Williams, he's swiping his hands and I called him and he told me his family have been there since the Revolutionary War. I've got more people than I can do stories on, but I pull up twelve including Josif Landowski and Ben and wonder how the heck I'm going to pull them all together in a theme.

That's why I end up here at the historical society.

"Is this the same one you're taking for the photoshoot?" Linda Keeton Young asks me. I'm not sure what I'm looking for. Jimmy resent all the information to my e-mail and it's a lot to digest in three days.

"Yes, kind of. There's been a twist," I tell her. "So I'm trying to lock in on some area information for a story. It's not something I usually do, a storyline, so I'm winging it."

"I've heard a lot about it." She walks over and tugs back on the railing making an opening. Then she waves me inside. "Take a closer look, if you'd like. This town needs all the P.R. it can get. I probably get ten people in here on a good summer week. I'd like to keep my job."

"Who is the woman in the photograph?" I ask, walking up to the picture in the frame and pointing toward the right side.

"That would be Delilah Gray. She was somewhat of an activist for her day, striving to help veteran soldiers find jobs so they could support their families. It is believed that is why she and Dexter started the mine here. That is the only picture we have of her. She was Dexter Black's companion. Some speculate that they were married. I'm sure you've heard the legend."

"Yeah. Any truth to the legend?" I ask. I look at the image. Yes, she was beautiful, with the kind of facial features magazine companies strive to find for their covers. She is posing with one arm on the camera, looking out like she is examining the horizon.

"We know very little about Dark Pines or Black Jack as it used to be called. Few of the men working there could write, much less read."

"Was she a photographer?"

"I don't know about that," she says. "I can't say that question has arisen when I have school groups in here or the treasure hunters come looking for the carpet bag of coins the two lovers in the legend were supposed to have stolen. Most folks just think she's posing next to the camera to give a sense of wealth to Dark Pines."

"I find it interesting that she would use a camera and not a big horse and buggy or any other expensive prop." It's true. I use props often and it has to do with the scene or image that I want to portray. And what photographer would work his way to a mining camp full of the poorest of the poor to sell pictures?

"Well, regardless, I'd love to get my hands on an old Civil War camera, that's for sure," I finally say, backing up from the picture. "Even to see one up close."

"We have that camera here, Piper," Missus Young tells me. "Would you like to see it? It's under glass and has been preserved that way since it was donated by Dexter Black's business partner in the 1900s. And if you want to take a few minutes to walk around, I can look up some things on our notes for the area history and see if I can find out if she did photography too."

"I would. That'd be great."

It is while I'm staring into the glass at the wooden box camera twenty minutes later, I see my own image in the glass. I've never liked the way I look. I don't know why. People always told Peyton she was so pretty. Nobody ever told me that and I'm her mirror image. I'm figuring, maybe, there's something wrong with me inside that makes people see me differently on the outside.

"That's the original camera."

I jump when Linda Keeton Young breaks my concentration. She chuckles softly, apologizes. "I'm sorry, sweetie, I thought you knew I was back here. It's seen its share of dead on the battlefield. I suppose your camera and this camera have a lot in common. I'd say you and Delilah Gray have a lot in common."

"What do you mean?"

"Lookey here." She holds up an eight and a half by eleven sheet of copy paper. On it, there's a couple newspaper articles. "I looked up her name on some historic newspaper sites and sure enough, Delilah Gray was a photographer. They talk about her in several newspapers and how it was so strange to see a woman on the battlefield, much less handling the large camera."

It's almost eerie. I guess I feel a strange kinship with this woman I've never met and who shares this same occupation of taking pictures of the dead.

"Do you know if the legend is true about her death on the waterfall?"

"I only know she's buried in some old cemetery up in Dark Pines. There weren't any local papers back then, so after her stint taking pictures on the battlefield, she kind of disappears in history."

"So let me ask you one more question." I wince-smile when I ask it. "I've scoured the historical archives of every newspaper and every historic document I can find about a little Jewish boy who may have escaped a Nazi death camp in Poland and moved to the United States. I even managed to, perhaps, find a picture of him in a Louisville newspaper in the 1940s and in a yearbook." I nibble on my lip. "But the trail stops there. Timothy Nicholson was his name on the yearbook. I got no clue where to go from there."

"Did you check family genealogy sites or historic newspapers?"

"I could only access information to 1921 in the newspapers and all of the sites charge a fortune. It's the same with the family genealogy sites."

"Well, come into my office. I might be able to help with that."

Timothy Nicholson was a boy adopted by John and Nancy Nicholson in 1941. There's no adoption papers available, just a note from a family member celebrating a protestant baptism of a little boy, age six who had come from Germany. Germany? I see pictures of him on a genealogy site from age six to well into his forties. *Uncle Tim-Tom*. That's what he was called. He was somewhat of a joker, I guess, and was constantly playing pranks on his small family of four.

"Look, he may still be alive," Linda Keeton Young says. "There's no death records, no obituary, and no grave. And, oh, my! There's an address."

Chapter 33
Untangling Tangled Webs

And these signs shall follow them that believe; In my name shall they cast out devils; they shall speak with new tongues; They shall take up serpents; and if they drink any deadly thing, it shall not hurt them; they shall lay hands on the sick, and they shall recover. Mark 16:17-18

"Papaw?"

I open the door to the hotel room and clasp the bible I was reading in the cleft of my arm. I'd heard three sharp knocks, ignored them at first, so engrossed in finding a quote within the hotel bible I found in a drawer.

"What are you doing here?" He's standing there, walker and all. I see him look at the bible, then turn his blue -eyed gaze up to mine. He's a big man, my grandfather, with thick shoulders and a stern face. He's always wearing a cowboy hat, dingy and gray. Probably the same one he wore when I left years ago. My little brother, Will, is standing next to him. He gives me a grunt, waves his hand. "I'll go sit in the car." He turns, walks away. He's as skinny as Papaw is thick. And tall. He grew up. I think he was only twelve the day I walked out the door, a little dude with red hair and freckles and ornery-mean as a cat with bells tied to its tail. Yeah, he had a black eye and a bloody nose that day. Got in a fight at school. No surprise to me.

I knew even before I answered it, the bang of knuckles wasn't the woman who'd been knock-harassing my door all last night. I know she thought I'm some sort of transient prostitute vying for her johns. I would have thought she'd noticed I'd nearly run screaming to my car when her first job of the night hopped out of his semi-truck and scared the heck out of me. But, I'd met her accidently while I was walking to my car at six-forty-five in the morning and she was slinking out of one of the hotel rooms with her shoes in her hand. I took her picture just as she looked up. I think she was going to punch me until I just walked right up to her.

"Look. I take pictures. I'm a photographer." I point to the picture on the flat panel display on the back of the camera. "See. I can even make you beautiful at seven in the morning. I do it with models all the time."

"Really?"

I nod. She thought it was funny and laughed.

I tell her: "I'll buy breakfast uptown if you don't knock on my door tonight."

The only place close that had breakfast is J.D.'s Corner Bar. She tells me everybody calls her Bammy because she came from Alabama and has an Alabama accent, the girl I'm treating to breakfast. We both sit at the bar eating greasy eggs and a thick slice of ham with sides of grits sprinkled with mozzarella cheese. She talks, talks, talks. I suppose when you do nothing but listen to men grunting over top you all night, it's nice to have some company to answer *uh huh* every now and then when it can be fitted between the chatter.

"I heard you're the one taking pictures of the crime scenes." I'm in mid-fork of a squirmy egg white and look up to see this huge hulk of a man. His head's shaved and he's got a blue dragon tattooed from his right ear until it disappears into his button up shirt. He reminds me of a pug dog with a tiny nose and angry eyes.

"Yeah, I'm Piper LaRue."

"I know who you are. I saw you riding around town with the cop."

"That's me. I've suddenly become his sidekick." I take a bite of the egg, try not to notice the big guy's really defensive.

"You know who's killing those girls?"

"No."

"That's J.D," Bammy offers while she chomps down on a piece of toast with red jelly on top. "His dad owns this bar."

"Yeah, and I told you not to come around here."

"She's a paying customer," I tell him. "Let her eat."

He leans in just across from me, elbows planted on the bar counter and gets right up in my face. "I know where you came from. I remember you from high school. You're from Copperhead Creek."

"What gave you the clue?" I ask with a dull look to my eyes.

"You can take the girl out of Kentucky, but—" he starts.

"—you can't take the Kentucky out of the girl." I end for him. "Yeah, I've been hearing that a lot."

"I played football. You were always on the sidelines taking pictures. You're one of Lee O'Sullivan's little sisters. You used to scream at me whenever I tackled your brother."

"Yeah, you were fast and I had a hard time not watching the games while I took the pictures."

"So, you're one of us. Who killed Jody Mills? You know that yet? Because it wasn't speeding home from working here in her car."

I've been deadpan staring him hard even though my heart is pitter-pattering in my chest. "How do you know she wasn't speeding home from here?"

"For one, she'd been borrowing my car because her car's fuel pump went out. When she parked it to get it fixed, the battery died. She didn't have the money to fix it. And her parents, they'd pretty much disowned her when she started working in the bar. The only time they'd give her money was if she went to church with them."

"That wasn't her car they found her dead in at Dark Pines?"

"Yeah, it was her car. But I'm telling you and you can ask Dee Williams down at Tanner's Garage, that car wasn't working. It was dead."

"Why are you telling me this? Why didn't you tell the cops this?"

"They didn't ask. And I wasn't telling and then getting Dee Williams involved."

"I didn't ask," I say softly. "Why are you willing to throw Dee under the train now?"

"You know why you'd get tackled once in a while at those games, don't you?" He jabs a finger hard at the wood between us. "Because you had a mouth on you just like you do now."

"Answer my question."

"He owes me cash."

"You think Dee did it?"

"Oh, hell no," J.D. pushes himself up, gives me a pickle face with pursed lips and furrowed brow. "He just knows that car was sitting in the garage lot that night. It was out back and deader than a doornail."

"Can I take your picture?" I ask him, whipping my camera out of my backpack. He blinks like I just said *boo* to him, folds his arms at his chest and stands back stoically. I suppose I did bring that question up out of the blue. I get his photo before he moves, three quick shots with our messy plates still on the counter and his beer taps all lined up in a colorful display behind him. I even got a bit of Bammy taking a bite of her grits with her spoon.

"Do I look like a crime scene to you?" he grunts.

"Rumor says you were going out with Jody, that true?" Again, I catch him off-guard and he tips his head to the side.

"If going out is a couple one night stands, I suppose," he tells me. "Were we a couple? No. Did I want to be a couple with that crazy woman? Absolutely not."

"Crazy?"

He leans over, looks left to right. "Yeah, crazy and slicker than a snake with oil on its back. Everything she did had some sort of a threat to keep silent tied to it in the end. She stole cash from my daddy all the time. I caught her. She told me she'd tell him I did it."

"Why wouldn't your daddy believe you?"

"Because he's my daddy?" J.D. Junior snaps back quickly.

"I get it," I mutter.

"I know you do. That's why I'm telling you this. I know about the money at your house. I heard about it when you left. I remember thinking that you were way too smart to steal money like that. Maybe you'd rob a bank and know all the computer codes and stuff, but I didn't think you'd just take money from a tobacco tin and walk off. I figure you know I'm not lying and I can tell you that before that cop starts knocking at my door thinking I did it."

"The ham and grits are really good. Will you sign a photo release so I can submit your picture for a magazine?"

"I know, I made them. And, sure. Make me a star."

Fifteen minutes later, I've got Bammy in tow and I'm taking the sidewalk three blocks to Tanner's Garage.

"I'm looking for Dee," I announce just inside the open door of the ancient brick building with gas pumps outside.

"Yeah, I knew you was coming." A man comes out slapping a dirty red towel on his fingers. He's fortyish and has a grayish tone to his skin. His hair is mussed like he was underneath a car. "Junior said you'd be here. He called."

"Giving you a heads-up, I take it," I mutter.

"You're right," he says. "And yeah, Jody Mills had her car parked back behind the gas station in a little lot I store the cars before I work on them or, in her case, when they ain't gonna work no more."

"You know how she got it, then?"

"I've got no clue. I don't recall if it was back there the day she died, but it was there two days before because I took the battery out of it. It was new. I put it in there when I was working on her car and I left it in until she told me she couldn't afford to pay me for the fuel pump and the alternator it needed. I asked her if I could take the battery. She said it'd be alright as long as she didn't have to pay for it. I do know that there was no way nobody could drive that thing. It had to be towed out of there and it had to be sometime between eleven that night and six in the morning. I had a whole crap load of cars to work on. I was doing fifteen hour days and—" He turns, points toward the glass windows that surround the building on three sides. "I can see that parking lot and I didn't see anybody take that car."

"Maybe she took it." Bammy has snatched up a celebrity magazine sitting on a glass stand beside a faux leather couch in the makeshift waiting room. She's flipping the pages and looks up. "Hey, Dee."

"Hey, Bammy," he answers with a sweet smile at her. "She didn't take it. Georgia Burns saw Jody with her mama at church that night."

"How long was she in church?"

"Long enough to get the money to pay for her car, I reckon, and not a second more. Jody didn't like her mama's church. It was too strict for her liking. She liked Preacher Young at Holy Trinity and started going there. That's why she went with her mama, you know. Her mama used church like it was a job for that girl. If Jody went to church, she'd pay for her car to get fixed. You don't know what church they go to, do you?" He laughs and Bammy laughs. I turn to look at her and she bobs her head up and down.

"No."

"It's the Church of Holy Pentecost." Dee kind of gets this smile on his lips. "You know, the Holy Rollers."

"Oh," I nod. "Yeah, my mamaw on my mama's side went to one of those churches off Goose Creek Road. So did most of her family. My daddy didn't like any of us going and he'd get mad at Mama when we stayed all night at Mamaw's and she took us." I don't add that after I was eleven and Will's prank putting snakes in my bed, it would take a lot of coaxing to even get me out of the car for their services. "I'm assuming you're telling me she was there on an all-nighter."

"Yeah. They were there two days. I remember my uncle saying they ordered pizza at Big Al's Pizza for lunch the next day."

"Do they use the snakes at that one?" I ask him. I remember going with my mamaw and my cousins to church. Before I was eleven, I liked to watch the preacher and some of his congregation bring out the snakes and weave around the room. That the snakes were poisonous didn't have much meaning with me, then. Mamaw said they did it for faith because the bible said they would be safe. We saw cottonmouths, rattlesnakes, and copperheads on my daddy's property once in a while. We'd give them a far walk around or if we were in a foul mood, toss a rock at them from far away. But at Mamaw's church, they held them to test their faith.

"Yeah, they do." Dee looks behind him. "I caught a rattlesnake up on the creek last spring and gave it to them in a pillow sack. I got to get back to work. You need anything else?"

"You know anybody else that was there that night besides Georgia Burns?" I ask him.

"I don't. I just remember her telling me that when I changed the oil in my car. It's a good hike up the hill and that's after you slip and slide up an old dirt mining road. Anybody that went was probably younger."

"Where's it at, this church?"

"Up in the Dark Pines."

The Dark Pines. It must be the old Dark Pines church where Ben took me on his horse. I feel a strange twinge. The woman. Who was she? And why was she there? "Do they still bury folks up there at the cemetery?"

"Not that I know of." He shrugs. "I think everybody's buried down at the Whispering Hollow Cemetery."

"Can I take your picture?"

"For the cops?"

"No, I'm a photographer. I like to take people in the places they fit in, like you right here."

So he lets me and Bammy and I leave and go back to the hotel. I dig up the bible to see if I can find out the reasoning behind snake handling in church and right as I read the verses, that's when my papaw and Will pull in.

"What do you need, Papaw?" I ask him, helping him jimmy his walker through the door. He stops halfway and shakes his head.

"I don't need to come in, Sugar." Sugar. My heart aches right then to hear him call me my nickname. Sugar. He used to sneak me teaspoons of sugar when he was making his coffee and my mama wasn't looking. "Peyton was all upset last night. Said you wasn't going to give your daddy that money. Said you was taking off again."

"I'm going to pay. I just don't have the money, Papaw."

"I don't care so much about that, Piper," he tells me. "You need to come home no matter what your daddy thinks, you hear me?"

"I heard you the other day when you bonked me in the head." I rub my head.

"Are you getting sassy?"

"No, sir."

"I miss you. I'm just gonna say it. It just ain't the same family without my Sugar." He sighs, looks up and I don't know what he's concentrating on because it's just the deep brown ceiling to the upstairs balcony. It's got spider webs and bubble gum stuck up there. "Why'd you take it? Why'd you take that money from your auntie?"

I stare at him. What if I told him for the hundredth time, I didn't take it? He still wouldn't believe me. "I don't know."

"You don't know? You tore our family apart, Piper Juliet LaRue O'Sullivan. You ripped it right down the middle stealing—"

"She didn't steal it, Papaw."

I lean to the right, look around Papaw's left shoulder to where Will is settled into the driver's seat of an old white truck. He's got his left arm hanging out and he's banging it on the door absently. Papaw turns.

"Shut up, boy, you don't know nothing."

"Yeah, I do."

I watch Will open the door to the old truck. It squeaks before he slams it with his arm. "I took it."

"What?" *Poo-plaw, poo-plaw.* Papaw does this crooked step-bang of his walker to his left ninety degrees and stops, stares at Will. "What are you talking about?"

"Aunt Tammy showed me the cut plug tobacco tin she kept on the shelf when I was eight or nine, I don't remember exactly. She was teaching me how to count money because the teacher called me stupid at school. She had me climb up the bookshelf and bring it down and we counted out one-dollar bills and five-dollar bills." Will walks the expanse between us, stops just short of Papaw. He won't look at me. "So when I was twelve, I wanted to buy some Milk Duds. I figured nobody'd know it was gone. I used five bucks for candy at the store. Then I started to feel guilty and I went to Harley and told him about what I'd done because I knew if anybody counted it, there would be five bucks gone. He was the only one that I didn't think would tell on me. We all know Piper would." He taps his finger on Papaw's walker. "Harley said he'd come up with a five dollar bill and put it back in the tobacco tin and he'd stick it back up on the shelf. But when everybody saw it was gone and I was going to say something, he beat me with the shovel in the barn and said he'd kill me if I ever told anybody he'd done it. He'd stole it. So it wasn't Piper who tore up the family, it was me. I don't know why anybody ever thought it was you," he says looking at me. "You never take chances. You're always careful, think things out. They should have know'd it was me. I'm tired of living with it. I'd rather die by Harley's hand. And I'd rather have Daddy look at me like he's been looking at her than carry this guilt. That's all."

So Papaw turns again, the *poo-plaw, poo-plaw* of the tennis balls making that funny sound when he walk-bumps back. He doesn't say anything for a long time. Then he just reaches out his hand, exposes a knuckle and bangs it hard on the top of my head. "Well, it's your fault for not saying anything."

We sit in Will's truck ten minutes later. "I'm not going to tell Peyton her husband bought her wedding ring with stolen money. She's got kids." I say softly. "And you guys need the money. Just let it go. I've got the cash."

"That's wrong, Piper," Papaw says. "It's wrong."

"You know it's right. You know I didn't steal it and that's what matters." I'm more afraid of what Harley will do to Will, I really am. He beat a twelve year old with a shovel, for heaven's sakes. "So I'll give you the five-thousand and Daddy will be happy. Peyton's babies will have a daddy—"

"And you'll be alone." Will says. "You was my favorite person in the whole world. I wrecked your life."

"No, baby, Harley wrecked my life. It's all behind us."

"I want to go to college like you. I don't want to work at the gravel pit or the mines," Will says. "Remember when you used to read to me?"

"I do." I smile. Cuddled up with Will on my bed and under a blanket after Mama and Daddy sent us to bed was the highlight of my evenings. "I taught you how to read. It wasn't that stupid teacher you had."

"I'm good at math like you."

"So you'll go to college. You can come live with me."

I got out of the truck, leaned into the window. "If you give me a couple weeks, I'll get the money. What's done is done. Nobody knows the wiser. I got so much money," I lie. "It's coming out my butt. Five-thousand dollars, it isn't even a bite in my wallet." Then I stop, turn my head. "Let me ask you something, Papaw. How do you get rid of a stick man curse, the kind with the doll made of pine sticks and wax?"

"You can't, baby," he answers. "Your mamaw always says that the curse don't go away until the maker of the doll passes away."

Chapter 34

Sorries and Handing Out Miracles

Boom-boom-boom-pop.

That's not me shooting the hoops at one-thirty. It's Ben Landowski. I've been standing in the shadows for a good two hours thinking he might come out. I startle him when he sees me walk up. I see him jump, try to cover it up.

"Go away, Piper," he says. Ben looks so different right now and in the light, almost like he was when I first met him. His eyes are glazed, his mouth set in a frown. I hold my hands out, force a smile.

"Play with me."

"I don't want to play with you." He's standing straight and tall and his face is almost lost in the shadows now. "And from what I hear, it sounds like you've got a new set of friends, the druggies and prostitutes who hang out at the hotel off the highway. Or are you working out there with them?"

I just stare at him, then say: "I'm sorry."

"Sorry for what? Ruining my grandpa's business?"

"Yeah, whatever."

"Just leave."

"I'll touch a snake if you stop being mad at me."

He doesn't answer, just gives me a blank stare.

"Okay, I'll go." I start to back up. "But you know Jenny Young isn't as sweet as she lets on, don't you?"

"You're a piece of work, Piper." He sniffs a mocking laugh. "You jealous? Is that what this is all about? You got a crush on me, too?"

Do I? Crud. I struggle with some comeback and can't think of anything. Then I remembered what I wanted to tell him. "Well, um, I found out how Dexter Black made all his money, Ben." I lean in a little. "Civil War wet-plate photography. He took pictures of the soldiers, both living and the dead. Did you know that?"

"No."

"And he sold them. He had a wagon full of darkroom equipment, chemicals, and his cameras and he drove from battlefield to battlefield and took pictures of the soldiers they could send home. Then after the battle, he went out on to the field with this huge box camera and got the images too. He sold these to magazines and newspapers."

He doesn't do anything, just stares at me. "Is that all?"

"No. He wasn't married. The young woman who accompanied him to start his mine was his consort, like a friend."

"So the legend isn't true." He nods his head, sighs.

"I didn't say that. In fact, here is something that you may not know. The woman who was with him was Delilah Gray. She was a sister of one of the soldiers missing in action. Dexter Black met her on the battlefield while she searched for her brother. She offered to ride with him from camp to camp helping him in return for the ability to find her brother. Then after the war, they stayed together."

"She ever find her brother?"

"I don't know. I do know, however, she's buried in Dark Pines cemetery where I saw that lady behind the church. I was thinking we could hike it, see if we could find it. Maybe we can see if she really jumped off the waterfall."

"You go ahead. I'll hang on to the story I have. It plays out better for the horseback riding trip."

"Yeah, okay." I work up a smile. I know it's lame. I realize for all it's worth, I've surpassed liking Ben

Landowski. I've never felt this way, this horribly wonderful ache in my chest right now while I tear myself away from the light and walk out into the shadows.

I see the porch light come on. It douses me just as I succumb to the darkness. I can see Josif stepping out on to the porch, squinting until his gaze stops on me. He takes two steps to the end of the deck. "Please leave my grandson alone," he tells me. "It isn't that you're not a nice girl. It's that you're the kind who leaves. He needs someone who sticks around."

I listen to the sound of the ball bouncing again, then the *twang* as it floats through the hoop. I reach around, tug on the papers I tucked into the back of my shorts and I pull them out. I walk up to the porch and get stabbed by Josif's straight-line expression. "Here. Here's your stupid miracle, Josif. He is not a ghost, your brother. That's why I came. Not to bother your grandson." I hold out the papers. "The trail ends with Timothy Nicholson. He's got records that show he came from Germany, but I think he probably didn't know he came from Poland. Missus Young at the historical society said she thinks maybe they told him to say he was German when they snuck him out so they didn't suspect he was Jewish. It just continued when he came here because he didn't know who to trust. His phone number's on there." I look up and Josif is slowly, tediously accepting the papers. But his eyes are on me. "I'm giving you the path. It wasn't that difficult to follow so I'm assuming you were just scared of what you'd come to find—the fear of the ghosts or grandeur of a miracle. He's not the ghost. So, it is the miracle. We think he's alive. I found a recent newspaper article about him celebrating his sixtieth wedding anniversary. Josif, he wasn't with the orphan kids who got on that train. The boy in the photograph is still alive."

Chapter 35

Dodging Death on the Highway

Detective Phillips knows what I was told by Dee Williams and J.D. Junior. I texted him when I got about a mile from the Landowski's. I could see I was getting service and paused along the road. I thought it would be cut and dry, but he starts texting me:

You still thinking that wasn't her in that car? He texts me back.

You can't drive a car that doesn't have a battery. She was at church. Then nobody knows where she went. Do you know Georgia Burns?

Yeah. She's in the nursing home in town.

Dee said she told him Jody was at the church the night she got killed. How's that work? You can't be in two places at once.

The wreck was late at night. Way after church was over.

Dee said it was a shutdown, all-nighter. Church has snake handlers???? Didn't her parents say she was at work? Did you ever question her parents?

Church. Work. Home? Not sure. Parents were distraught. How'd you get this stuff? What about snakes?

Snakes at church. Got it hanging around with Bammy. The nice thing about being redneck, nobody judges me. Or if they do, I don't care.

So you're claiming redneck now?

Never denied it. Nobody asked.

The light from my cell phone is bright and I blink, thinking I hear a car coming. I step to the right of the solid white line on the side of the road and shake my head, getting ready to run again. I'm tired tonight, I—

BAM!

He hits me like a ton of bricks at the same time the glare of headlights blinds me and the roar of tires skid across the road. I feel someone grab me, rip me off the road and just as my thighs slide skinned-flesh along the gravel and grass on the edge, the car comes sliding sideways only two feet away.

"Run." It's Ben's gruff whisper and he jerks me so hard off the ground, my neck snaps and my shoulder pops hard. It forced my feet to do a wobbly run-walk across the grass until I can get my footing. We slip-slide while I try to figure out what happened between my last text to Detective Phillips and the moment the car high beam lights splashed across my body and the spray of gravel hit my back. The front bumper of the car had been so close to my left hip, I felt the warmth of the engine.

"Were they trying to hit me or was it an accident?"

We tumbled down the hill and then ran deep into a cut of mountain. I hear the sound of creek when we stop. I kneel down, catch my breath. I can hardly see Ben in the moonlight, hands on knees and head bobbing up and down searching the horizon for the car.

"That's the stupidest question I ever heard."

"No, dumbass, here's the stupidest question," I hiss-whisper back. "What are you doing here?"

He laughs sarcastically. "Do you like want to die or something? You're standing there texting on your phone and completely not looking anywhere else. That car has been following you—"

"Shut up, butthole. I hate you."

"Well, you know what? I hate you too."

Silence. I'm shaking. Ben's rubbing his forehead with his hand. "Somebody is trying to kill you."

"Maybe they are trying to kill you."

"Alright," he opens his eyes wide. I see the whites against the moonlight. "Why?"

"Because you're mean and you're an idiot."

"I wouldn't be so judgmental considering I just saved you from being a pancake on the road five minutes ago. You're a real case, Piper. Everybody knows you've been asking questions around town about Jody. Leave it alone."

"You're the one that asked me to look into it. What kind of car was it?" I couldn't see. I only caught the silver bumper and a splash of gray or green.

"It was a truck and that was before I realized somebody's trying to stop you for some reason. Snakes, breaking into your cabin to leave hexes, trying to blow you up and run you down. Isn't that enough to leave a hint for you? Maybe that's why they've been leaving the bodies, a warning."

"It looked like a car."

"Are you going to fight me about this? Why do you always fight me about everything? You asked me. I told you."

I haven't cried since I left home. I suppose seeing Papaw today and seeing Willy and knowing my little brother nearly got killed by Harley to keep a secret has been laying on me all day. We agreed not to say anything to my family. The timing was bad. Peyton just found out she's pregnant with her fourth. But while I sit here, for the first time in so many years, I don't feel alone. Even with Ben staring hot vinegar at me and knowing he hates me but he's still here, it sends a jarring right through my soul. So, I cry.

They are hot tears and thick ones spilling down my cheeks. I'm making those goofy *harrumph-harrumph* sounds in perfect timing to sniffles. And all I can say is: "I fell into a dead girl's coffin and—and scared the crap out of old ladies and my week turned to crap."

So what does Ben say? "I know. I heard. Detective Phillips has told the story around town twice over, showed everybody the picture." Does he not have a soul? That's when the crying turned to bawling and I know his t-shirt is wet with my tears because he hunkers down next to me and shoves my head into his chest and lets me spill it all out.

We walk the side of the road back to the hotel. It takes a good hour and not just because we jump off the road each time a car passes. Ben keeps leaning over while we walk, trying to get a fix on my expression. I turn away. I'm afraid he's going to tell me I'm not such a badass anymore. I text Detective Phillips: *Someone tried to run me over with a truck tonight. It could be my brother-in-law. Long story. I'm not sure.* He sends me one text and it looks like he either accidently hit the send before he was finished or he went out of service. It just says: *Snakes and—*

"Well you got more men coming to your door than I do, Piper," Bammy says from the chair she sits on by her door in the upstairs balcony when we get to the hotel.

"What's she mean by that?" Ben asks. He gives her a wary wave.

"My papaw and my little brother came today. Now you."

"Not Bucky? He's got it bad for you."

"No, he doesn't," I tell him. "He was trying to save his sister from you. I don't think he wants to leave you in the same room alone together. I believe Bucky and I were going to be your chaperones."

"You're kidding me, right?"

"He said you were a player."

Ben rolls his hand through his hair. He gets this sheepish look on his face, then turns it to the far wall. "You know, I'd really like to tell you I'm a player. Who doesn't want to be that guy who's got a girl on every corner, I guess. I'm just not. But girls like that, right? They like a guy who's been around."

"I don't know. Not really. I don't."

"Well, it seems to me, they do. Because I'm like an idiot when it comes to girls. Bucky's the one who's got girls coming and going. I got the idea you figured that out, that's why you didn't go out with him. You don't seem the type, but he's nice looking, you're hot. It's the perfect match. Piper, you know me. You know me better than anybody. It doesn't matter, though. You're leaving." He shrugs. "So did you know all along we really weren't going to get the shoot?"

"No. Abe Starling had Tessa and Marcus on contract. He had to use them for the shoot unless they were being used elsewhere. I was elsewhere. Me, I was getting replaced by Delta Raines. She's from a big company and Abe got her. He can't afford us both."

"You knew this?"

"I found out yesterday. I was more stunned than you, Ben."

"I'm sorry. I shouldn't have jumped before I asked."

"Not as sorry as me," I say. "This project sucked out my entire bank account including maxing out my credit cards. I'm more than dead broke. I'm so in debt, I don't know what I'm going to do."

"You don't have to pay us back unless you gave

Grampa a heart attack tonight with all that info on his brother."

"Oh, no, I do." I snatch my keys, nod to my car. I'm shook up. "I called the company that Abe is doing the project with and they are letting me send in my own work, vie for one of the magazine layouts. The odds are slim, but I'm not going down without a fight."

"You're shaking. You want me to sit with you?" Ben is looking at my hands. I'm shaking. I'm scared. I'll admit it.

"I don't know who it could be. It could be my brother -in-law. Hell, it could be Missus Mills, Jody's mom. I don't know."

"I'd blame it first on Harley," Ben sniffs. "Missus Mills is alright. She used to be my art teacher at Whispering Hollow High. She was a bit weird, but no weirder than any of my other teachers. She wouldn't hurt a fly."

"An art teacher?" I ask.

"Yeah." Ben nods. "Until she had the nervous breakdown when Jody died."

I'm strangely fascinated with the idea of that beautiful rendition of the black cat on the dead girl thighs. Of course, it could have been painted on with a stencil. I'll have to bring that up to Detective Phillips. "Maybe you're right. Will fessed up and told Papaw he took the money and when he tried to put it back, Harley stole it. We don't know what we're doing. It's been a weird day. Oh hells bells, it could even be your angelic Jenny."

"You know, I've got a confession to make." Ben shoves his hands into his pockets, rocks back and forth. "I got the feeling Jenny was—kind of a manipulator."

"What makes you say that?"

"She kept saying stuff about you, like little things. They were mean. She was doing it to my grandpa too."

"Like what?"

"Like you're a hillbilly and come from the wrong side of town, if you know what I mean. She said you have like twenty boyfriends. You were always running around with some guy named Zane and Tucker. Little jabs here and there."

"How would she even know that?" Zane and Tucker? Those were Romeo's buddies I went with to the beach last summer. I've got their pictures—oh, in my wallet.

"I don't know. I know they aren't true, Piper. It ticked me off she'd say that about my friend even if she thought it."

I know where she got my information. The little witch stole my wallet. I excuse myself, walk a few steps away and text Detective Phillips about my conversation with Ben.

I'll go talk to her. Going in and out of cell range. Call you later. Did you get my last text?

What text? Did you know Missus Mills was an art teacher? Maybe she drew black cats—?

Nothing.

Chapter 36
Holding Hands and Digging up the Clues

When Peyton was fifteen, she told me she'd loved Harley McCarthy from the time she was ten years-old. I remember her words, I remember the shine in her burnt orange eyes that were just like mine. She reached out and she grabbed my hand and she said: *I love Harley McCarthy and I ain't never gonna let him go. I know'd it from the second I laid eyes on him when we all walked to the bus that first day of kindergarten. I feel it in my gut. He's my soulmate. Do you know what a soulmate is? It's a connection. It's like our spirits are all tangled together and even after we die, we'll be together like two angels holding hands in heaven for eternity. He kissed me on the lips in the barn, Piper, and it was like a movie kiss. I'm gonna marry that boy. I'm going to be with him forever.*

We were sitting in one of Daddy's big old maple trees in the back yard. She said there was nothing more beautiful than that kiss and it sealed their fate together. While I look up at the pine trees in the forest surrounding us, I think of Peyton and I think of Harley. Are there really soulmates or are all relationships one-sided? Or is this kind of what it feels like, holding hands and fighting and making up and laughing, crying—

"What are you thinking about?" Ben is walking beside me. We're hiking to Dark Pines this morning to find Delilah Gray's grave. We're almost to the top of the mountain. I want to see if Delilah Gray's grave is really up here, find out if she really existed. It didn't take too long to get this far. We parked on an old service road and hiked from where it was cordoned off.

We're holding hands. I'm wearing a little red flannel

shirt and jean shorts and he keeps tugging on the flannel flaps and tickling me in the ribs. Every time he does and I jerk to the right, the little camera backpack on my shoulder slides down and almost hits the ground. Funny, I don't tell him to quit it even when a couple lens caps fall out. I guess I like him more than my camera. *Hmm.*

I got on my beanie because my hair looked like crap and he keeps tugging it over my eyes. He just started that a second ago. Just came up beside me, slipped his hand over mine. Soft flirting. I like it. My heart jumped, my tummy tickled. He spent the night, fell to sleep on the couch. I tiptoed out at three in the morning. I asked him if he was awake. He wasn't. Still, he said we could both fit on the couch. And he held me. That was it. But it was so much more, I suppose. Because I can't stop thinking about his body pressed to mine, his fingers twining in my fingers. His lips every now and then, kissing my head or my cheek or once in a while, my lips. Then, I got up about five to work on the layout to send to Jimmy Bean. Ben got up too and I sat on his lap while he helped me write the storyline.

"How do you know if you've got a soulmate?" I answer his question with a question.

"A soulmate." He chews on this a second and reaches up, pokes my beanie hat. "Aren't you hot?"

"No."

"Soulmate," he says it again. "I can tell you by all the literature books I've read, it seems to end with the girl riding off with the prince into the sunset or both of them dying. So in other words, it is deep. Why?"

"Well, because I always used my sister's definition and that's kind of stuck in my brain. But she loves Harley and said he was her soulmate and he was crappy to her."

"I don't know if they are true soulmates if he's

abusive, you know?"

"But what if he abuses her and it is still undying love?"

"You're goofy."

"You always tell me that."

"Stop."

I do what he says. He twists around so we're facing each other. He's tall. I have to look up. "So while I was trying to be mad at you yesterday thinking that this photo thing was all a big scam, I couldn't understand why my instincts kept telling me nobody could be that good at being—I don't know, everything you are—funny and smart and beautiful. I mean, that's all the kind of things that let girls like you get away with crap, scam people, whatever. But it's like I see past that in your eyes, in that sparkle. I don't know where you're going next. Maybe you'll come back someday. But right now, we got this right now. Maybe—part time soulmates."

I laugh right when he kisses me. It doesn't matter, he's laughing right when our noses bump. The next time, he's right on track. Best kiss ever. Soft lips that taste a bit like peppermint bubblegum and his fingers tangling in my hair.

"Sorry, that was kind of off." He looks at me sheepishly.

"Feel my heart and you won't say that." I reach up, snatch up his hand and press it to my chest. It's banging so hard, I swear he must hear it. Yeah, that worked. He's got a smug look on his face.

"Let's walk. We'll kiss later."

So everything's going fine. We're standing in the cemetery and lo and behold, Delilah Gray's headstone is a beautiful sandstone marker. It states:

Delilah Jane Gray

Born: July 3, 1840 Died: Jan 5, 1867. Drowned.

And these signs shall follow them that believe in my name shall they cast out devils; they shall speak with new tongues; they shall take up serpents; and if they drink any deadly thing, it shall not hurt them; they shall lay hands on the sick, and they shall recover."

"Okay, that's weird. That's the same saying from the bible they use to condone using snakes in the church."

I should have taken that as a warning. But my curious gaze slid to the right of the grave instead. "Hey, Ben, look." I hunker down on one leg and read the headstone next to it. It says: *Ezekiel Hiram McGraw.*

Born: November 27, 1832 Died: Jan 5, 1867. Drowned.

"It's got the same date. And the same epitaph underneath," Ben whispers, pushing away the overgrown grass at the bottom. "I never even stopped to look at the graves. But I wouldn't have put two and two together. So the legend is true? Delilah met this Ezekiel McGraw and tried to run off with him?"

"I don't know. It's cool." I grab my camera from my little backpack. I start to dig out the lens I need. It's not in there. "Aw, dude, when you were playing footsie with me up the last hill, my lens must have fallen out." I start to hand him my backpack. "Hold this. I'm going to go look for it."

"Footsie?" He grunts a sarcastic laugh, winks at me. "You seemed to like it then." He shrugs. "Look around. See what else you can find. I'll go take the walk. I'll find it in five minutes or less or you have to go out with Bucky."

I furrow my brow. He must have been able to read the distress in my eyes.

"I was kidding. I was going to make fun of you always losing stuff, but it's still a sore spot with me, you and Bucky flirting when we looked for your purse." He throws out his hands, rolls his eyes and I watch him disappear into the pines. Dark pines. I made a note to myself to take a picture there. Then I gently drop my backpack and walk over to look at some of the other graves. There's a newer grave in the far back and nearly hidden in the brush. I mean, not new, but not so old the ground is furrowed like the other twenty or so graves still visible. It's got a homemade marker on it made of cement. It just says: OUR GIRL. J.E.M. There's also some more writing beneath, and I squint and lean closer. It's difficult to make out, but it is the same epitaph as Delilah Gray and Ezekiel McGraw.

"Mills," I say the name to myself. "Mills. J.M. Jody— Mills. Oh." It takes me two seconds to reach over, delve in my backpack and pull out my phone. This high on the mountain, I've got service.

"Hey, Detective Phillips."

"I thought you would have left by now. You on the plane?"

"No, Low Po, you're not that lucky. I'm actually up at the top of mountain at the old Dark Pines Church. Hiked up here. There's three graves here. All of them have the epitaph from the Gospel of Mark in the bible, you know: *They shall take up serpents; and if they drink any deadly thing, it shall not hurt them.*"

"And—?"

"Well, don't you think that's strange that they have this on a dead person's grave?"

"In comparison to someone who's alive?"

"Think about it, smartass," I grunt. "Dee Williams told me that they used Dark Pines Church for snake faith services. What if people were being tested for their faith or doing something the people of the town didn't like and they died from poison from a snake bite?"

"There's no way we could know that if the dead were buried a good hundred years ago, LaRue. There hasn't been a burial there since probably the 1940s."

"Not so. There is a grave here and it says—" I hunker down on my knee, push the grass away. The wind kicks up so I don't think anything of the sound of leaves behind me. "J.E.M. It's newer. What was Jody Mills's middle—?" Then when I hear the footsteps, I smile and start to turn to make light of the Bucky joke and he must have run back up so I didn't take up the offer.

"Oh, no—" But it's not Ben standing there. One second, I'm slightly turned and staring at woman. The next thing I know, I feel a dull thud on the side of my head. Then, there's only blackness.

Chapter 37
Death by Snakes and Waterfalls

"—okay, you know it isn't about the snakes, right? Piper, look at me."

I keep coming in and out of gray. There's oozy orbs. I feel sick to my tummy. I blink. "Snakes," I mutter and look up. "Why'd you hit me on the head?" Ben is staring at me from across a room and right down the center of two sets of church pews. He looks concerned. His voice is soft like I'm a little girl. I look up, look to the sides. Oh, I'm in a church. I look to the right and the big boxes with blankets. The blankets are on the floor. I must be in the Dark Pines Church.

"I didn't hit you. I just saw the door to the church open and—this—"

This. I blink. Snakes, snakes, they are everywhere around me crawling on the church floor. It is like someone tossed thirty of them into the air and let them drop. I start to rise, press my back to the little podium.

"Easy, easy, easy." He's stopped at the door. I don't understand. There's warmth on the back of my head. I rub it, pull my hand in front of my face. Blood.

"Piper, listen to me. Is that—blood?" He keeps looking down at his foot, his ankle, then back to me.

"Yeah. My head hurts, Ben."

"You got knocked out. I don't know what happened. But it's going to be okay. Just focus on me." I am looking at the floor. I make a funny mewling sound. Snakes. Snakes, snakes, everywhere. I remembered looking in the window the day we came here on horse. I remember the boxes along the wall covered in blankets. What I didn't realize then that

I know now is that they were glass fish tanks filled with snakes for the church and carefully covered from prying eyes. Now they are empty. Their contents are all over the floor amidst broken glass of the fish tanks. All of them are poisonous, I just know. And Ben, he's leaning in, trying to get eye contact.

"Piper, listen. It's not about the snakes, your phobia. It's about the trust. It's easier to use something you can see instead of something you don't understand. What happened the next day after your brother put snakes in the bed?"

"They all laughed at me."

"So you felt betrayed by Will when he put the snakes in your bed and everybody laughed. You get it? The snakes didn't bite you. They didn't hurt you. They are just an easy thing to put a wall up because your little brother made you feel like an idiot. Did they bite you?"

"No." They were cool against my skin. The thought makes my own skin crawl. I shake it off with a shiver.

"Because you were warm and felt safe. They weren't scared of you. They were cuddling like Teddy bears, baby. These snakes aren't any different. If they don't feel threatened, they aren't going to hurt you. So, if you just walk across the room really slowly, you'll be fine."

"What if I don't want to?"

I know he doesn't want to tell me there's one slip sliding its way along the wall. I know it is there. I've been watching it out of the corner of my eye, hearing the sound of its skin make a muffled scuffing. I'm imagining it sliding to my foot, my calf, my ribs, my shoulders.

"Do you want me to tell you?"

"That there's one crawling at a healthy pace toward my foot? And it's going to crawl up my leg?"

"No, goofy," he says it softly. "I'm going to walk

across and get you. I'm not afraid to walk through a bunch of poisonous snakes for you. But my foot, it is sitting right on a trip wire. So I'm going to get shot. Then I'm going to have to do it with a bullet in me. I just don't want you to jump when it goes off because it will be loud. Look." I catch his eyes, then follow them down to his knee, his calf and then his ankle. Sure enough, I see a flash of thick fishing line there. I follow it up to the wall and the shotgun sitting there. "When I move, that's going off. I'd rather be going backward than forward. However, I will do what I have to do to get you out of here away from the snakes."

"Will you call me badass again if I walk it?"

He laughs softly and I see his eyes get this sparkle. "Sure. You name it. I'll flip cartwheels for you, Piper, if you want. Can you walk? Are you too dizzy?"

"I'm okay now. My head hurts a little." There are times in my life I've been standing on the edge. I always take a step back, get to a safe place. But Abe's not right. I do take risks. I always figured I wouldn't have ever left home if my daddy hadn't showed me to the door. But when he opened the door, he never told me to get out. I just walked and kept walking. I take risks all the time. It's just thought out well ahead of time.

It isn't something I get the opportunity to do right then, though, struggle with how the odds will lay out on which path I should take so I have the least falls, the least skinned knees. Stay. Walk. Because I have to run. Right now, there is no choice. There's a murder getting ready to occur right before my eyes. And it comes in the form of a woman with a loaded shotgun taking the two stone steps up to the door behind Ben. I look up. Ben is giving me a forced, but coaxing smile. What he doesn't see, but what I see is her stopping like she's surprised then hauling up the gun.

So I just let out the most horrifying scream. I take off

in a forced knee-snapping, march-run like a football player sprinting through car tires during a fitness drill, trying desperately to dodge the snakes but knowing I'm doing a wonderful job of both ticking them off and scaring them at the same time. I lunge the last three feet and slam into Ben who is wagging his head back and forth. He takes one step back and simply bows to my weight, half-crumbling and half sitting down on the woman behind him.

We slide, the three of us to the crackle of shotgun above our heads as the tripwire fired the gun. I'm splayed on my belly. Ben is sideways, eyes confused when he snaps his neck to the right, sees the woman, sees the gun.

"I knew you'd come back." She's looking at me when she says that.

"I don't know what you mean." I'm trying to come to my feet. Ben's rising, dragging me with him backward.

"Missus Mills, that's Piper LaRue. She's the photographer that came to take pictures of the mountain. Are you okay?" Ben is holding out one hand partway between us as we step back one step, then another while he lays out introductions like we're sitting in a restaurant and another couple has walked by that he knows. "Piper, this is Jody's mom—"

"I know who you want me to believe she is. I know all about her house being right here where the church was built." Missus Mills tips her head to one side, smiles slyly. She's gray long hair held high in a bun on her head and modest tan skirt and white blouse. "I know you're testing me, Satan. I know you conjured this beast up again just like you did when you took over Delilah Gray's body and killed her too. My grandpa told me the stories. I know what you did to them."

"Delilah Gray died, Missus Mills." I'm still taking a step back for each one she is taking. I don't want the gun in my face. I don't. "We just saw her grave. The stone said she drowned."

"Because the people of the town drowned her! She was wicked. They threw her off the waterfall along with the man she seduced. That's the only way to kill demons like you. That man was my great, great grandpa—Ezekiel McGraw. And that woman took him from my great, great grandma. Now you've come back with your camera. Same as the woman, you like dead people. You take pictures of them, talk to them. You may have walked through the snakes unharmed, but you'll never live through the waterfall. I sanctified the water. Now you're going to be baptized in it, burn! And this time, you're not coming back."

"What's your biggest fear?" I whisper to Ben. I feel his hand clasp my own while she walks forward, we walk back. Because I know where she's herding us. I don't even think she hears me. She is ranting and raving. "You're afraid of falling, right?"

"Yeah." His hand is tight. I look up. He's got his head turned, watching the edge of the waterfall.

"Well, my greatest fear is losing you." I give him a little shove with my butt to get him to take two steps to her one. We need more space. It's hard and he just takes two steps. "I'm not going to lose you," I say it. I take two steps back and just come at him, unlatch my fingers. Then I turn like I'm just scared and going to hug him with both hands on his chest. He takes two steps, latches on to my arms with his hands and I see him looking at me. It's been raining. I know it is a crazy drop downward. I also know the pool is full from the rain. I make a wide circle of my eyes. He shakes his head.

"Please trust me." Damn. He nods. Trust. Oh, maybe that is my greatest fear, seeing the trust in his eyes while he nods, grabs me and we jump.

Chapter 38

I Want to Be a Badass Enough to Kill Him to Get It, I guess

I hit the lake below. It jars my body. But I come up. My head pops through the surface. I take in a breath. Silence. I'm doggy paddling, cupped palms slapping the water. I see nothing but lake and trees. I don't know what to do. Where'd he go?

"Ben!" I call out his name. "Ben!" Then I scream it. I look to my left. It is nothing but stone and muddy bank. I don't know what to do. I look up wildly. I don't see Missus Mills. I look left to right. I don't see her. I don't see Ben.

"Okay, dive down. Find him." I kind of make a flip-doggy-paddle forward and kick hard with my legs. My arms, I'm splaying and splashing. *Do people just go to the bottom of a lake when they drown? Or do they float? I need air. I'm not going up. I need to find him. I need air.*

I go up and down two times. I'm sobbing outwardly and loudly and trying to take deep breaths. *I killed him. I made him jump.* I hit the bottom, push up. I don't know how deep it is. Twenty feet? No, I couldn't go down that far. Is that something—?

A shirt. I feel a swatch of clothing tickle the tips of my fingers. Is it him? My hand is spread wide. I pull, I tug, I kick until I make it to the surface. Then I see his head come up. Dead. Is he dead? I'm still sobbing and dragging him with my stupid doggy paddle strokes. "Ben, Ben, Ben," I'm chanting. "Wake up. Don't die. Breathe. Breathe. Breathe. Breathe. Breathe." It's not fast enough and man, he's heavy when I get him close enough to the shore I can stand and drag him by the shoulders.

I roll him on his back and watch the water just fall out of his mouth. I push on his back. I'm still making wild head jerks to make sure Missus Mills is not coming. I roll him over, start mouth to mouth resuscitation. There's no blood, barring a little cut on his cheek. "Breathe," I'm whispering. "Ben, I'm begging you." I sob. "Breathe."

And he breathes. It's an enormous gulp of air. Water is running from his nose and he's trying to wipe it away while he looks wildly up at me, the fingers of his hand waving at me violently. I snatch them up and he's trying to sit up.

"You're okay. Oh, God, just lay there. You're okay."

"Y—y—you're—" Ben's trying to say something.

"Don't talk. Just breathe." I'm laying overtop him, he's choking and coughing and gagging.

"But—you're—"

He tries to sit up again, chokes and gags. He leans over and throws up on the muddy ground. I take off the flannel I'm wearing, shove it to his face. Then I push my arm around him and pat his back like he's a three year-old awakened from a nightmare.

"Okay," he says, breathing deeply three breaths. "You're badass."

I gawk at him.

"You told me if you got across the snakes, I'd say you were badass. You—are badass."

Chapter 39
The Truth About Jody

"Hey, LaRue." Detective Phillips reaches out and nudges the ice pack from my head and rubs the bump. I'm sitting on the back bumper of the police cruiser off the main road and only twenty feet from where the two bodies were dumped. He takes something from his pocket, drops it in my lap. "Nice bump. Here's something for your troubles." I look down. It's my wallet. "Now, I'm going to bang the other side for scaring the holy hell out of me." He raises his hand and sure enough, he knocks the other side with a good swipe of his knuckle.

"How'd you find this?"

"I stopped in at Preacher Young's church this morning like I said. I went inside and talked to Jenny, told her about the wallet. She started bawling like a newborn calf and said she found it in the parking lot of Potter's Church. You might remember it—" He chuckles and holds up his phone with my contorted face right before I slide into the casket. I glare at him. "Preacher Young goes to these little remote churches and does services on Saturday nights. She was with him and went for a walk, found it up by the cemetery."

"Wait, I lost the wallet before we went to Holy Trinity to—"

"She found it in a paper bag. She still had the wallet and the bag stuffed hidden in a shelf of her closet. The brown paper bag was full of trash from somebody's car." He smiles at me. "Most likely, it was whoever dug up those graves because there were receipts for two shovels and garbage bags from DeMarco's Dollar Store. And there were purchases of rubber gloves from Handel's Hardware in town. And a gas receipt which Eddy at the Whispering Hollow Quick Stop and Carry Out identified as belonging to—"

"Missus Mills."

"Girl, you're smart for a hillbilly." He shifts on his seat on the bumper. "When we were talking and you just cut off like that, I heard Missus Mill's voice. I tore out of there and called for backup—which in my case, is the fire department and a couple guys who've got ATVs. We got Jody Mills's dad part of the way up the hill. He was parked out off an old forestry road." Detective Phillips nods up toward the hollow of Dark Pines. "The wife, Maddy, fell about forty feet and hit a rock ledge. They're still trying to get her out. She must have jumped. She's dead. Ralph Mills said his wife has been getting worse and worse with her mental illness, won't take her pills. He said she saw you taking pictures and something just went south."

"Wait—" I hold up a hand. The Stick Man outside my window at the cabin, he had a certain scent. "Tell me something. Did you notice if Ralph smelled like—"

"Ginger? He's constantly chewing on ginger root sticks for his stomach. Yeah, it was noticeable. Is that what you mean? My old man did it too. It's an old home remedy."

"Within a day of my wallet being stolen, somebody was outside my window. I smelled ginger." I sigh. Ralph Mills was my Stick Man.

"From what I got from Ralph, a relative of his wife was entangled in a love affair and the family's always blamed it on the witch curse and Stick Man. The black cats, she used a marker to put those on the girls as a warning. Ralph, he played along."

"Okay, that makes sense," I say. "There was a Civil

War photographer that came here and lived in the coal mining town. Her name was Delilah Gray. I found her grave—that's one of the three I was talking about. It's right next to Ezekiel McGraw's grave. They both allegedly drowned on the same day. Story goes that the two were running away together. Delilah jumped off the waterfall thinking Ezekiel had fallen. And Ezekiel found her bag and jumped too."

"Yeah, I know the story. Did you see the bag on your way down? Or maybe in the water. You went for a dip. It's supposed to be full of cash."

"Nope. I'm not sure there's a bag at all. I'm guessing they were tossed into the waterfall by people of the town because of their sins. I'm not telling anybody that but you."

"The secret's safe with me. You remember Preacher Young saying Jody had a stalker? It was her dad, trying to scare her with the Stick Man story. He'd told it to her all the time, that if she didn't repent her ways, the Stick Man was going to get her. I guess he was the one following around Kayla Delray and you. He didn't break into her apartment. He's the plumber they contracted during the renovations at her apartment. I figured that out when I saw his car on the road up there. It has: *Proud Christian Construction Worker*. She said the contractor bugging her had the same thing. He was telling her to repent her ways. He just snuck into her room when she was gone and took her clothing."

"That's Jody buried up there."

"Yeah, LaRue, I talked to Georgia earlier. I suppose my phone call set this off. She called Maddy and it all went downhill from there. The Dark Pines Church gets used for some of the Church of Holy Pentecost services, the ones with the faith snakes. Now, it's been illegal since the early 1940s for poisonous snake handling in religious services. But it's been going on here for a long time."

"Dude, I get it. My mama's side of the family are Holy Pentecost. You don't need to explain it. It is what it is."

"I could no more arrest Preacher Harkins for using snakes than I could arrest Josif Landowski for being Jewish. Sometimes our faith is dangerous. Ask either of those men and they'll agree."

"You're preaching to the choir, detective."

"You're funny." He reaches out and knocks me on the shoulder. "Here's the nutshell. Jody Mills and her mom attended one of Preacher Harkins's services up in Dark Pines a little under four years ago. Whereas Jody was trying to get away from her mother and father's church, they were trying hard to pull her back in. That's one of the reasons she was seeing Preacher Young, trying to deal with all the changes. Jody went to church that night, why I don't know."

"Dee Williams said it was because her mama told her she'd help pay to fix her car if she went. It wasn't working."

"Well, that explains why her mama was in so much pain. Jody got bit by a rattlesnake and her mama refused to take her to get treatment. She said God was testing her. Jody didn't even make it down the hill. Dead. Ralph and Maddy were so scared they'd get arrested and the church would get closed down, the two dug up a grave in Hazard. Why? They knew the coroner would do an autopsy on a young woman to check for foul play. He would find snake toxin in her. So they pulled the body out, went down and towed her car from Tanner's Garage. They burned her up inside and rammed the car into the guardrail, burned it up too. Then they buried Jody up in the Dark Pines Cemetery."

"What's with the dead bodies dumped here?"

"From what I gather from a twenty minute conversation with Ralph, he really thought when you showed up in Whispering Hollow, you were here undercover to investigate the truth about Jody. I'm sure he's been watching the crime shows on TV. He got paranoid and it only provoked Maddy Mills more. They dug up the two girls. One from Potter's Church and Holy Trinity so somebody thought that it was a serial killer. They thought it was okay to do it, you know, because the girls had both committed suicide. They believed they weren't going to heaven anyway. The other skulls, we still have to assume, are from a family burial plot there."

"All this is making my head hurt. Can you take me back to my hotel room?"

"Yeah, come on." Detective Phillips waves me to his car. "Hey, by the way, when you're feeling better, I want to hear the whole story. I got Ben Landowski's side of the story in the ambulance. He made it sound like he was a superhero. Now I'd like to hear yours—" Did I cringe? Because the detective laughs. "Naw, it was the other way around. He said you saved his butt."

"So Jody Mills's mom is dead and the curse is broken," I say that softly more to myself than Detective Phillips. I think of those two wax stick men and I heave a sigh of relief. He gives me a hard stare and a tip of his chin.

"A curse? Am I missing something, LaRue?"

"Just superstition," I mutter quickly. "I mean, because everybody thought Dark Pines was cursed because of the bodies. You know, the Stick Man story."

"Yeah, she's dead. There's no Stick Man, just a girl that got bit by a snake and whatever people have conjured up in their minds about this old ghost town. What curses folks thought this old piece land held, were nothing more than the Mills family trying to cover it up and old legends we'll never know are true or not."

Shay Lawless
Chapter 40
Saying Goodbye

If you want to get a taste of what its really like to live in rural U.S. you got to sample Kentucky. Whispering Hollow, Kentucky, that is. It's four hours from the city and thirty minutes off the highway. It's beautiful mountains and creeks. It's ham and grits with cheese at J.D.s and if you need your car fixed, Dee Williams has you covered—

"I don't know how to say goodbye, so I won't. I can't." That's me leaning against my rental car two days later. I'd finished the Midwest Farmer's Magazine submission, sent it next day air to Jimmy Bean. Ben did most of the writing while I sat on the side of the bed in the hospital knocking ideas off him. But I had to add our adventure, had to put in something about Josif's quest to find his brother. They made him stay twenty-four hours. He was a bit hot about that, but I stayed with him.

Then one more day and I'm leaning against the rental car.

"What happens with your family?"

"I'm going to send them a money order when I get back."

We just stand there hugging each other against the car. I've got my forehead pressed to his chest. He's wearing a t-shirt and I can smell his aftershave on it and his sweet scent. "Does your grampa still hate me?"

"No, he's just—it freaked him out, me getting hurt. Will you—come visit? Before school starts or something. You promised me you'd touch a snake, remember?"

"Yeah, well, I jumped over twenty of them for you. That ought to account for something." We know I won't come back. His grandpa is right. I'm a leaver. "As soon as I find a job. I got to go." I just push away from him. I don't want him to see his badass girl crying. "I'll—I'll, um, text you, right?"

"Yeah," he sighs. "Right." Then he stops. "Why do you think they put that bible verse on Ezekiel and Delilah's grave. I mean, I'd like to think they jumped for each other. I don't want to think that the people of Dark Pines put it on their grave as a warning—they died because they weren't pure."

"So maybe they believed the two were tempted by the serpent, the devil," I offer, "by seeing each other in a world that found it unacceptable for a married man and an unmarried woman to find love. So by jumping and dying, God showed they were committing a sin. It was punishment. Like Jody's mom thought she was being tested and punished for working at the bar and seeing all those men. I think it was a warning from another time. Don't play with fire. You'll get burned. Don't go out with a married man. We're not married. We lived through the serpents and the waterfall, right?"

"Yeah, right."

Chapter 41
Finding Home

HOLOCAUST BROTHERS REUNITED AFTER 75 YEARS. It is a big deal. I saw it in all the newspapers even before I landed at the Louisville airport five weeks later. They are doing a big piece on it on national television, the reunion of Josif Landowski and his biological brother, Timothy Nicholson. Because yes, it was him and he was alive. It seems that the night before the orphans were taken away, Josif's brother snuck out to find him. He was halfway across the city when the other orphans got on the train. He was left behind. When he couldn't find Josif, he was eventually taken in by a woman who helped Jewish children escape the Warsaw Ghetto and find adoptive parents that were in America. In the end, he found a home in Louisville, Kentucky.

I wanted to be there to see them so I talked my sister into meeting me in a diner just outside Louisville afterward so I could give her the five-thousand dollars they still believed I stole. Ben left me a couple messages. I didn't have time to get back with him. Then, it was so crowded, even when I tried desperately to break through the crowd, I couldn't. I leave. I'm trying to figure out how I can make an excuse to visit Whispering Hollow. I want to go back. I want to talk to Ben. I'm not sure, he wants to be with me.

I'm early meeting at Spencer's Country Kitchen. I get a booth in the back and order a coffee. I can't see out the window, so I keep turning to look up at the doors anticipating Peyton. I'm praying she doesn't bring Harley. I don't want to see him. And it isn't that he just used me and he used my sister. It is that he almost killed my favorite little brother.

I'm nervous. I suppose the coffee isn't helping. I've had three cups My sister's late getting here. For five-thousand dollars, though, I assume she'll come. *Poo-plaw, poo-plaw.* Strangely, I think I hear my papaw's walker.

"Hey, Piper."

I am typing on my computer, e-mailing Jimmy Bean from Midwest Farmer's Magazine when she slips into the booth. I stand up. She's got Papaw and Will and Lee and Daddy with her and I know my eyes are big while they all plop down and slide in like we hadn't missed a beat since eight years ago.

"Hey—Daddy," I say. I'm sitting across from him and he's rubbing his hands together. It isn't a good sign and I feel like a six year-old again who just got caught with muddy Sunday school shoes.

I take the envelope with the money from my backpack. I push it across the table to him. "Here's the money I stole. I'm sorry—"

"He knows, Piper, knows you didn't take it." Peyton shakes her head, looks at Will. "We all know." They are all staring at the money with eager eyes. I know it is a lot. I know they need it. There's always stuff in Daddy's house breaking down. There's always grandbabies to feed.

"We want you to come home."

"Just take it. I can just see how this would work out at family reunions, Peyton. Harley stink-eyeing me," I try to kid them, but Daddy's shaking his head. "This is it guys, I'm not coming back. I—"

"Baby, don't go again. Daddy's sorry." My daddy said that. He's got tears in his eyes when he snatches up my hand while I'm pushing the money toward him. I see him and his big, round face and gray hair. I see him break and I've never seen him do that before. I just burst into tears right there at the table with one of my heaving sobs. I know everybody's looking at us like a bunch of crazy hillbillies when I jump up from the booth and wobble-walk my way to Daddy and hold him tight. "Don't leave, baby," he keeps saying while I chuck up about a million happy sobs.

"I choose you. I told Harley to get out." Peyton holds up her left hand and wiggles her fingers. I see the little white mark where the ring had been and the sun couldn't shine on it to tan the rest of the skin. "It was hard. But he don't love me like I loved him. Not in the same way. And you don't hurt kin like that. I know when he goes huntin' all the time, he ain't going out to catch no deer. Mama and Daddy, they're going to help us out until me and the kids get settled, until the baby's born." Peyton reaches down next to her, drags up a grocery bag and slowly slides it across the me. I open it. It is Aunt Tammy's old plug tobacco lunchbox. "She'd want you to have it. I thought you'd want it." I did. I smile.

"One day at a time," Papaw says. "One day at a time."

It's probably more scary for me driving to the Landowski's house later that night. By the time I get to Whispering Hollow, it is eleven o'clock. I don't see Ben's car. But there is a car at every cabin and a couple extra next to the house. I knock at the door and Josif answers in his nightclothes and he's knot-tying a belt around his bathrobe.

"Piper, it's so good to see you." He waves a hand for me to come in and I shake my head. "We just got back about an hour ago. We looked for you—"

"I was there." I hold out my hand, shake my head. "My flight was late and I couldn't get through the crowd. No, I don't want to bother you this late. I just wanted to see Ben." I hold out my hand. "And give you this."

"Well, we would have liked to have you there with us. It was you who made it happen." He takes the envelope, twists his head to look at it in the sparse light. "What is this?"

"It's your payment on your invoice," I tell him. "Twenty-two thousand dollars and fifty-two cents."

"Oh, my. That's way too much."

"No, it was the ballpark figure I gave Abe at the beginning. He paid it out to me a week ago. I was just waiting, hoping I didn't have to get an attorney."

"And you didn't?"

"Naw," I say. I didn't. Delta Raines isn't working out so well for Abe Starling. She's flighty and didn't have a clue how to figure out what her customer needed. Her entire photo shoot for the magazine proposal in Florida was completely off the grid of what Jimmy Bean and Midwest Farmer's Magazine was looking for in their theme. They took hundreds of pictures of models in yellow bathing suits on the beach with white horses. I don't know what kind of country living that embodied. And they liked the ones I sent of Ben digging out the mud in his old horse's hooves much better.

I tell Josif that and I also tell him the money is his. Abe Starling is trying to get back on my good side. I'm letting him sweat it out a bit.

"So is Ben here?" I ask.

"He's back at his apartment," Josif tells me. "In town. He's going to go back and forth. School's getting ready to start. He's busy, you know. Back and forth, back and forth."

"Will you give him something for me?" I ask.

"Why don't you give it to him yourself?"

"You asked me to stay away from him."

"And it didn't work, did it?" Josif chuckles. "Are you still a leaver?"

"I don't want to be. My apartment in Washington State is lonely. I met with my family today. Daddy said he wanted me to come home."

"That's good to know. Okay, he's at the Randall Cove Apartments in town. Apartment 3B." Josif starts to close the door when I tell him goodnight. "You're always welcome here. But after the magazine ran, our cabins have been filled up and I've got bookings for the next six months."

"No kidding." I laugh.

He leans out the door and gives me a kiss on the head. "You be a stayer, you hear me?"

Boom-boom-boom-pop. There's a basketball court at Randall Cove Apartments. I'm shooting baskets. Ben's not home. At least, he didn't answer the door or his texts. I'm thinking maybe he knew I wasn't coming back. Maybe he's out with Jenny. It was kind of dumb to think—

I see him in the shadows even before he struts over and snatches the ball from my hands. "Okay, one game of around the world. If I win, you stay a couple days." He acts like he's tossing it at me hard, doesn't.

"You still irritate me. Do you ever notice your games are always one-sided?" I pretend to be snotty. He rolls his eyes.

"So, give me what you got. What do you want if you win?"

"I stay for more than a couple days. Whispering Hollow is my home base."

"Seriously?" Ben's looking at me. He was rolling the ball around in his hands and stops. Then he steps up to me. "Like—forever?"

"Like, yeah, I'm kind of offering you a job. Jimmy Bean liked our proposal so well, he wants us to go all over the Midwest and the South and do stories on small towns and what makes each unique."

"You're kidding."

"I'm not. They are completely changing the format for the entire theme of the magazine because they liked the layout of our story so much. They liked your writing. They liked my pictures. They loved the entire format. They said they've got more readers in the last month than they've gotten the entire twenty years they've been publishing and their stocks in the outlet have risen eight percent."

"You didn't have to put my name on it. You did most of the work."

"No, we did it together, dumb butt. We make a damn good team."

"I've got school."

"And so I go and take all the pictures. We go together on the weekends so you get a feel for the area. We write it together." I reach out and knock the ball from his hands. "You know I love you right? I feel like I'm going to be a yoyo coming back here. I mean, if you feel the same way I'll dump the Washington State apartment and stay here."

"I love you, too." He says that and gets that goofy grin on his face. He takes a couple steps up, chucks me on the chin and then gives me one of his tummy jerking kisses. "You're my soulmate, you know. My badass, girl."

CPSIA information can be obtained
at www.ICGtesting.com
Printed in the USA
LVHW072054230623
750625LV00002B/259